"I looked for that girl at other competitions that season," Nathan said. "Never saw her again."

Harper's gaze had deepened. She had tears in her eyes. Something he had absolutely not meant to draw from her. "That was in San Francisco," she said, and he nodded.

"That was me, Nathan. It was the first time I ever took first place in my division..."

Her? Harper? He gave his head another shake. But...

His mouth opened. Nothing came out. He just stared, bouncing mentally from past to present, memory to current sight.

She held his gaze steadily, and something settled over him. Within him.

They'd known each other then, on a level that had worked, and they'd met again.

Two loners meant to be friends.

Sometimes life really did hand you a gift.

Dear Reader,

Welcome to Ocean Breeze! And to a very special story. Harper and Nathan grew up in the dance world. It's a world I lived in for many years, traveling to competitions, learning to read judges, looking forward to watching the best of the best perform. I learned what to look for in terms of technique and also entertainment value.

And I witnessed the heartache, the body aches, the soul-searching that never appeared onstage but were rampant behind stage, during hours every day spent in the studio, on the dance floor, learning, practicing, dancers pushing their bodies to extremes. Those times were the highest highs and the lowest lows.

They were also some of the best moments of my life. My own less than stellar hours at the ballet bar and the many, many classes I observed. I once sat in a small rehearsal studio in Burbank, watching as my daughter rehearsed a tap dance number with Jerry Lewis that later aired on his telethon.

And from deep inside me came Harper and Nathan. Both gifted dancers who had very different views of and experiences with the dance world. I hope you'll read their story. And that you'll come away with some of the very real joy that lights up my heart.

Tara

THEIR SECOND CHANCE DANCE

TARA TAYLOR QUINN

SPECIAL EDITION

If you purchased this book without a cover you should be aware that this book is stolen property. It was reported as "unsold and destroyed" to the publisher, and neither the author nor the publisher has received any payment for this "stripped book."

Harlequin® SPECIAL EDITION™

ISBN-13: 978-1-335-18026-1

Their Second Chance Dance

Copyright © 2026 by TTQ Books LLC

All rights reserved. No part of this book may be used or reproduced in any manner whatsoever without written permission.

Without limiting the exclusive rights of any author, contributor or the publisher of this publication, any unauthorized use of this publication to train generative artificial intelligence (AI) technologies is expressly prohibited. Harlequin also exercises their rights under Article 4(3) of the Digital Single Market Directive 2019/790 and expressly reserves this publication from the text and data mining exception.

This is a work of fiction. Names, characters, places and incidents are either the product of the author's imagination or are used fictitiously. Any resemblance to actual persons, living or dead, businesses, companies, events or locales is entirely coincidental.

For questions and comments about the quality of this book, please contact us at CustomerService@Harlequin.com.

TM and ® are trademarks of Harlequin Enterprises ULC.

Harlequin Enterprises ULC
22 Adelaide St. West, 41st Floor
Toronto, Ontario M5H 4E3, Canada
www.Harlequin.com

HarperCollins Publishers
Macken House, 39/40 Mayor Street Upper,
Dublin 1, D01 C9W8, Ireland
www.HarperCollins.com

Printed in Lithuania

A *USA TODAY* bestselling author of over one hundred and thirty novels in twenty languages, **Tara Taylor Quinn** has sold more than seven million copies. Known for her intense emotional fiction, Ms. Quinn's novels have received critical acclaim in the UK and most recently from Harvard. She is the recipient of the Readers' Choice Award and has appeared often on local and national TV, including *CBS Sunday Morning*.

For TTQ offers, news and contests, visit www.tarataylorquinn.com!

Books by Tara Taylor Quinn

Harlequin Special Edition

The Cottages on Ocean Breeze

Her Christmas Wish
Beach Cottage Kisses
Christmas Cottage Getaway
Their Second Chance Dance

Furever Yours

Love Off the Leash

Sierra's Web

Not Without Her Child
A Firefighter's Hidden Truth
Last Chance Investigation
Danger on the River
Deadly Mountain Rescue
A High-Stakes Reunion
Baby in Jeopardy
Her Sister's Murder
Mistaken Identities

Visit the Author Profile page
at Harlequin.com for more titles.

To my daughter, Rachel. I was there for you then, now and forever. I love you so very much.

Chapter One

Standing at the barre attached to the wall in her spare bedroom, across from the full wall of mirror, Harper Michaels let the music take her as she ran through pliés, tendus, dégagés and ronds de jambe, warming her body up, preparing it for full movement. Working toward the frappés, which came next.

She was sweating by the time she'd finished the grande battement that ended the morning's opening regime.

Her daily routine. Every morning except Sundays since she was ten years old. When her friends were spending an hour in the bathroom experimenting with hairstyles and makeup before school, she'd been at the barre in her bedroom. She'd looked forward to getting out of bed to get there. And had proudly worn her thirty-second, tight ponytail and makeup-free face to the bus stop.

Both bus stops. The one she caught from her mother's house, and the other one, from her father's.

Two bedrooms. Two ballet barres.

Pulling the small towel off the end of the barre, Harper wiped her neck and shoulders.

She'd had two of everything, except families. She hadn't had even one whole one of those.

The thought might have been depressing, once upon a time.

Harper had long since found her joy in life, and in spending time separately with both of her parents—once she'd aged out of their constant custody disputes and had made it clear that if they continued to put her in the middle of their anger toward each other, neither of them would see her.

She was living her dream.

Still performing onstage when she wanted to. And spending most of her hours creating movement pieces and setting them on other, beautifully positioned, professional dancers. Allowing her inner vision, her spirit, to be heard. With a growing reputation that was already promising work far into the future.

A lifetime of it. With the success of the pieces she'd already created, in tandem with her own onstage notoriety in both ballet and modern dancing, she could always open a studio and teach. Making enough to support herself. Security for life doing what she loved.

It didn't get any better than that.

But the cottage she adored was getting even better—starting that morning. She showered lickety-split and dressed in leggings and a thigh-length flannel shirt with the sleeves cut off. Harper grabbed one of the elastic bands off her wrist, pulled back her hair and looped it into a ponytail, then pulled up the tail and looped that around, too. Called for Aggie, with the kissing sounds her girl always responded to, and watched as the 100-pound, big-boned four-legged family member stood, turning her soulful eyes up for approval.

Aggie never left a room until after Harper did. Unless it was to investigate unknown sounds that could signal alarm. "You're just my big, majestic babysitter aren't you, my girl?" she asked bending to plant a kiss in the thick black fur at Aggie's neck. "Mama told you that you're getting a new outdoor room, and today's the day the guy comes to go over the details and sign the contract with me." She talked to the Bernese Mountain Dog as she walked.

Talked as she always did when alone with her furry family member. "His name's Nathan Connolly. The guy Gray and Sage told us about…"

The dark eyes glanced up at her, and Harper swore the girl raised an eyebrow at her. Grinning, she patted the head next to her and went to the kitchen for a protein bar before the contractor she'd called was due to appear out back.

"Hopefully he'll be able to get the work started right away," she said as she handed Aggie a three-inch-long treat bone, before unwrapping the bar she'd pulled out of the cupboard for herself. "I want it done by the time it gets warm enough for us to sit out there for breakfast."

Aggie chomped. Harper saw the nod there, too. And, sitting on the floor beside her girl, pulled her knees up and started in on her breakfast. Smiling as the big fur-covered girl looked over at her.

Her and Aggie. That was her homelife.

And it was perfect.

Talk about perfection. Blue skies, sunshine, sand waves and…privacy! Standing on the beach behind the cottages on Ocean Breeze, Nathan Connolly took a deep breath of sea air. Pulled the salty life-sustaining coolness deep into his lungs.

Early for his appointment, with his zipped leather pouch tucked between his elbow and his body, he put his hands in the pockets of his cotton painter pants and walked down toward the sand wet by the tide. He'd been thinking about the place since he'd done his final inspection on the Bartholomew deck, and that morning, before leaving home, had sat at his computer and looked up listings on Ocean Breeze. There'd been a place for sale halfway down the beach last time he'd been there. Chances of it still being available had been slim.

It hadn't been. And would have been more than he'd be comfortable spending. Not that he couldn't afford it. He just didn't like to dig too far into his capital.

But another cottage, yet to be renovated, had come on the market, selling as is. The price was much lower. Still hefty. But less.

And worth it, he determined, even from afar.

He'd make some calls. The project appealed to him. So did living on that beach.

He bent to pet Morgan, Scott Martin's corgi, as she trotted up to him, and then looked over to wave to Scott standing up on his deck as Nathan passed. He continued across the acre that separated Scott's place from Harper Michaels's cottage. His potential new job.

He'd met Scott and Iris, Scott's fiancée, at the Bartholomew place. Sage Bartholomew was Scott's twin.

And that friendly wave, the four-legged greeting...and the beach's privacy...had Nathan feeling pretty good as he headed up the beach toward the cottage he'd been instructed to meet behind at 8:00 a.m.

Clearly Harper Michaels wasn't going to invite him into her home—through it—to get to the back deck. He'd had to park out front, in her driveway, and walk around. So he'd arrived early for a little walk on the beach.

The woman must have missed the memo about neighborliness on Ocean Breeze...

"Nathan Goldman?"

Head shooting up as he heard the name, Nathan's eyes narrowed, and his system froze. The woman approaching him was wide-eyed. Model gorgeous, even in what looked to be a work-around-the-house outfit and no makeup.

For a split second desire flared, and he floated naturally into come-on mode. And just as quickly stopped it.

"Are you looking for me?" the woman asked, almost upon him. A dog—a big dog—came down from the deck he'd been approaching, as the woman continued forward, smiling. "Nathan Goldman, I can't believe it."

He wasn't Nathan Goldman. Not like that. Not without the Connolly. Not anymore.

"I'm Nathan Connolly, here to see Harper Michaels." Gray Bartholomew had told the woman about Nathan, not the other way around. He had no idea what the Michaels woman looked like.

"That's me, you've found me." The woman had reached him. The big dog had, too. Was gazing up at him with eyes that said they saw too much. "I can't believe it's you. What are you doing here...wait, did you just say Connolly?" The smile dropped from her face as her brows drew together.

Pulling forth his portfolio, he unzipped, reached in and handed her a business card.

She read the card, looked up at him, still frowning. Read again. "But..."

"You called my company saying you were interested in a custom-made deck, but only if I designed it myself." Off-kilter, business was all he had. "You want it similar to the one I did for the Bartholomews."

She was half squinting as she looked up at him. "Sage and Gray, yes, but..."

"I'd like to get right to it, if you don't mind," he said, his tone brusque. "I've got a packed morning." He'd have moved toward the deck if not for the monster guard she had. He looked at the huge animal instead.

The thick-furred creature didn't budge, or even seem to blink during the stare-down.

"This is Aggie," Harper Michaels said, as though they were all friends meeting for the first time. They weren't friends.

She wasn't going to be a client, either.

And the whole personal-cottage-renovation-on-the-beach thing had just faded into dust, too.

Nathan Goldman?

No way he could live there.

And Nathan Connolly didn't need the work being offered to him on Ocean Breeze. He'd just wanted it.

"Aggie, this man is the best dancer Mama has ever seen. Hands down."

Nathan's gut rocked for a second as his gaze slowly lifted to Harper Michaels. The awe in her expression was nothing new to him. The knowing that seemed to be shining out of those brown eyes most definitely was.

No one knew him anymore.

And denial was not going to get him out of there. "You've seen me dance."

"Are you kidding? You're why I'm a happy healthy adult living a great life on Ocean Breeze." The woman's direct gaze, her warm tone, tried to nail him where he'd sworn he wouldn't be hit again.

Once a heartless womanizer, not always a heartless womanizer. He'd grown up. Become a man he could live with.

Her words slowly seeped through the macho muck racing from his eyes and ears to his groin. He studied the woman. Not sure she was for real. "How did I possibly help you become healthy and happy?"

He hadn't slept with her. He was certain of that much. Hadn't ever met her.

Maybe that's why she was unharmed by who he'd been.

Her shrug shut him out of a place he suddenly wanted to go. Needed to go.

"Seriously, how?" he asked, taking a step closer in spite of the big, brown-eyed threat sitting next to her.

The dog, Aggie, didn't lunge. Didn't move. Her watchful gaze slid slowly back and forth between the two humans in her presence.

Shrugging, Harper said, "You don't know who I am, do you?"

Oh, God. *Had* he slept with her? Or dated her during a show and dumped her?

Nathan's gaze dropped to his feet. And then rose, meeting her eyes head-on. He'd take her job. Do it for free.

And get the hell out.

"I'm sorry, I don't." He was an honest man. One who was slowly gaining back not only his self-respect, but his soul. One hard truth at a time. "And whatever I did…"

No. He didn't get off that easy. No global apologies. Atone one wrong at a time.

"I'm Harper Cecelia."

Looking her right in the eyes, he shook his head. So Michaels was a married name. The maiden one didn't ring a bell, either.

She pulled out her phone. Going to call the cops on him?

He was a creep. But had always been a law-abiding one. Had never forced anyone to do anything. Had merely accepted what was being thrown at him. And, often, on him.

There'd been times over the past several years that Nathan had almost wished he could be charged for a crime.

Have his day in court. Be convicted. Serve his time. And be set free.

As it was, after so many years of living a different life, there he was, a walk on the beach turning into a nightmare.

Harper Cecelia Michaels wasn't lifting her phone to her ear to speak to whomever she'd dialed. She was holding it out to him.

Showing him a photo that carried a brand whose logo had once been an outline of his posed body.

It only took him a second to realize that the logo wasn't meant to be the main source for his attention. It was the likeness of the ballerina. And the credits listed.

It was the likeness of Harper Cecelia.

He read. Every word. Didn't want to. Couldn't not.

And then with a half nod, he looked at her again. She, a woman, had reached a pinnacle that so few female dancers had the opportunity to touch. A height that took incredible talent and a lifetime dedicated to hard work for the men in the field, too. But one with so much less competition the feat would never be the same. Not to Nathan, at any rate.

He'd been there at seventeen. Given all the advantages because he'd been gifted. But also because there hadn't been many others vying for the same path. He hadn't had to look for invitations or hope to get auditions. Hadn't had to face regular rejections. The offers had come to him.

For jobs. And a lot of other things, too.

Too many things for a kid his age to handle well. Taking a deep breath, he prepared to atone to an artist who was probably far more gifted than he'd ever been. One who'd most probably been one in hundreds to him. "Where did we meet?" he asked, needing to know all of it, to take it on fully, to have even a hope of making it right.

Shaking her head as she pulled back her phone, Harper

smiled again. That friendly, sexy smile that had hooked his groin before. How could he not remember the woman?

Even as he asked the question, he knew. His vision had been focused on himself. That was how.

"We've never met."

He saw her lips move. Heard the words. Stood there confused.

Her gaze turned inward, but still with a grin, as she said, "I was thirteen the first time I saw you dance. You were at a competition I was in, senior category. I was still junior. I'll never forget that day. You took first place overall."

Could have been any of a dozen states. And nearly a decade of years. He waited.

"When I saw you onstage... I just couldn't stop watching..."

And he'd blown her off without even giving her the respect of an introduction. There were probably hundreds more like her.

"You changed my life that day. You showed me that dance wasn't just about the technique, the lines and timing, the perfectly executed moves, though, of course, those are critical. But to be good, the best, took something that couldn't be learned. It had to come from inside. And flow out to the audience. An emotional art. I felt it. Emanating *from* you. And in me, too."

Wait. Eyes narrowed, he stared at her. She was telling him that she wasn't happy and healthy because of some horrible lesson he'd taught her young enough for it to shape her life for the better? His offstage actions in those days rarely resulted in happy endings for others.

"You're telling me my being onstage made you happy?"

"Your being onstage made millions of people happy."

Millions who hadn't known him.

Her words brought him back full circle.

With a difference. Those years onstage, and on the circuit…he'd actually managed to be a genuine positive influence on a female dancer.

One who'd done what he couldn't do, apparently. By the looks of things, Harper Michaels had made it big—without becoming a jerk.

Heaven help him, but he couldn't just walk away from that.

Not if she chose to hire him to design her deck.

And judging by the smile that was still lurking at the corners of her mouth, he figured chances were pretty good that she would.

Chapter Two

Harper couldn't believe Nathan Goldman was standing on her property. She had no idea how or why Nathan Goldman, renowned ballet dancer, had become Nathan Connolly, contractor/business owner.

He'd just disappeared. And no amount of internet searches had brought anything up on him. He'd been from San Francisco, as she remembered it.

And now was living in San Diego?

"Like I said, I'm somewhat strapped this morning, so if we could get a look at your space, and you tell me what it is that you're hoping to achieve, I can get to work on a design specific to you…"

The man walked while he talked, stepping around her on the side opposite of the one Aggie occupied, and she and her girl fell into step with him. Aggie in the middle.

A circumstance Harper applauded. Figuring Aggie knew that she would.

Nathan Goldman.

She'd thought of him so many times over the years.

Had a ton of questions to ask. So many things she wanted to know. And, as a choreographer, to discuss with him—the most accomplished male dancer California had ever produced.

His disappearance from the dance scene had seriously rocked her world.

But he was clearly not wanting to enter that sphere again. Hannah understood needing to protect one's privacy, and so she spent the next half hour talking cottage decks—treated woods, foundations, types of railings, and then they were down to the actual design.

"I want it to be shaped like Sage and Gray's," she told him. Straight along the length of the cottage, and then an L-shaped abutment that was more circular than straight, giving views of the ocean no matter where one was on the deck.

Nathan's focus as he walked around, taking measurements, making notes, attracted her. He'd given the same concentration onstage. As though he was in his own world, seeing things, knowing things, and she wanted to see and know, too.

Not in a creepy, or sexual, sense. It had never been that for her. She'd heard the stories, and had seen too much, to ever think of him in that way. The awareness went deeper than that.

Beyond human imperfections.

Ballet—all dance—was about being as perfect as you could be. The more accurate the form, the pull-up, the centering, the muscle control, the more balance was maintained, which allowed for exquisite movement. Nathan had come as close to reaching that flawless state as anyone she'd ever seen.

"If, instead of rounding, we give another support here, and one here, we could create a space that would not only allow anyone on the deck a view of the ocean, but if all seats were occupied, everyone could still see each other, too." The way he moved from spot to spot, stopped and turned toward the ocean from each one, and then, from every perspective, spun just enough to face every other space on the mock deck, had Harper visualizing him onstage, setting a piece for the dancers.

He was talking about the deck.

But his form, his straight back and shoulders, pulled-in core, the way he carried his weight, stepping as though he had none…not something most people would notice.

Not something she ever noticed in most people.

"Would you rather we go another route?" He'd stopped moving. Was watching her, his gaze clearer than it had been since she'd called his name.

"No," she told him, relaxing into the smile that she'd learned to wear onstage and off. "I love everything you've shown me."

More than he knew. What she'd give to be able to set a piece on him. To have her work brought to such exquisite life.

To meld her inner voice with his and watch him take her vision to levels higher than even she could see…

"Then if there's nothing else, I'll get this drawn up and should have a quote to you later today." He'd stepped away from the space where her new deck would be, and was heading toward the side of the house. "Email okay?" he asked.

He had hers. She'd had to leave it, and a cell number, when she made the appointment with his office. "Fine," she told him, following a few steps behind him.

And when he would have walked off, she said, "How soon can you have a team out here starting work?"

"If you like the quote, we can do a digital signing today and I can have a crew out within the next couple of days."

She nodded. Smiled bigger.

Needed so much more from him.
Had no right to ask for it.
And watched him go.

He should have just walked away. The second she'd called him Goldman.

At the latest, before talking to her about the deck she wanted added to the back of her cottage.

Why in the hell hadn't he walked away?

He'd changed her life. That damned phrase had hit him hard.

He'd assumed at first he'd done her wrong. So he'd planned to build her the deck she wanted, for free, because it was the only thing he had to offer her that could in any way make up for hurting her. Giving her a lifetime of peaceful moments on the ocean to make up for the despairing ones he'd given her in the past.

When he'd heard that he'd actually helped her…

He'd stayed for himself. Because he hadn't been able to walk away from a dancer who'd actually benefitted from having known him back then.

Giving to himself what he'd sworn he'd spend his life giving to others.

Or…

Maybe he was facing the ultimate test.

Could it be that he'd grown so much, improved himself to the extent that his resolve was ready to be tested? To prove that he'd not only meet the challenge, he'd succeed beyond his own expectation?

What that success might look like, Nathan had no idea.

Didn't stop him from pondering its existence, though, while he sat at his computer with lunch and built a virtual rendition of the deck he'd envisioned on the beach that morning.

He enjoyed his work immensely. Had everything he wanted.

Except maybe the wife-and-kid thing.

He'd eschewed public life for private, had spent years redesigning himself as he perfected a craft he'd always been curious about: building. Mastering the trade, learning design, getting his contractor's license, investing some savings in his start-up business.

And the past year—his decision to abstain from sex—was a starting place for becoming the person he wanted to be, had solidified the rest for him. He wanted a real relationship, not the casual associations that had always come easy to him. He wanted to be attracted to a woman, seek her out, not simply go out with her because she was fun and making it obvious that she'd like to be with him.

Even leaving the stage and all it entailed behind, he'd found himself going out with the same kinds of women, doing the same things, because women still gravitated to him. They issued clear invitations, and he responded naturally in the way he'd learned since puberty.

Only difference was, the emptiness left behind by those encounters had begun to far outshadow the highs he obtained from sex. Maybe they always had. He'd just been too full of himself to realize it.

He'd never had to think about whom he might want to ask out. Or to look for someone he'd like to be around. Would like to get to know better. Those who wanted to have fun, who came on to him, blocked the way for anyone else to get close.

And he hadn't stopped them.

After watching the Bartholomews rekindle the love

they'd almost lost, seeing them on the beach with their precocious little four-year-old, the way Gray looked at Sage one night while she'd been standing in the sunset, he was more certain than ever that he wanted something he'd never had. A real, meaningful relationship.

And, eventually, a homelife. Which, in his mind, meant parents who loved each other raising their kids.

Maybe.

If he found a woman to date. And then marry.

What in the hell was he doing thinking about dating while working on a quote?

Or putting that furniture around the deck space on the virtual drawing he'd made while filling in specs? And a built-in propane fireplace?

Harper Michaels had most definitely not asked for that.

She'd asked for his vision.

And there it was. Complete on the screen in front of him.

Nathan spent the next hour chewing random bites of a sandwich that had gone dry, biting off pieces of the browning banana on the paper plate he'd brought in with him, and working up a cost estimate.

With and without the fireplace.

She'd accept the quote or she wouldn't. Either way, he wouldn't have to see her again.

Unless he wanted to.

And therein lay the rub.

Could he do it? Take on California's dance darling and stay true to his own course? Be a man he could trust? And respect?

Thinking about the way he'd felt that morning when Harper had told him that he'd made her life better shot him right back to where he'd been then. Catapulted backward a decade, attempting to rewrite his own history. To make himself look better.

A dead-end street that could kill everything he'd worked so hard to achieve.

Kill the man he wanted to be.

He should price himself out of the job.

But what if he passed the test? What if he was just a contractor on a job, completing the project and leaving another satisfied customer in his past?

He wouldn't have to be on-site much. Just inspections and maybe a couple of times during early construction, to make certain that the shape was as exact as it was going to have to be to achieve the desired effect.

He wouldn't be able to guarantee that he could schedule those visits while Harper was away. He couldn't work his crew to a dancer's schedule.

Or even ask her schedule.

He should price himself out of the job.

He'd worked too hard for too long to risk failure.

He'd worked so hard for so long and he still didn't trust himself.

The only way to be the man he's sworn he'd become was to prove to himself that he had what it took to be that man.

Lunch hour had passed. As had the hour after it.

And Nathan had just hit Send.

A fireplace. She'd never even thought about the option. But Goldman had known. And the quote in front of her had just put a big bust on her resolve to find someone else to do her deck. She'd been online all afternoon, researching possibilities, looking at finished deck projects, reaching out to other deck builders who were willing to drive down the cliff to do the work. All of them had been.

It wasn't about the money. It was about the deck. An extension of the home that embraced her every single time she came home. She'd love to come home and have a place to be outside that was as comfortable and usable as Sage and Gray's was. She'd only been on their deck once, but couldn't get over how much it enhanced their daily lives.

The quality of living.

Her cottage, Aggie—they were Harper's immediate family. Her neighbors on Ocean Breeze were the closest she'd ever come to having real friends. Ones that she trusted.

The deck was like…adding a member to the family.

And Goldman had nailed her addition even beyond her own expectations.

Sitting on the floor of the private studio she'd purchased in a strip mall before she'd bought her cottage on Ocean Breeze, scrolling through the document on her phone, Harper wanted to be shocked at the sense of perfection coursing through her. Or even a little bit surprised.

Instead, she clicked to accept the quote without any further battle with herself. The man had come into her life at a critical point before. His essence had reached into her soul and made her way clear. And had resulted in her making a decision that probably saved her life.

One that had most definitely made her bone-deep happy.

The idea that he'd done it again, come into her life at a critical point, just wasn't a question.

How she was going to deal with having the man around was.

She revered the messages sent by the man's soul, his talent, his ability to tap into things that mattered far more than money, job or fame. Even in the form of the warmth and life added to a deck with a built-in fireplace.

But she didn't care for him outside of the professional world. Didn't like him as a person.

Even less after having met him.

And yet, on that deeper level, he still called to her.

It was like having an idol and seeing it smeared with clay at the same time.

What in the hell did she do with that?

The answer was clear as she quickly agreed to the quote, with fireplace, signing digitally so that the work could begin as soon as possible.

Accept what he had to offer. And steer clear of the rest.

She had no idea why Goldman had left the dance world. Could made an educated guess, though. He'd either suffered an injury that, in a regular walk of life, wouldn't phase him a bit, but had prevented him from executing the perfect moves that had made him famous, worshipped in the dance world.

Or he'd finally played with one too many women and gotten himself in trouble somehow. Maybe he'd broken the heart of someone with enough money to sway the cancelation of a distinguished career. Perhaps just by threatening to go public with Goldman's heartless choices.

Either way, it was none of her business.

While he'd been reticent, to say the least, he'd treated her with complete respect that morning. Even when her younger self had started the meeting off wrong by gushing all over him.

She'd just been so happy to see him alive and well.

There'd been a lot of talk about him at ballet barres that first year after he'd disappeared. From him dying in a motorcycle crash, to being on Broadway under an assumed name, though there'd been no explanation as to why he'd need to change his name.

Rumor had it that his mother had sold her studio, too.

All of which should not be fodder for Harper's thoughts. Determined to keep such meanderings at bay, she stood, took one last sip of water, restarted her music and, as she counted beats and the music rose, started at the beginning of the seven-minute piece she was creating to set on a premiere ballet company in Utah later in the month. She'd watched a plethora of tapes of the dancers. Knew their strengths—and weaknesses to stay away from—and was filled with possibilities as, still in the leggings and cut-sleeved shirt she'd donned that morning, she pirouetted, leaped and spun across her workspace.

Stopping now and then to make a note. Most of the piece would only ever be in her head and muscle memory, but where she might consider another choice as she watched others perform the various parts, she'd give herself some suggestions, things to watch for, substitutions that occurred to her as she was dancing.

And she stopped, about three-quarters of the way through the piece, to glance at her phone: 4:45 p.m. End of business day.

Had he responded?

Was she on his schedule?

When did she owe money, and how was she to make the payments?

She'd left her email app open. Nothing had come in. She saw her text notification icon active in the bar at the top of the screen. Clicked on it.

Breathing hard from the work she'd been doing, Harper still felt a leap of excitement as she read the words.

Crew ready to start tomorrow. Need your choices. Meet at Builder's Wholesale this evening?

Her thumbs flew on the screen as she responded. Time? Payment link?

She was hiring the man. Not bonding with him.

But when his response came back, suggesting they meet in a couple of hours, and included a link for her to click to make the down payment she'd agreed to in the quote, Harper had to take a minute. She leaned against the wall, staring out at the mirrored walls around her, at the dance floor, and her mind's eye saw Nathan Goldman there, as he'd been onstage so long ago.

She'd known all his competition pieces. One in particular, to Jeff Buckley's rendition of "Hallelujah," came to mind. The lyrics of the song, about love being a cold and broken hallelujah, had spoken so strongly to her she'd been unable to breathe.

It was as though he'd been in her home, watching from above. And the pain he'd emanated as he'd moved, she'd felt that, too.

The piece had ended with him on one knee, his other foot extended out in front of him, and his arms rounded in second position, a questioning look as, face tilted upward, he seemed to beseech powers stronger than he to show him his way.

He'd known the truth about love. That its power to conquer all, its longevity, was a fantasy.

And yet he'd shown her that a lack of true love didn't mean lack of life. There was still more out there. Things worth seeking.

He'd stood as the music ended and, after a completely silent pause, applause had exploded around her. His face had broken into a huge smile that had seemed to spread around the room to each and every person there. That smile had made a promise to her twelve-year-old heart.

Joy existed.

Right there.

In having done the dance.

Blinking, shaking her head, Harper reminded herself that the ability to see and execute movement had been inside her before she'd ever known Nathan Goldman existed.

He'd merely been the conduit who'd lit up the path before her so that she could see it clearly.

They needed to talk about lighting for the deck. Did she need to hire a separate electrician, or could he take care of that, too?

Texting back that she'd meet him at seven, Harper clicked the payment link, accessed her digital wallet and paid the bill.

She'd hired a business. A conduit.

Not a man.

Chapter Three

The woman showed up in the same clothes she had on that morning. A shirt with sleeves so roughly cut, it was obvious she'd taken about a minute to do them herself. Or someone else had.

The beige cotton fabric was big on her, hanging down past her thighs. And her flip-flops had paint stains on them.

As he watched her approach him at the entrance to the several-acre contractors' outlet mall, he figured everyone there would think she was the contractor, and he was the client. He'd taken the time to shower, change into black jeans, a button-down short-sleeved shirt and slip-ons.

No matter what the woman had said about his positive influence in her life, she'd clearly heard about his less stellar offstage behaviors. She was most definitely not out to impress him.

To draw him to her.

To hit on him.

He understood.

Was still insulted.

"I'm so sorry, did I keep you waiting?" she asked, rushing up to him. "I was in the studio working and time got away from me. And, of course, this would be the night that I hit every light…" The smile that accompanied her words set Nathan's world right again.

He didn't like that, either.

"You're in rehearsal?" he asked, holding the door for her to enter in front of him. The words came naturally. He knew what "in the studio" meant that late in the day.

And just that quickly had fallen back into a persona he'd vacated long ago.

So noted.

Determined to meet the challenge, to pass his test, feeling as though he could graduate from atoning to head into the next phase—living free in a decent life—Nathan's mental walls shot up, were in place, even before Harper had a chance to answer him.

"Utah City Ballet has commissioned me to set a piece for their seventy-fifth anniversary spring show. It's an original score, written by Dominici, and tells the story of six principals, each with an unreachable dream, who, through twists of fate that bring them together, all have their dreams come true."

Dominici. A modern composer already reaching Pachelbel levels of worldwide fame.

They entered the first shop they came to. An indoor lumberyard. He'd never done business with the place before because he had his own supplier. But showing different wood qualities to his new client distracted him from any thoughts about the world he'd once inhabited.

He talked about the hardness of different woods. Showed her examples.

Leaning in to run her finger along a particular board at the top of the pile of jarrah he'd been discussing, Harper asked, "What would you choose if you were making your own deck?"

A simple question. Nothing that could possibly explain his sudden step back. But Nathan played like he had to look around him to ponder that one. Before turning back to indicate the two-by-twelve she was still touching.

"This would be it," he said. "Not only because of the curled lines, bits of lighter yellowed color and grain. But because of its resistance not only against rot, but also insect attack. It's a type of eucalyptus plant and is imported from Australia." Back in his groove, he gave estimates of how the jarrah choice, along with various others, would raise or lower her overall cost. Talked about longevity. Ways different woods would need to be maintained.

And took notes as they moved from store to store, looking at railing styles, fireplace inserts, and rock, hearth and mantel choices. Like him, Harper seemed to know exactly what spoke to her, what she wanted, paying attention to the practical as well as to the aesthetic.

After they'd left the last store, and since he had a couple of brochures to go over with her before she made final choices, he suggested that they head across the street to finish up at a Mexican restaurant that he frequented fairly often.

While he most generally met with clients in his office, or their homes, he'd occasionally done business over lunch hours in the city.

And after his stale sandwich and banana he hadn't finished for lunch, he was hungry.

"Unless you need more time to ponder," he offered, as he held the door leading them outside to a sky that had darkened while they'd been inside.

Parking lot lights stood tall and bright, surrounding them, and still, as Harper smiled at him as she walked past him through the door, he felt as though the world had grown more intimate.

A public restaurant had to be it. Not her home. Not his office.

Not anywhere he'd be alone with the woman who'd been set in his path for his own growth. Temptation, familiarity with a former life, even that smile, were not going to stop him.

Failure wasn't an option.

Harper allowed her smile to disappear as she sat in the booth across from Nathan Goldman and studied the menu. All the delicious scents coming at her were a distraction. And the enchilada plates, garnished with a hefty scoop of sour cream, tempted her mercilessly.

She was being bombarded with the smells of all the food she wasn't going to eat. Not only did reading the menu offer her a chance to get through the physical onslaught, but it also gave her a break from being fully, one hundred percent completely aware of the man sitting across from her.

So she stayed engaged, in spite of the fact that her choice had been made before she'd walked in the door, right up until their waitress came, tablet in hand, ready to take their order.

"I'll have the chili lime salmon," she said. "Sour cream on the side." She'd have a taste, but couldn't have the stuff melting all over her plate, saturating the food beneath it.

Her dinner companion ordered the enchilada plate. Just to dig at her.

The thought flew in, and then right back out again. He had no reason to taunt her.

But as a dancer, he'd know how hard—and critical it was—for Harper to have a healthy relationship with food, and still maintain the body through which she created beauty.

And when they were alone again, and he nodded at her

and said, "Salmon, unsaturated fat, with anti-inflammatory properties to help reduce swelling and aid in muscle regeneration as well as being a good source of protein," she was back to thinking he'd ordered his dinner quite on purpose.

To taunt her?

The stories she'd heard about him, the tears she'd witnessed in women's dressing rooms, had painted a picture of a man just that heartless.

She had no hint of a smile on her face as she stared over at him. How could someone with so much artistic talent that it even oozed from wood creations be without soul?

"So, what? You ordered the enchiladas just to be mean?" She shook her head even as she said the words. Couldn't believe she'd really uttered them.

"It's my standing order every time I come here," he said, as though taking no offense at her rudeness.

Leaving her feeling like she was the one filled with too much self-importance.

"They why make the comment?" she continued anyway.

With raised eyebrows he seemed about to say something. Stopped. Then with a shrug, said, "My mom. She was a fanatic about everything she put in her body. Trying to preserve, for as long as she could, the only thing that made her happy. Being able to perform. We had salmon three times a week when I was growing up."

She'd heard stories about his mother, of course. Had seen her, many times, from a distance. Had even seen her onstage once, in a production of *The Nutcracker*, when Harper had been about four.

"Was it only you and her?" she asked. She'd heard that it had been. Just hadn't known if that was just the public persona the two traveled with. Like the name Goldman for him.

Cecelia for her.

"Yep. My dad died before I was born."

He showed no emotion at the words.

Because life had started that way for him? He'd never known anything different?

"I'm sorry."

He shrugged again. "Don't be. They weren't married. From what I've gleaned, he was one of my mother's benefactors. I was the result of a kind thank-you, not a relationship. He was decades older than her. And left his entire estate to the Metropolitan Ballet."

Wow. She *hadn't* heard that.

And felt like a total creep. Wished she could take back the harsh words she'd blurted. She said "I'm sorry" again, instead.

"No reason." He grinned then, and looked nothing at all like the smiling man she'd seen on the big screen as she'd stood in the auditorium and watched him dance live from a distance. Most particularly when he sobered, glanced down, then back up, and said, "You know, it *was* kind of mean. Me knowing your situation, and ordering the enchiladas."

Her mouth dropped open.

"Not purposely so," he quickly asserted. "I grew up eating with dancers. I know that diet is an acute part of the life, I just never adhered to it when I went out to eat. Even back then. At home, I had no choice. There was nothing else in the house. But..." He shrugged again, a movement that was so expressive in itself, and said, "I never even thought about how hard that must have been for those who couldn't indulge." He stood.

Left the table without a word.

Shocked, Harper stared after him. Had he actually just walked out on her?

Was leaving her to eat alone? And foot the bill for both

meals? Did he think, if he wasn't there to see, she'd have some enchilada? Or have it taken away so it didn't tempt her?

The idea was ludicrous. She cared far more about living the dream than she did about food. Trying to pretend that her feelings weren't hurt, that she wasn't hugely offended and embarrassed, too, she looked for their waitress. She'd cancel Goldman's order and ask for hers to go.

And if anyone felt sorry for her for having been walked out on…well…they did. Having spent most of her life with the barbed looks of jealousy stabbing her back, she'd perfected the art of letting things roll off her.

Onstage, the bright lights prevented her from making out faces in the audience. Only she, the music and other dancers in count with her existed. And in the rest of her life, she'd learned to not look.

Which was why she didn't immediately see the black jeans and white shirt heading back in her direction. She was only just in the process of comprehending that Nathan Goldman was still there as he bent to slide back in across from her. "Two chili lime salmons coming up," he said.

He was smiling.

She smiled, too.

And then quit looking at him.

He couldn't help that everyone in his sphere had revered and spoiled him from birth. Couldn't change or have stopped the adulation he'd been receiving from strangers since he'd won awards at his first national dance competition when he was five.

And a grown man making excuses for himself, rather than taking responsibility, did not point him in the direction of success.

Driving home after dinner that night, Nathan pictured the celebratory cocktail waiting for him at home. He'd done it.

Met the challenge. Come out…not behind.

He'd learned something key about himself. That he sometimes had a lack of awareness of the personal needs of those around him. He'd corrected the failing in the moment. And would do his best to be aware of his shortcoming in the future.

He'd also finished all business with Harper Michaels. There'd been no hesitation in her decision-making. All brochure items she liked were circled. He knew she preferred lighter to darker in terms of color scheme. And wanted the best underside supplies, those that wouldn't visible, used on her deck as well.

He'd learned a valuable lesson to propel him into his future as a better man. Perhaps one of the most critical. And last.

The time with her that day had allowed him to step back into his old self through a different perspective. To see something he'd missed in his self-improvement project.

Meeting her *had* been a test. A challenge.

He'd gone back into his old world.

And he'd come out an improved version of himself.

Challenge met.

He was still feeling pretty damned good about himself—looking forward to a real future—when, out on his own deck in a gated San Diego community, looking at the privacy walls surrounding his backyard, his phone buzzed a text message.

Clicking almost eagerly, thinking it was his most recent client with a last-minute change, he glanced at the unknown number. And read the text.

From a Realtor. One who'd gleaned his information from

a form he'd filled out that morning online before heading to Ocean Breeze. The one who had made the cottage's information more fully available to him.

Had that only been fourteen hours ago?

Seemed like part of a lifetime had passed.

Because he'd fully left one behind?

The Realtor wanted to know if he was interested in seeing the cottage. She could show it to him the following morning.

Shaking his head, he held his phone while he took a sip of his one shot of Scotch, mixed with a good dose of water, mentally preparing his polite refusal. Then it hit him—he was going to be at Ocean Breeze anyway. Had arranged to have his crew meet him on-site after Harper Michaels had left for the morning ballet class she took three times a week.

He wasn't going to buy the place. Obviously.

But he could take a look. Get some ideas of what he wanted. And...thinking of others, not just himself...he wouldn't be wasting the Realtor's time because he'd give his ideas to her as they came to him, have her look for a different place on the water for him.

Lord knew he was ready to get out of the walled enclosure he'd called home for the past decade. All he'd been after when he'd bought the place had been privacy.

And comfort, of course. He had a pool with an outdoor fireplace. Had a fireplace in his large bedroom suite upstairs, too.

He'd never used either one of them.

But on a beach...with ocean air blowing in...

Clicking the response bar, Nathan smiled as he set up the meeting.

Chapter Four

Harper skipped her morning ballet session. While attending class was as necessary to her equilibrium as sleeping at night, she could do a full-out hour herself once she got to her studio. Or take an afternoon class. And work later that night.

She just didn't feel good leaving Aggie home alone with strangers arriving to work on their cottage. Nor did she want to be a problem neighbor. She'd be present to see who was taking on the job, and to make certain that they knew to park on her property, or across the street, and to stay up by her place.

Things that Goldman would know. And likely tell his crew.

Harper just wasn't one to trust her homelife to others.

After doing her wake-up barre, she showered, dressed in a short-sleeved green leotard with multicolored flowered leggings and took Aggie out for her beach walk. Telling her about the day's plans. Figuring she'd hang with the soulful creature while they both acclimated to having their space invaded.

And then, "You want to come to work with Mama today?" she asked, her heart warming as Aggie's big black head turned up to her. Taking in every word.

"You want to go?" She clarified the answer she determined she'd just received. Smiled as Aggie's tail wag verified her translation.

And she was just turning back toward her place, waste bag properly disposed in one of the cans on the beach for that purpose, when she caught movement out of the corner of her eye. Up at one of the unoccupied, and as yet unrenovated, cottages toward the middle of the two-mile stretch along Ocean Breeze.

The place had clearly been vacant since long before Harper had moved in. Old boarded-up windows were the giveaway. She'd never ventured up toward the building, nor had she heard anyone else ever mention it.

So why was a guy, based on build, cropped hair and pants with tucked-in shirt, walking along the side of the run-down home before eight in the morning? Pulling her phone out from the pocket in her leggings, Harper kept her eye on the old cottage, or rather, the being moving around it.

No wait, not one. There was a second. A woman who'd just appeared around the corner of the building from the far side. She was in the sand in a skirt and loose blouse, her shoes dangling from the fingers of one hand, her other hand reaching for the man, linking her arm through his.

Had they just…in the sand…

Tapping her phone screen, she opened her camera, snapped some pictures. Just in case they needed evidence. She was ready to call the police.

And was aware that she tended to overreact when it came to the sanctity of Ocean Breeze. Strangers on the beach wasn't unheard of. Hell, she was bringing three of them down for the next many days as they built her new deck. And residents had visitors.

But so early in the morning? Outside a dilapidated and deserted property?

Moving slowly toward home, she watched the couple—alert for any signs of vandalism—until they were out of sight. They'd headed toward the front of the cottage. The street.

Aggie didn't seem bothered by the disturbance. Just to be sure, Harper tapped her phone screen, opened her photo gallery, enlarged the most recent picture.

And felt like a fool.

She knew the man. He was on the beach, primarily, because of her. And the woman? Goldman was a womanizer, to be sure, but he'd always had a level of class about him. She didn't see him doing it in the sand on private property that didn't belong to him.

Nor would he be damaging anything.

Obviously, he'd hooked up with someone after their dinner the night before. The hours had become a new day sooner than the couple had wanted to part, and he'd brought her along to see that his crew was there and settled in before taking his current arm weight out to breakfast. They were passing time until his crew arrived.

Feeling as though the photos she'd taken were burning her eyes and fingers, too, Harper quickly deleted them. Admonished herself for having taken them.

And even more for letting them get to her.

Letting *him* take any space at all in her thoughts.

She was buying a deck.

Goldman no longer existed.

Aggie needed her breakfast.

And Nathan Connolly had a right to his privacy. Even if he made choices that left broken hearts in his path. In the years she'd followed Goldman around the circuit, she'd never seen or heard of him approaching women. Or coming on to them. He'd just callously, though from all accounts gently, accepted what was offered. And discarded it when he was done.

None of which had anything at all to do with Harper.

Or her new, very expensive back porch.

Could she be any more obvious?

The Realtor, Nancy Harshman, held a hand up to Nathan in the driveway, silently asking for him to steady her as she stood on one leg at a time to put her shoes back on.

She'd been using any excuse she could find to touch Nathan since about ten seconds after they'd met in front of the cottage for sale on Ocean Breeze.

From holding his hand too long in their original shake to holding on to his elbow as they'd walked on the uneven sand in the back.

She had lovely red manicured toes.

Perfectly shaped calves. And everything else.

And…he had absolutely nothing.

No desire whatsoever to explore what she was clearly offering. He wouldn't have done so, regardless. Not as close as he was to reaching his self-imposed personal goal of celibacy. But the fact that he didn't have to fight with himself to turn away…or even remind himself that he chose to do so, was telling.

Holding the graceful fingers in his hand while Nancy bent over, exposing her slim skirted backside to him, Nathan…didn't even hint at growing hard. Panic infused him. A wave of cold, followed by hot. Hints of nausea. Had he gone too far? Disciplined his psyche to the point of losing all desire to…

Was that it, then?

He'd sought to have a better life, only to be left with less than he'd ever had before?

His smartwatch vibrated against his wrist. Snatching him away from irrational mental wanderings to remind him of his upcoming appointment.

With ballerina Harper Cecelia.

Harper Michaels.

He had a flash of memory of her at the dinner table the night before, lifting her napkin to her lips. And knew that he still liked women. He hadn't wanted *her*. She was way too much. But he'd definitely experienced a momentary fondness for those lips...

And...the way he'd reacted to the woman when they'd first met...yeah, he was fine.

Nancy had both feet back on the ground. Was still holding on to his hand as she smiled at him and said, "I know you said you've decided you don't want this particular property, that you want something on a private beach, but maybe not with quite as much land, or the steep drive down, but I seriously think you should consider buying this place as an investment."

She still held his hand, but her tone, the look in her eye, had definitely sharpened. For a second there he saw her going in for the kill.

She'd been playing him. Using her wiles, thinking he was being taken in by them, to get a sale. He dropped her hand, but before he could politely thank her for her time and head to his car, she said, "Just hear me out a second, Nathan."

Something sincere in her tone caught his attention. He looked up at her. She met his gaze head-on. "You're a contractor," she said. "You could do the work yourself, or with your crew, at half of what it would cost someone else. If you've got materials left over from other jobs, or are able to get them at discounted rates, even better. It'd take what, a month, or so? The bones of this place are excellent…"

His words. He remembered saying them to her as he'd taken one last look around, absorbing the place, before they'd headed off to inspect the outside.

"…and then you put it up for sale. I can guarantee you, fixed up, I'd have multiple buyers for this place today…"

And she'd make a hefty profit. Commission for selling it to him in the first place. Then at least selling Realtor's commission, and probably buyer's, too, if all went as smoothly as she seemed to think it would.

Assuming he listed the place with her when he was ready.

Meeting her eye to eye, he considered her words. Ran some mental calculations. Trying to ignore the rush of enthusiasm that was attempting to be put in the mix.

He was always jazzed to make a good profit. Fairly.

There was close proximity to Harper to consider.

But…not really. Not if he had work going on her deck and his own place at the same time. He'd only be around Ocean Breeze a few weeks longer than planned.

"It's the time of year to take on such a project," Nancy said, still eye to eye with him. "April's nice balmy weather, you'll be indoors so the rain won't be as much of an issue, and you'd be done in time to sell before water and outside temperatures make spending time on the beach more of an option."

She knew her stuff.

And having worked on outdoor decks in the area for a number of years, Nathan recognized the accuracy of her assessment.

Her gaze softened into more of a friendly tease. "You aren't saying yes."

He wasn't saying no, either.

"Give me some time to think about it."

"I've got another showing of it this afternoon." Such an obvious sales pressure tactic. Nathan was a bit disappointed in her.

Gaze narrowing, he stared her down.

"It wasn't on my radar until you'd sent the message. The brokerage I work for just got the listing and I hadn't yet seen it. But I check our message board more regularly than most. I have another client who's been looking, who is ready to write an offer, but because I saw you first, I had to give you a chance."

She hadn't known, until he'd met her there that morning, that he'd had no intention of buying the place.

"And I make you more money than someone who wants to buy it to live in," he caught up quickly. She'd get more than three times the commission as the second sale, post renovation, would come with a much higher price tag.

"Selling it before another agent does makes me more money than if I don't get the sale."

If he didn't commit immediately, he was going to lose the chance.

After confirming that there were no pending offers ahead of him, he made a full price offer on the spot. With the caveat that they get the paperwork in immediately and ask for a two-hour response time from the seller. He didn't want to be embroiled in a bidding war.

They might not get the quick response. Sellers were only required to adhere to buyer's conditions after the contract was accepted and signed.

But, once committed, Nathan was going to do everything he ethically could to ensure that he got what he wanted.

Harper didn't speak to Nathan alone that morning. Her decision to make sure that she didn't—a fallout from the private fool she'd made of herself on the beach that morning—hadn't even come into play. He'd been all about business. Introducing her to his crew. Giving a rundown to them in front of her, referring to her for any input, and then leaving them to it.

He'd had an important meeting to get to.

A personal one, she'd known.

She'd seen the woman waiting in his car as she'd pulled out of her own driveway while he was marking off postholes with his men.

She'd had the harebrained thought to warn the woman, but had come to her senses even without the questioning glance Aggie sent her from the passenger seat as she paused before switching gears from Reverse to Drive.

She didn't hear from the contractor all day.

Other than a text from his company letting her know the crew had left for the day, giving a basic summary of the work completed, and the time they'd be back the next day.

A message she'd been told to expect. All part of the Connolly package.

She refused to allow herself to think about the man himself, even as her mind wandered anyway, wondering if he was with the same blonde that night whom she'd seen him with that morning. Were they, right then, sitting across a booth from each other in some plush restaurant overlooking the ocean? She put a sweater and flip-flops on to head out to the beach with Aggie. After dinner was one of her favorite times to be out, to breathe ocean air, listen to the waves and reflect on the day. Stepping carefully down the temporary steps the Connolly crew had erected for her use during construction, she had another flash of the man she'd once known as Goldman, walking on the beach with the blonde's arm through his, her shoes dangling...

And turned to Aggie. "You want a run or walk?"

The girl had been cooped up in the studio for most of the day, and while she had a big comfy bed, a basket of toys and a doggy door that allowed her to come and go in their private courtyard, the space was hardly big enough for one lawn chair.

She could squat and go, but doing her business was a side product of Aggie's outdoor time. As big as she was, the girl needed exercise if she was going to stay healthy long into the future.

Taking Aggie's even steps beside her as a choice not to run, Harper headed down to the water, to walk along the ocean.

Scott's place next door had the light on over the kitchen sink—but otherwise looked dark.

"Looks like you'll get to see Morgan and Angel," she said to her girl, her tone bright and eager.

Since Iris had moved in with Scott—her place was closer to his sister's, but his was bigger—that light on usually meant the couple was out on the beach with their two four-legged girls.

Turning those gorgeous brown eyes on Harper, Aggie wagged her tail. She knew the tone of voice, even if she didn't comprehend all the words.

Harper was certain that Aggie also understood that Morgan and Angel stood for the corgi and miniature collie.

Both less than thirty pounds, but Aggie's closest friends, too.

Could also be that the couple was all the way down at

the far end of the beach with Sage, Gray and little Leigh. While Harper adored the little girl, and was quite fond of Sage, she didn't ever head down that far.

She'd been friendly with Gray when he'd first moved in with Scott, but he'd been going through a hard time, had not welcomed company, and Harper had never really gotten to know him all that well.

She'd heard great things about him, though.

Just didn't feel comfortable invading their family unit.

When there was a gathering on the beach, though, she grabbed up as much Leigh time as she could get. The four-year-old was smart as a whip. Even more astute. And filled with a sense of adventure that Harper envied.

Aggie's single *Ruff*, followed by tail-wagging so robust that Harper's backside was taking a soft beating, drew her attention from the dusk-shadowed stretch of beach along the water where they'd been walking to the answering barks coming from up in the sand by the cottages.

Juice, Dale's apricot-colored standard poodle service dog, stood wagging her tail, while Morgan and Angel darted down to Harper and Aggie.

Scott and Iris were on Dale's deck, clearly having a beer with the bearded, athletically built writer—based on the bottles visible in their hands.

She was about to keep walking, to mind her own counsel, when Iris called out and waved her up. At first, Harper hadn't thought the other woman liked her much—something she was so used to she almost took it for granted now—but since Iris had nursed Scott after a surfing accident, and subsequently moved in with him, the photographer had become the closest female friend Harper had ever had.

Not that they were all that close. Harper wouldn't know how to pull that off.

But enough so that Harper didn't want to turn down the invitation, didn't want to offend Iris or risk losing a relationship that mattered to her.

As the four dogs played in the sand, Harper chatted with her neighbors, declining the beer offered to her. But she sat a bit, enjoying the conversation.

Right up until Scott said, "Did you all hear another cottage sold? The boarded-up one mid-beach."

"Who bought it?" Dale lifted his beer as he spoke, as though to toast the new owner.

Shaking his head, Scott replied with, "No clue. Sage thought Leigh might be running a fever after preschool and called Cassie…" The pediatrician on the opposite end of the beach from Sage and Gray, one of the first residents of Ocean Breeze, who always seemed to have answers to questions before anyone else. "…Leigh's perfectly fine, but when Cassie went down to take a look at her, she said she'd heard a guy looked at the cottage this morning and made an offer on the spot."

Harper stared at him. Feeling heat creep up her skin.

As dread filled her stomach.

Chapter Five

Nathan found out just how quickly news spread on Ocean Breeze when he stopped at the Bartholomews' after inspecting his last jobsite Wednesday night. Harper's place.

He'd hoped she'd be there. It was only polite to let her know that he'd be an Ocean Breeze owner, but only for a couple of months with no plans to live there.

Instead, he'd passed by the cottage he'd paid cash for that afternoon and made his second planned stop. To let Sage and Gray know the same.

Only to find out that they'd known the place had sold. Just hadn't known to whom. They'd been thrilled, though not as much when they'd heard that he didn't plan to live there. Gray had driven down with him, though, eager to take a walk through the place with him once he'd known Nathan already had the keys. The title work would take a few days, but the current owner had offered the keys as soon as the cash had been transferred.

He had no idea who the person was. He had wanted to thank him or her, but had only seen the corporation name under which it had been owned. Turned out to be the same source from which Gray, Sage, and he'd been told Scott and Iris, too, had all bought their places over the years.

Gray had had some good pointers, having just done a lot

of the renovation work on his place himself the previous fall, and Nathan was eager to get started. He'd driven his truck, with tools in the bed to do some basics that night, but as soon as he dropped Gray off, he headed back down to Harper's place.

He had no obligation to her other than quality work on the deck she'd ordered. Owed her nothing. But he didn't feel right, being on her private beach without her knowing he was there.

It was just a thing…maybe something she'd put out the day before, or something he'd gleaned during his years being absorbed by her world…but for someone who lived onstage, privacy was as important to survival as food.

Food kept the physical body going. A secluded space fed an emotional state that poured itself out to hundreds and thousands of strangers under bright stage lights week after week, year after year.

She didn't answer his knock. Thinking she was outside with Aggie, he walked around the cottage, taking another glance at the work his men had completed that day, and saw her just sitting there. On the makeshift steps he'd built to spec himself the night before, and had the Connolly delivery truck pick up from his garage early that morning.

"It's after-hours," she said, when she saw him standing there. Aggie, who was on the sand in the middle of the Connolly framework, lifted her big head. Stared at him.

Neither of them looked all that friendly. But then, it was dark, and the shadows left by the moon's glow made faces hard to read. "I know."

"If you think you're going to come down here and find the kind of welcome you're used to getting with women, you're mistaken." No *mistaking* the tone of voice that time.

And while, granted, the man she'd known in the past

had given her reason to form such an opinion of him, her comment still rankled.

More than it should have.

Standing his ground, he folded his arms and said, "Pardon me?"

"I saw you this morning with the woman I'm now assuming is your Realtor since I've just been told that a man saw the place this morning, wrote an offer on the spot and has already taken possession of the place. It was like a blast from the past. Seeing whoever was partnering you onstage staking claim off it as well." She was looking out toward the ocean. Not at him.

Nathan felt stabs that shouldn't have mattered as much as they did.

"Of course, back then, I was also privy a time or two to the tears when you walked away. And heard stories of a whole lot more."

He'd assumed. The confirmation was still a blow. For no reason other than that he'd left that life behind and since meeting Harper on the beach the morning before, hadn't been happy about the commingling of his past and present.

Obviously, his celebration the night before had been premature. He had more to get through before he'd completed the atonement obstacle course that would set him free. At least he hoped it would.

Meeting Harper in his current world had to be that last challenge.

Fate didn't just screw with people for grins.

Nor did words erase years of negative behavior.

"I can't help how women react to me," he started in. Stopped when she made a sound of disgust and looked straight at him.

"Seriously?" she asked, her tone brimming with not good things.

With an acknowledging bow of his head, he continued. "However, I can assure you that this morning, I did not respond, nor do I intend to do so. I was invited out to dinner tonight, to celebrate the sale, and declined."

At which Harper's gaze returned to the ocean, and he said, "I appreciate you voicing your concerns, however, and guarantee you that I will not be looking for anything but deck feedback and payment of my bill from you. Nor will I respond in kind if you suddenly find yourself sucked in by my irresistibly powerful force and try to get friendly with me." The last was most definitely tongue-in-cheek. A barb headed in her direction. Small retaliation for speaking a truth that hurt. And also the complete truth.

Turning her head again, she smiled at him. Like she had the night before when he'd returned to the table after changing his order. "I deserved that. And I apologize."

Perching himself on top of a four-foot pile of deck boards, he said, "So when did you hear that I bought the place?"

"Fifteen minutes ago."

"I stopped by to tell you." He owed her nothing. And yet he'd known cluing her in was important. "I probably should have called."

"You don't owe me anything."

"But it bothers you, doesn't it? Having someone bring your professional world into your private one?"

Her mouth opened. Closed. She didn't look away.

Neither did Aggie.

Nathan sat there, under scrutiny from both of them. "Which is part of the reason I got out," he told her. More than he'd ever told anyone.

Or had intended to share. Ever.

"I love what I do," she said, seemingly speaking to the night air. "And I use up every ounce of energy I have doing it."

She could have been making small talk. Telling him she was too tired to be having a tentatively deep conversation. That she had nothing left for his presence in her space that evening.

"This is where you fill back up," he said softly. Because he knew.

"No one here has seen me dance, or seems to have any interest in or knowledge of the performance arts. I'm not even sure how many of them know what I do for a living."

That in itself was telling. And called out to a part of Nathan he'd forgotten was there.

"Or maybe they just respect your space," he offered, though he had no idea why. The response didn't speak to what she'd been telling him. It spoke to what he wanted to tell her.

That he'd respect her need to just be Harper on the beach. With her neighbors.

With him.

He felt like he'd scored a victory when his response seemed to draw another look from her. Until she said, "Why here?"

For the investment. The words were there. True. "The walls around me feel too tight."

What the hell? He was spewing private thoughts now?

"There are other beaches."

Right. Nancy Harshman had already called him with a couple of possibilities. At the same time she'd offered a dinner meeting to go over the listings.

"I saw a place for sale here when I was working on the

Batholomew deck. Kept thinking about it. Looked yesterday and it had sold. But the cottage mid-beach was available."

All fact. Which was where he chose to reside. With the facts.

Letting in other aspects, esoteric things that would never be pinned down, understood, controlled, was forbidden to him. *By* him.

He knew better than to allow the free-for-all.

"It speaks to you, too." Harper's tone had changed noticeably. Softening. Filled with a confidence conceived through understanding. "Your spirit craves the sense of okayness that breeds down here."

No. Nathan studied the postholes, twelve inches in diameter each, filled with cement holding firmly to the four-by-four posts that would support the deck. He wasn't getting all woo-woo. Knew better than to trust any part of himself that filled him with his own importance. Like he was better…more…than others.

Finding out the truth, that he'd become less as a person than everyone else he knew…

"I'd like to make a deal with you." Her words drew his attention. Not his gaze.

"Our deal is already signed."

Harper just kept on speaking, as though he hadn't. "I don't tell anyone here about your first career, or anything I know about you from that world, and you don't ever mention me in my professional capacity. Not ever. To anyone. Here or otherwise. Except Aggie. You can talk to her, though I'd rather you didn't. But not Morgan or Angel or any of the others."

Her deal…was beneficial to him as a contractor who didn't want his past life to become present in any way. He'd had no intention of talking about her to anyone. She was a client. But it was her mention of the dogs that had Nathan still sitting there.

"I mention you to Morgan or Angel, both of whom I know at this point, and our deal is off?"

He should be smiling. He wasn't.

More so, when Harper turned her gaze on him. He couldn't see much, pinpoints of light where her eyes were, but the steadiness of those little arrows held him steady as she said, "Canines don't speak English, they speak spirit and soul. Aggie tends to mine. I don't need the others aware of things that don't call for their gifts. Their full attention is needed elsewhere."

He wanted to laugh. With her, not at her. To believe that the woman was living in a world as make-believe as the stories she portrayed onstage.

For some reason, he didn't crack a smile as he said, "Deal."

Then he stood up, told her to have a good night, and left without letting her know that his presence on her beach was only temporary.

He'd intended to.

He just hadn't.

And didn't know why not.

Key members of the Utah City Ballet were in town on Thursday and with Dale covering Aggie duty for her, she left for the studio before any Connolly crew had arrived, and was gone until well after dark. She came home to find Aggie fed and waiting to greet her, and, after a quick and very short walk on the beach, fell into bed with movements running through her mind. She'd barely glanced at the deck in progress. Only enough to get around it in the dark.

Aggie, who always knew when Harper was lost in work, jumped onto the queen-size mattress and lay down gently, up against Harper's back.

Harper's last waking thought was Aggie's good-night sigh.

Then she was startled out of sleep by the sound of the girl's low, threatening growl.

Disoriented, she stumbled out of bed in a T-shirt and panties, and grabbed for her phone and a vial of pepper spray. She'd brought up Scott's contact, with her finger hovering over Call, by the time she reached the door of her room. Waiting for emergency crews to get down the hill didn't seem prudent in the immediately dangerous, befuddled moment. And Scott and Iris were right next door.

Ahead of her by several bounds, Aggie was standing at the kitchen door. Ears alert, head cocked.

Not growling.

That's when Harper looked toward the window and saw that dawn had arrived. Just barely. The sun wasn't up yet, its glow had begun to spread over the new day.

She felt as though she'd just laid down. Grabbing a calf-length black sweater off the hook by the door, she wrapped herself in it and then peeked outside.

Goldman was there. In jeans, a short-sleeved white T-shirt and a camel-colored leather tool belt strapped across his hips. He wasn't being noisy. Running power tools or hammering. He was going through boards, one by one, laying some in a pile by the newly roped-off deck space. And tossing others, one at a time, to lay by themselves in the sand.

She was considering heading back to bed, where she could put a pillow over her head and pretend that there was no world out *there*. But Aggie let out her half cough half bark that meant she wanted to do her business. And the sound was apparently loud enough for Goldman to hear. He froze, board ready for launch, and glanced toward the window.

He finished his throw. She'd give him that. Hadn't looked again.

But he'd seen her.

And Aggie was certain it was her time to pee. Almost an hour ahead of schedule.

With another intense day stretching ahead, before the Utah dancers left to catch a plane home late that afternoon, Harper needed that hour in bed. Instead, grabbing a pair of sweats from the dirty clothes in the laundry room, she pulled them on and, sweater flowing loosely around her, took Aggie out the front door, as she'd done the night before.

And also just like that journey in the dark, the girl ran around the cottage to the patch of artificial turf made for pets that she and Scott had had installed on the acre between their two cottages. And then headed out back.

Harper, who couldn't just leave her out there, followed her around to see Aggie standing at attention, directly in front of Goldman. Not threateningly. Just…watching him.

He, on the other hand, picked up another board, seemed to be looking it over from end to end, flipped it, looked at the other side, and then tossed it.

"Good morning," she said, and before he could respond, she added, "What are you doing here?"

"Working." The word came out in a bit of a huff as he picked up another board and tossed it without any inspection at all.

Duh. Working. Better question would have been, *Why?* She needed to get in the shower. Shake up her brain a little.

He just…looked so good. Tight jeans. That tool belt thing, drawing attention to…yeah well, everyone knew where tool belts hung.

"Your crew call in sick?" *Go inside, woman.*

Too tired to pay heed to the silent admonishment, Harper approached until she was standing right next to Aggie, her hand resting lightly on top of the girl's neck. Goldman threw a glance in their direction, but barely. "Nope."

She should go. "Can I ask what you're doing?"

Without even sparing her a look, he picked up another board. "I'd say you just did."

Of course she had. Was the man trying to be annoying? She continued to watch him exclusively as she asked, "Are you going to answer?" She wasn't annoyed.

But he might be.

"Every delivery has bad boards. We put them aside and get credit for them." He continued to go through the pile as he spoke.

"And you go to every new job, every delivery and inspect the boards?" Seemed like overkill to her, but what did she know about running a construction business. "You don't trust your crew to know what boards are good ones?"

At that, he stopped, stood the board in his hands on end beside him and held it there. "They know to discard those that are warped or that have serious gouges or bad spots in them," he assured her. And continued to stand there, looking at her. Almost as though daring her to ask the next, painfully obvious, question.

She suddenly didn't want to disappoint him. "So why are you here at dawn, doing it for them?"

With a challenging jut to his chin, he said, "Because I have a client who is delighted by the jarrah's yellow hues and I want to make certain that every board on the one-of-a-kind deck we're building gives her what will bring her the most pleasure. In addition, she likes the curl design, also inherent to the jarrah, and since she's paying top dollar for the imported wood, I need to make certain she gets what she pays for."

She stared at him. Had nothing pithy to say. Aggie moved beneath her hand, and she loosened her hold, petting the thick fur of her housemate's neck. "Oh, well, I have to go get showered. I'm due in the studio at eight." An hour and a half into the future. Turning, she took a step toward the side of the cottage from which she'd come. But turned back toward the total silence behind her. "Thank you," she told the man who was watching her, not his wood.

"Class this morning?" he asked, not acknowledging her gratitude in any way.

She shook her head. "Principals from Utah Ballet are here. Yesterday and today."

His expression changed. Sharpened. Softened. Then tightened. "You're setting the piece on them."

Not a question. She nodded anyway. Caught a glint in his eye. Not of longing, but of…knowing. Understanding. Without another word, she turned her back and left him standing there with his wood.

Her wood.

Wood. She'd once heard an angry, crying dancer make a derogatory comment about what Nathan Goldman could do with his "wood."

No wood.

Just boards for her deck.

Chapter Six

He'd been purposefully quiet. Had hoped to be there and gone before his crew arrived ready to work, but also without disturbing the home's occupant.

His crews were used to him budding in for what they called "esoteric" reasons. They didn't question his choices.

And he hadn't wanted to have to explain them.

To anyone.

He hadn't factored in the monster dog.

A mistake he would not make again.

The early morning stop gave him a head start on his day, and by eleven, Nathan was heading back out to Ocean Breeze. Not to Harper's place, but to his own. His mind was spinning with ideas, and he didn't want to be anywhere else.

Until Juan, the foreman on the Michaels project, called to say that the order that was to have been delivered at the beginning of the next week for Harper's chimney was on back order. Either she was going to have to wait a minimum of a month, or make a different choice. Juan rattled off product numbers for several similar options that could go out immediately.

And, of course, it was Friday. If he didn't get the order in that day, it wouldn't be processed until Monday—the scheduled day of delivery. Add on another two days for the rock to ship and…

With resignation to his fate, he dialed Harper's number, expecting to leave her a message. But, of course, the irritatingly intriguing woman picked up.

"I thought you'd be working," he said by way of hello. "Was going to leave a message." As though she'd hang up and give him a do-over. One that went his way.

"We're taking five. What's up?" She sounded not out of breath, but…winded. As though she'd just come offstage. Was standing in the wings, her mind filled with what came next. And Nathan regretted the call for another reason.

He didn't want to interrupt her process. Those moments, when a dancer was alive inside, where only music and movement existed…sacred.

"Nathan?"

His name on her lips. He liked it.

Of course he did. She represented a lucrative job. And so he quickly relayed what Juan had told him.

"Can you bring the brochures by here?" she asked him, then gave him the address of her studio. A short fifteen-minute drive from Ocean Breeze.

Instant irritation flared. Not because his sojourn to his cottage was being put off, though it was, or because his afternoon had to be adjusted, which it did. But because there was no way, after all those years, he was going to be forced back into an environment he'd left behind.

Another test? Forcing him to go back so that he could see there was no longer any pull? That the world had no hold on him?

"What time?" he asked.

"Now's good. We'll be breaking for lunch after one last run-through. Should be done by the time you get here."

The tension in his gut easing, Nathan agreed to the plan. She'd be on break. Could meet him in the parking lot.

He didn't have to enter the ethereal halls of a top-rated studio filled with mirrored rooms with sprung wood floors, dancers in hallways stretching, choreographers, instructors, physical conditioning gurus all focused on their art. Sweats and leotards and all the expensive, well-worn shoes with elastic and ribbons browned from use.

The bare feet with permanently calloused, corned and knotted toes.

So maybe the feet he couldn't escape. He took a pair with him everywhere he went. Including the shower. But the parking lot…he didn't even have to look at the building it serviced.

Pulling in where his monitoring system told him to turn, he glanced at the brochures on the seat next to him. From the stash he carried full-time in a bin in the back of his tonneau-covered truck bed, and then ahead. To see traffic coming and going. Nondancers. He wasn't in the parking lot of a studio. More like a medical complex. A nice one, he'd had that part right. Sprawling.

What the hell? Had she given him the wrong address?

Pulling into a spot on the back end of the lot, he pulled up the text message she'd sent after their call. Checked it with his dash system.

And then saw the second message she'd sent. Telling him to come on back when he got there.

Irritation flared again. A little more prepared that time, he didn't give it any brain time. Just grabbed the brochures and exited the truck. He'd delivered plans, contracts, brochures to places of employment many times in his career.

Get over it. Because if it was an issue…him going into a studio…what did that say about him? That he wasn't who he thought he was? That he hadn't succeeded in becoming the man he wanted to be? Was only pretending to be someone he wasn't?

The last thought rankled. Pissed him off, actually. Gave impetus to his step as he sought out a site directory, found the suite he needed and made his way there.

For a quick brochure handoff. She could text him her choice.

Heading up the walk toward his destination, he heard the music before he registered the open door. The studio was located in the middle of a row of four doors, two on either side, leading to indoor storage units—per the sign on the building.

It wasn't like you could play loud music with doctor's office appointments happening on the other side of shared walls, the thought occurred.

His mother's studio had been freestanding, on its own lot.

Harper wasn't standing at the door. He hadn't texted to say he'd arrived, but he'd figured the door was open so she could watch for him. Had hoped, anyway.

As he approached, he heard the music, a haunting melody, one that he felt in his bones, and he slowed. Figured he'd leave the brochures outside the door and slip away to avoid any chance of interruption. Text her to let her know they were there.

Saw the cowardice behind the justification, the temptation to give into it, and straightened his shoulders.

He was a grown man. Not a kid who'd never had a choice, never seen the life coming. A man who'd made the choice.

Taking those last steps to the door weren't all that hard.

One foot in front of the other. He was in the doorway. Looking in.

At a single room, not a studio filled with them. Not a hallway. One mirrored room the size of two major theater stages, with sprung wood floors, a ballet barre mounted to a wall and a single dancer executing the most exquisite leap, to land in a quadruple pirouette with one muscled arm raised straight in the air. As the music faded, the fist jerked downward, to beside the man's chest, and he fell down to one knee, his upper body arching over, head bowed.

Nathan swallowed in the silence. Hard.

"That's it!" Harper's voice was like a glass of iced water on the moment. "You nailed it. Exactly," she said, coming from a space along the wall beside the door. She'd been standing just a couple of feet from Nathan, and he hadn't known she was there.

The dancer she'd praised stood. Nodded. Strutted toward her in his tights and tank, a smile on his face. The tights... worn so that his choreographer could see every line.

And, if a man was feeling his maleness in very immature ways, they were a way to show off his endowment, too.

Sliding the brochures just inside the door, Nathan quickly and quietly took his leave.

Harper hadn't heard Nathan come in. Danny Bloomington, her male principal for the Utah piece, was the one who'd noticed the brochures sitting on the floor just inside the door.

As soon as Danny left, leaving her to finish the lunch break he'd interrupted, she'd looked at the rock, texted her request, and had just finished the fruit salad she'd been munching on when the Utah dancers were back for one more run-through. Watching her piece come to life, she had tears in her eyes as she clapped one final time.

Gave a few last-minute reminders and critiques.

And then she shared brief hugs with all of them as they filed out the door, wishing them a safe flight back, and telling the assistant director who'd traveled with them and learned the piece as well to reach out if they had any issues when they got back.

She was flying as high as she got, and was a little sad, too, as she drove home that afternoon. Tired from her short night—but more so from the letdown of adrenaline and creative energy she'd expended in the past two days—she really wanted to take a sleeping bag out to the beach, up close to her house where she'd have privacy, and just smile at the sky while she lay there.

Knowing that she had a crew working in the midst of her privacy nixed the idea.

And as she walked into the cottage from the garage and heard the saw and nail guns going out back, any thought of lazing around inside flew out the door, too.

Aggie's big brown eyes stared up at her expectantly, just inside the door, her tail wagging, and Harper accepted the inevitable. She was in for some beach time. Far enough away from her cottage to escape construction sounds. To wallow in the serene sense of having created something that would carry to an untold number of hearts. And to say goodbye to another piece of her own.

A surreal floating from one sphere to another. Something that neither of her parents had ever understood. No matter how many times they'd seen her choreograph, rehearse and perform. They weren't artists.

Heading out, she saw Iris and Scott on the beach a quarter of a mile in front of her. Recognized them from the corgi and miniature collie running back and forth in front of them, as though urging them to hurry. Friday night on the beach. In April.

Folks would be out.

Chances were good someone would start a bonfire at some point. Chairs would appear. A cooler of drinks.

And it was all more than she could contemplate at the moment. Too much coming at her. Too loud.

Not that any of them got overly raucous.

Keeping a slower pace than her neighbors, she talked softly to Aggie. "Mama just needs quiet surrendering to what is." The girl had to have seen her friends ahead. Still, she gave full attention to Harper. Staying close. Glancing over at her often as they walked. "But then you know that, huh?" she asked her sweet and gentle family member.

Choosing to believe that Aggie's glance at her in that exact second was a confirmation, not a coincidence, Harper made it to the destination she'd subconsciously known she'd been heading toward since she'd left the studio.

Had one of her first two options been available, she might have settled for one or the other of them. She'd told herself she would, at any rate.

She'd seen Goldman's black truck half a mile down the road when she'd pulled onto Ocean Breeze. Didn't mean he was still there.

He owned the place, but it wasn't like he could move in. The cottage was a disaster.

She could see lights on in the place from down by the water. Even with the sun still shining. Figured he might not want her intruding on him.

But she headed up anyway. Needed to talk to him, as though there was unfinished business between them.

A confirmation that he'd gotten the rock ordered and Monday's delivery was still on?

He'd probably already texted that much. She hadn't looked. Didn't want to see more of his cryptic, professional notes.

Not then.

Not feeling as she did. In the state she was in.

Not knowing that he'd stood at the door while Danny was dancing.

And then left without a word.

He'd been there. That day. At her studio. But in the spiritual place she was in, too. He knew the highs and lows that mingled together into almost a catatonic peaceful state. He had to know. It wasn't possible that he could dance as he had, speak to her young heart from across an auditorium, if he didn't have pieces of himself in that realm.

And…he was Nathan Goldman. The most exquisite male dancer she'd ever seen. She wanted to know what he thought of the piece she'd created. Of Danny's execution.

"I'm not ready to entertain guests." The words came at her from the kitchen window as she approached a dilapidated back porch.

"How about just a spectator, then?" That's who she was in his life. And all she wanted to be. The rest, the other parts of his world, were of no interest to her.

No, that wasn't right. She wasn't callous. Selfish.

She was interested. Just didn't want personal involvement in the rest.

Unless it meant, "I can help clean," she told him. "It's something I'm really good at." Which would be a piece of information he wouldn't know about her—even if he'd spent hours on the internet reading everything he could find. "It calms me," she continued, stepping carefully on first one then the other two porch steps. Behind Aggie, who'd taken them first.

He could order her off his property.

Or politely ask her to leave.

Maybe he'd already tried with his first comment.

She didn't feel unwelcome.

"Wiping away dirt and grime…making things shine…feels good." True. It was also work.

She didn't owe him. Was paying him quite handsomely for the job his company was doing for her. But all day, in the midst of her deep focus, glimpses of him studying every single board for grain and color…for her…kept floating just beneath the surface.

He hadn't answered her. Not to accept her offer. Or decline it. He was cleaning the windowsill. Checking out the state of the wood underneath years of collective dirt?

She wouldn't go any further than the porch. Not without an invitation.

Stood there and watched him work until he said, "You coming in?"

Then she smiled, opened the door, waited for Aggie to enter first and followed her girl into Nathan Goldman's new digs.

Chapter Seven

Nathan hated cleaning. Had planned to hire a service to do the initial gutting of dirt for him. But he'd wanted to see the quality of some of the wood he was hoping to be able to preserve. And to remove the lime and tarnish on plumbing fixtures that, if in good enough shape, would add to the ambiance of the cottage he'd be putting up for sale before summer.

So he'd picked up a couple of buckets of cleaning supplies.

Not sending Harper away had been a matter of practicality. No professional cleaning service he knew of would come out on a Friday night.

And she was there…offering.

She was already in the door before it hit him. A woman offered. He accepted.

Maybe that was just who he was. A guy who'd spent over a decade fighting a losing battle. Yeah, and if so…he'd be spending the next six decades doing the same.

Harper had already spied a bucket of supplies, and was reaching into it. "Hold it," he told her, more harshly than he should have. "You can see the place, if you want. I'm assuming that's why you're here. You're as curious as Scott and Iris were, as Sage and Gray and Dale were…"

And some others on the beach who'd stopped by during the few hours he'd managed to be at the cottage on Thursday and Friday.

"They've all been here already?" she asked, grabbing a brand-new cleaning rag from a pack of them and the spray bottle she'd chosen after checking out the array.

"Yeah."

Rag and bottle in hand she said, "Do I get the same tour?"

He hadn't said he'd given any of them tours. He had, of course. In good cheer, too.

Waving her out of the kitchen he said, "Look around if you'd like. But you are not cleaning."

When she left without arguing, Nathan went back to work. For about thirty seconds. Then he followed her. Found her in the living room, perched precariously on a ladder he'd carried in the day before, working at a section of crown molding.

"What the hell!" The words escaped him before he could stifle himself. "No way you should be up there. One fall and your career..." He stopped when he saw her staring down at him, mouth hanging open.

"I apologize. I wasn't expecting to walk in here and see you straddling something that was not made for straddling." More like practically doing the splits between the ladder and a built-in shelf above the fireplace.

"I'm fine," she told him, pushing off with the leg on the shelf to get herself fully secured back on the ladder. "I just had to get a look at that molding. I was told all the cottages had it. Unfortunately, my place is one of the smaller ones, and one of the first to be renovated. I think, anyway, because it didn't have as many of the opulent touches. But I know it had the molding. I've seen a photo. It's gorgeous," she said then, pointing to the small area she'd cleared. "Way better even than I suspected."

She was right. The molding glowed.

As did the woman perched close to it. Nathan caught himself staring.

Stopped.

"You have to keep it," she said then, climbing down from the ladder. "Unless of course, you don't want to," she added, as though she'd just heard herself.

Or realized that she was speaking so familiarly to someone she'd only known a couple of days. A virtual stranger.

Who, according to her, had helped her determine the entire course of her life.

Unknowingly helped her, he reminded himself. With *unknowingly* underlined and in bold print, and a stern period on the end of the thought.

She was keeping her distance but watching him. "You left the studio without saying hello today."

And there it was. The reason he hadn't wanted her on his property. Or in his life. A situation he could hardly avoid. Reasons being twofold, and both of them on him. He'd agreed to work for her. And he'd just paid cash for a cottage on the private beach upon which she lived.

To pass his test, he reminded himself, somewhat desperately.

Lest he drown in his own admissions.

"To interrupt that moment would have been criminal." He spoke complete truth. Just not one he'd have chosen to share if he'd have had half a mind about him.

"You think?" The way she asked, as though she was holding her breath for the answer, drew his gaze.

Right into her smile. Where he got lost.

His opinion didn't matter. And he was no longer sure she really wanted it. Was she just being polite?

And that mattered...how?

"The moment I saw was everything you, or anyone, could hope it would be." He hardly recognized his own voice as the words came forth. He'd suddenly seemed to have developed a deeper, more vibrant tone.

Harper blinked. Once. Twice. And then three times. Her lips trembled. And he stood there watching, knowing that he didn't want to be in that moment, to be alone with her in that place.

And doing absolutely nothing to save himself.

Or save her from him.

Nathan Goldman had described a snippet of her work as a perfect moment. Granted, Danny's dancing had been a huge part of the mix. Bringing her vision to life in his own unique and gifted way. But the storyline, the movement choices, how they fit together, the ways they were joined, were all hers.

Confusing how she could reach the height of success she had, and still be the little girl who'd recognized greatness, who'd been swept to a world of unsurpassable beauty and grace for a few brief moments, and knew she had to spend her life revisiting that place.

In a few short words, Nathan had certified her presence in the world he'd shown her.

The man might have quit dancing, but the dance was still within him.

There were no words that fit that moment. Movement was about expression without words. Using the body to communicate that which couldn't be said.

And so she moved. Not toward the man, but in a state of

gratitude. Taking her rag and her spray back to the bucket from which she'd collected them, she picked up the whole thing—leaving the other in the kitchen where he'd been—and headed to the first bathroom she came to. He couldn't work without facilities. And she knew how to make them sparkle.

A gift she'd received from her mother—the ability to take joy in making things clean. First and foremost, the bathroom.

Which prompted the drive to learn all the ways to do it best.

Goldman didn't have all the supplies she'd have liked to use. But he had some good ones. Enough of them that an hour and a half after she'd entered the small, but full bath off the hallway, she was standing in a shining moment.

Walls that had been graced with quality, washable, moisture-resistant paint. Durable tile floor. Fixtures made of the best materials, allowing her to scrub away grime to expose the natural beauty. A tub that, while filthy, had been in great condition. Same for the sink.

She'd heard sounds come from the other room. A power tool. Clanking. She had lost Aggie a time or two while the girl went to check out the source of various unusual-to-her noises. She hadn't seen Nathan. Or heard him speak.

But he'd have heard her in there. She'd run water several times. First to see if there was any. And, before using it to clean, checking under the sink and around the toilet to make sure no water was spewing where it shouldn't have been. She'd had a sink leak once. Had lost all the paper supplies she'd stored under it. A lesson she'd never forgotten.

Just as she was never going to forget the evening. As exhausted as she was, she was wired, too. In a way she'd never been before. Like her life had just aligned. Her dreams and reality had become one.

Had Nathan's?

He'd recognized the spirit in the studio—and had quietly walked away.

The dichotomy was eating at her.

He was gruff with her, unwelcoming. And yet, he let her stay.

Dropping what was left of the supplies she'd used back into the bucket, Harper headed back out to the cottage's living areas. A living room, dining room, den/library, breakfast nook, kitchen—almost twice the space she had—all needing hours of attention just to see what could be preserved from what was trash. If Goldman chose to go that route.

Based on his life choices, the man might be all about leaving the past behind.

She'd be more apt to believe that if she hadn't heard his one-sentence response to a few seconds of performance art.

He was lying on the floor in the kitchen, his upper half under the kitchen sink. The cupboards she'd seen when she first walked in were no longer there.

So much for preserving the beauty. Her heart sank. The room she'd just hoped she'd started on its way to restoration, the time she'd spent on fixtures...maybe he'd be willing to let her buy them for his place?

She held back, waiting for him to notice her. Not wanting to interrupt. Aggie, on the other hand, walked right up to Goldman's chest, as though giving her opinion on the project. Or his progress.

"Can you move just an inch or two more to the left? You're blocking that light that's shining right in my eyes, and it helps."

Harper moved. Not even all that surprised that those would be the first words the man uttered to her in over an hour. All about him, not about the time she'd just donated, or what she might have accomplished for him.

Not that she'd stayed for any kind of praise. Still…

His hand, bearing a wrench, moved toward Aggie, and Harper took a sharp step forward, stopping when she saw the back of that hand gently push Aggie a little closer toward him. The girl took a step and stood, still watching.

He hadn't been talking to Harper about the light. He'd been instructing Aggie.

Who seemed perfectly aligned with being of assistance.

Mouth open, Harper stared.

Aggie knew. She felt the things that Harper and Nathan Goldman Connolly weren't saying. The connection on a different plane.

And on some level, the man was responding to the girl's awareness.

Which meant that Harper couldn't just turn her back and walk away.

She wasn't going to leave without her dog.

And apparently the mammoth fur thing thought she was an integral part of his drain trap repair. So he finished tightening. Wiping away excess plumber's primer and cement, before he shoved himself back and sat up.

He didn't wipe a hand through hair that was probably sticking up on end. He didn't care. Wasn't out to attract anyone.

And he had glue on his hands.

So he couldn't thank the dog, either, with the pat on her head she'd seemed to demand earlier. At least he'd figured that was why she'd come out and nudged her head under his palm.

Good news was, he could rinse his hands. Which was what had started the past half hour's worth of unexpected repair. He'd turned on the faucet and had heard the drips under the sink.

"I came in to tell you that you've got some great potential for preservation in the hall bath, but it looks like you're opting for all new."

Harper's voice came from behind him.

Peripheral vision while on his back had shown him that she'd come out bucket in hand. She was done helping him.

If her dog had been free, he could have hoped that she'd have slipped away and left him alone.

Turning toward her while he dried his hands on a mostly clean towel, he noted that the hunk creature was back where she belonged. At her owner's side. Not his.

The look in those big brown eyes was not going to guilt him into…what…he didn't know.

"I'm not opting for anything," he said, because the conversation was straightforward and in his wheelhouse. "First job is to assess. Then to opt."

"Kind of late to decide with the bottom cabinets all but gone."

He'd left the framing. Could work with that. And owed her no explanation, but he said, "The wood was rotted."

The concern on her face seemed genuine. "Really?" she asked. Turned and headed back into the living room, saying, "Then come in here and look. I thought everything was amazingly healthy, but it's not like I know anything about structural issues."

She'd left him no option but to follow her. To the hall

—that led back to the cottage's four bedrooms. Three to the left. One, the master suite, to the right. She'd turned left.

Stopped at the first door on the right. One of the three full baths. With so much else needing attention, he'd barely given the room a glance. Had used the toilet in the master suite the one time he'd had to pee.

She flipped on the light as she entered. But didn't come back out. Not eager to share the small space with her, Nathan rounded the doorway enough to see inside.

And then stepped in fully. Pushing past his uninvited guest to look into the claw-foot iron bath. And dropped to his knees to look under it, too.

"I couldn't get the tile under there as clean as I'd like. The tub might need to be temporarily taken out, but probably not. There's enough space—I'm pretty sure I could have finished the job if I'd had my long-handled scrubber."

And there he'd been thinking the area was spotless.

"And…it's not the tile I was worried about. You said rot. Tile doesn't rot. But the vanity…the scrollwork is lovely, and the drawers are bigger and solid—better than anything I've seen in my lifetime…"

She stepped back when he moved toward the sink. Not out of the room as he'd expected. Just back against the wall. Leaving him to slide in front of her. And with the drawer she'd pulled out, as much as he slimmed himself, his butt brushed against her.

Wood rot. Looking for signs of wood rot. And…

Everything shone. He'd been so intent on looking for leaks, most particularly under the tub as that could mean having to tear out flooring and walls. He hadn't paid a hell of a lot of attention to anything but the woman he was hell-bent on avoiding.

The fixtures…the old scroll mounted mirror…he felt as

though he'd stepped back into some 1950s movie, in full color, filmed in a million-dollar mansion.

He ran his hands along the woodwork holding the mirror. "This is incredible." Not a scratch in the sink's basin. Caulking needed to be redone around the drain. A five-minute fix.

Dropping down to one knee, he nearly held his breath as he opened the cupboard door directly beneath the sink, and couldn't help the grin that split his face as he noted, not so much the pristine cleanliness—though that was kind of impressive—but the lack of any buildup on the pipes. Or darkened spots on the wood.

"No signs of rot." He didn't even try to hold back the pleasure he felt. "And," he stood, slid quickly away from her to the doorway and turned to face the room, "good job on the cleaning."

Harper moved from the wall to sit on the rounded edge of the tub. "I'm figuring, since these places were originally kept for the rich and famous, that original choices were state-of-the-art for the times, and any necessary maintenance was tended to promptly."

"I'd been hoping so, but after the kitchen episode tonight, wasn't feeling as optimistic."

She shrugged, and he noticed the grace with which she'd completed the simple move. The lines of her shoulders up her neck, down her back, around her arms... "If this room is anything to go by, I'd say you have a good chance of preserving. If you want to."

He did. Yeah. He did. Preserving...

His sanity.

What the hell was he doing noticing body lines?

From one thirty-second phrase of movement?

It took him a second to realize that he was standing there nodding.

A glance her way told him she was glancing down at her fingers on the edge of the tub. They lifted, waved toward the tub. The room. "I couldn't imagine the artist in you would want to lose this."

Her words hung there...like a challenge.

Or so it seemed to him.

Because his life had become nothing but challenge to him?

No, that wasn't right. Designing came naturally to him. His ability to know just what wood suited which structure. Creating something big and heavy and lasting for others to enjoy...

"Why did you leave?"

The words yanked his gaze toward her. He couldn't believe he'd heard them. Couldn't let them hang there on the edge of her lips. Sent steely darts clear through them. Reducing them to silence in the ether.

"I'm sorry" Her next words were better. He glanced briefly at her eyes, and away. Nodded.

"But the question had to be asked, Goldman. It's hanging there between us every time we see each other. And since you've chosen to buy this place, it stands to reason that we'll be seeing each other more than I anticipated."

She didn't sound any happier about that prospect than he was. Which irked him.

He'd inspired her life. She'd reached the pinnacle, was living her dream.

And he was imploding the aura she'd built for herself on Ocean Breeze, the air in which she'd surrounded herself, for the downtime she needed to refill her well.

"I just can't stop wondering why," she said then. "Which

means I can't stop thinking about you. I just need to know why."

I can't stop thinking about you.

A swell of something fierce, and far too good, swept through him. While he rode the wave, the rest of her words landed softly. *I just need to know why.*

Because she didn't want to think about him.

And he most definitely could not have her walking around thinking about him. Not when he was at the critical point of freeing himself from the past so that he could move toward the future he knew—as deeply inside as he'd ever gone—that was right for him. A future he not only wanted, but one that he needed.

If he was ever going to be happy…truly happy…laugh-out–loud-just-because-the-sound-burst-out-of-him happy… he needed to get off her radar.

She *needed* to know why.

Chapter Eight

She never should have asked the question.

Nathan clearly wasn't going to answer it.

She would have stood and quietly walked out, leaving him to the solitude he clearly wanted, except that he was blocking the doorway.

And Aggie, lying on the floor behind him, didn't seem to get that there was a problem. That alone was enough to unsettle Harper. The girl had been her safeguard since the first day she'd brought her home.

A barrier between her and anything that might knock her off course.

"I was performing as the male principal with the American Ballet Theater. It was a one-night gig. A fill-in. I'd done the part to much acclaim from the powers that be and when ABT's principal came down with a cold, and it became known I was in town, I was invited to dance ahead of the understudy."

Mesmerized, not only by the words, by the picture they were creating in her mind, but by the fact that Nathan Goldman was giving her something of substance, Harper sat frozen.

Fearing he was about to tell her that he'd injured himself on the very night of his big chance…or…that he'd fallen… she could hardly breathe.

Her mouth had dropped open when he'd begun to speak. She didn't bother to close it. She had to breathe. Steady in, steady out.

"Everyone who was anyone in New York ballet was there that night. My agent, of course, and other representatives who'd been vying for me as well. And, of course, my mother…"

He didn't seem to be with her in the room. His body was there. His spirit had transferred him to another place. Another time.

As though he had to look back somewhere to answer her question.

Because he didn't carry the memories into his current existence.

"Everyone had offers. My mother was a mess. Flying high, crying with joy. Flaunting herself. She was in her glory. On the cusp of everything she'd ever wanted…"

His pause carried pain. She felt it. Because he'd fallen. Question was, had the injury been a career ender? Or were they getting to that?

Could she bear to sit there? To live through it with him?

She couldn't move. There was no way she could leave.

"…except that it wouldn't have been," he said then, slowly, as though only just seeing into a long-ago future. "Because what she'd always wanted…craved more than anything in life…was for it to be her onstage. For her to be the one agents and directors were clamoring for…"

Probably. Harper had assumed that Fiona Goldman had wanted for her son what she'd once had. Before she'd aged out and opened her enviously successful studio.

Because he'd been given the gift, too.

"I took a master class from her once," she said aloud,

shocked at the sound of her own voice. She sounded so normal. So here and now.

And quickly shushed.

Nathan's gaze narrowed in her direction. His chin tight. She wasn't sure if he saw her.

Or if she'd ruined the moment. "So what happened?" She had to ask. Did it as softly as she would have if coaxing a bird from a nest.

He shrugged. "I danced. Took my bows. Walked offstage and out of the theater."

With that, he turned, stepped around Aggie, and left her sitting there.

Mouth hanging open...again.

What was he doing?

Dredging up the past...thinking of things he'd promised himself he'd never have to waste brainpower on again... reliving...

No.

Back in the kitchen, he went to work on the windowsill again. His goal for the night had been to get the woodwork in the kitchen clean so he could determine if he'd be able to keep it, or would be forced to replace it. He'd made it no further than half of the windowsill over the sink before he'd discovered the leak.

Then the rot.

And had to know how much of it there was. To get it out as though, by just sitting there, it would contaminate what was still salvageable.

Like his past, if allowed to exist in the present, would rot his future.

He heard Harper in the living room. Or rather heard Aggie's paws traipsing on the floor and assumed Harper was with her. He'd never noticed Harper's light step. Not even when he'd been listening.

"Thanks for all the work in there," he said lightly, as the sound of the dog's paws entered the kitchen. With his face in the window, he continued to clean.

Would not turn around.

What had happened back there...

Never again.

Done.

"Consider it a trade-off for the time you spent vetting boards this morning."

Good. She'd gotten the message.

"Done," he said. Glad to have ended something that should never have started in the first place.

"So what happened next?"

Uh-uh. He turned. Purposefully avoided Harper's communicative expression. He wouldn't be burned twice. His gaze bumped into the dog's soulful eyes instead.

There was no question there. No judgment, either.

"You were going to tell me why you left." Harper's voice, soft and filled with kindness, said the words. So how could they possibly seem as though they'd come from her dog, too?

Was he losing all sense of reality?

"Surely everyone didn't hold it against you because you grabbed your stuff from the dressing room and ducked out to come down after a show?" The incredulity in her tone spoke volumes. "No way I'd ever believe that."

No way it would ever happen.

He needed her gone.

And she'd given him the way to make it happen. Back in the bathroom. As soon as he told her why, she'd be done with him.

He continued to clean. Hopped up on the framing that had survived his tear out, straddled boards he knew to be solid, and continued to wipe. "I didn't go back to the dressing room," he told her. "I walked offstage, out the side door, and disappeared. I made a phone call to my mother, telling her I was done. I emptied my bank account. And I spent the night in a cheap hotel room. The next day, I took a cab out of town. Had it stop at a box store so I could buy a suitcase and things to put in it. And then I caught a flight to Florida."

And there she had it. More of it than anyone else had ever had.

She wasn't leaving.

As far as he could tell, she hadn't moved.

"How old were you?"

The question was innocuous. Didn't matter. So he said, "Twenty."

The thirteen years between then and that moment seemed like thirty. Or had before she'd brought them back to life.

She had to go.

"Why?"

The one word nailed him to the wall. He stood there, doused rag in a hand reached up against crown molding he was beginning to think he could keep, and just froze.

Why.

He'd told her when. He'd told her how.

All she'd ever asked him was why.

Tense to the bone, Harper wanted to walk out the back door, down steps that needed to be replaced and never look back.

Aghast, confused, feeling strangely broken inside, she

stared at Nathan Goldman, and saw…a man in a tool belt wiping grime from molding.

She saw Nathan Connolly. A contractor who designed one-of-a-kind decks, and was straddling boards wide enough apart to unbalance most people, while he perched, in contractor shoes, almost on the tips of his toes.

Goldman in disguise.

And she couldn't go. Couldn't leave him trapped on those two-by-fours.

She should. She knew it. Leaving him in peace was the decent thing to do. The only right choice.

But she didn't move.

Aggie didn't nudge her into action, either.

"Why, Nathan?" *Nathan*. The one part of himself he'd kept intact. What it meant, if it meant anything at all, she had no idea.

He wiped, moved, wiped some more. Saying nothing. Acting as though she wasn't there.

Maybe wanting her to take the hint and leave.

But he wasn't telling her to go.

The man had a full vocabulary. And every capability of using it. And he wasn't telling her goodbye.

Or to get the hell out and never come back.

One word—*leave*—would do it.

Five minutes passed. Her back ached. Her feet hurt. She needed a hot soak and her bed. And she stood there. As though on guard.

Protecting something she couldn't see.

From what, she didn't know.

At some point, Aggie sat.

Nathan had reached the joining of two walls. Had both feet balanced on one two-inch board, his face tilted upward in the corner. "I didn't know at the time."

Chills passed through her. Her muscles felt weak, as though she'd pushed them too hard.

Nathan turned, sat on the corner joining of the framework he'd left, and looked at her. Shrugged.

Without conscious thought, Harper moved, too. Boosted herself up on the countertop he'd left on the opposite side of the wide galley kitchen. Remaining completely silent.

Feeling as though a breath could cause an entire existence to crumble.

Or to have heavy weights crumble it beneath them.

"I gave everything I had to give on that stage that night. And there was nothing left."

She listened. Knew exactly how he'd felt giving his all. Pouring every ounce of training, of need, of emotion and desire into a piece.

She'd come offstage exhausted. Completely depleted. Hurting, even.

But she'd always had something left.

Herself.

"You were young," she said, when he didn't seem able to elaborate. "Facing a lot of pressure that night…" Trying to find an explanation for something she'd never experienced and didn't understand.

He shook his head, cutting her off midstream. "No," he said, looking her in the eye. "I really was done. I didn't want the life, Harper. I had the talent. Looking back years later, I'd even go so far as to say that I got to a special place when I danced. But I didn't like performing. Entertaining an audience. All I really knew that night was that I had to get out. To leave it all behind. It was as though, if I didn't take control of my own life that night, I might never have one."

She stared at him.

"A life of my own," he clarified. "One shaped by my own choices."

Wow. Completely nonplussed, Harper had no idea what to say. Maybe there wasn't supposed to be anything. Maybe just sitting there was it. Accepting his right to choose.

Hoping he'd made the right one...

"I've had a lot of years to learn, to mature, to gain understanding, since that night," he said then, sounding more... real...than she'd heard him in the three days they'd known each other. "That last bit, me taking back the right to choose my life's course, it's true, but I can't tell you I was consciously aware of it at the time."

She understood the words. Couldn't imagine making the choice. Didn't even want to contemplate walking away from the world of performing arts. Of not being able to express that which she couldn't say, through song and creative physical movement. "Do you miss it?"

His shrug wasn't convincing. Either way. "I don't look back," he said.

A nonanswer. For which she had a rebuttal. "What about today? When you inadvertently walked back in?"

"I didn't walk in. I turned around and left."

Right. She knew that.

And wondered if he even knew the answer to her question. He didn't look back. Because he just naturally didn't? Because the past, his art, didn't pull at him?

Or because he'd consciously blocked the way?

"You felt something today. During that brief peek."

He shook his head, jutted his chin. "Just an appreciation for something I know a lot about."

Maybe.

In her heart, she didn't believe that, though. Who he'd been, the art he'd performed...hadn't come from the cerebral left-brain cortex, from which he seemed to be speaking to her.

"How long did it take your mother to come around?"

"She didn't. I haven't seen her in over a decade. She has a new protégé, one she's legally adopted, and I wish her well."

A stab of pain shot through her. She wished she could be shocked. But with the heightened awareness, heightened emotion and heightened drive for success at any cost that came with her calling, she wasn't.

Nathan had just described the reason she was close to no one in her field. And held her distance outside it, too. She'd never turn her back on family, not ever, for any reason—as evidenced in her relationships with her parents—but she'd pushed past others to get where she had to go. Had turned a somewhat calloused back to those who needed to make it right alongside her.

She'd never backstabbed. Never taken advantage.

Even when others had done it to her.

She'd just never let herself get to know the women who'd lost out to her. Didn't know their hopes, their dreams and motivations. And didn't know what had happened to them after they hadn't made it to the pinnacle, either.

Her bleeding heart would have stopped her from succeeding.

Which didn't make her the greatest person in the world.

Hence, her aloneness.

Still, she'd never, ever have turned her back on someone she loved. "Have you tried to reach out to her?" She dropped the question into the silence that had fallen. Not sure why she was pushing the point.

"I call her every month. She answers. I ask how things are going. She tells me about the awards Brent is winning, and I wish the kid well."

"Have you ever met him?"

"Nope."

"Maybe he could use your influence." Not that it was her place to judge.

He shrugged again. "She's keeping him healthy. In school. Off the streets. Away from drugs. Kid could be doing a whole lot worse."

"What about love? Is he getting any of that?"

Nathan slid off the board, seemingly perfectly at ease with a double conversation that was ripping her to shreds. For Brent. But for the young Nathan, too. "That's the future," he said. "A wife. Kids. Dinner together every night."

In a young dancer's world, one who had to rely on local studios for training, dinner was eaten on the floor of the changing room, or, if she was lucky, at a table in a studio gathering room. And once she reached a level of success, was actually in shows, or was a choreographer backstage... many nights there'd be no dinner at all.

Harper couldn't imagine not having that flexibility in her life.

But she wished the best of luck to Nathan Connolly. "I hope you find exactly what you most want," she told him, as she followed Aggie out the back door.

Glad to have known him.

But no longer sharing an unseen sphere with him. She'd thought they were kindred spirits, seeing and understanding things that others couldn't access.

Instead, he'd just been really good at putting on a show.

Not his fault. Not hers, either.

Just...life.

But her step was slow, her heart sad as she made her way home.

Her ties to Goldman had just been completely severed.

Chapter Nine

Nathan's little heart-to-heart with Harper—a person from the life he'd left behind—actually did set him free. He'd been honest. With her, with himself.

And oddly enough, found that talking with someone who understood what he'd come from really had been the closure he'd been seeking. Found in a place he'd been purposely avoiding.

His time with her had been the culminating moment he'd thought it to be. The last challenge in thirteen years of them. Just differently than he'd thought.

It wasn't a test of his resolve, of his sincerity and improvement. But rather, a chance to take his final bow. By accepting the challenge of being in Harper's company, pushed to the point of stopping by her studio right at the time that a man who was living the life he'd once led had been performing, Nathan had walked straight onto the path he'd been seeking.

He wasn't a used-to-be. And a trying-to-be. Or a want-to-be. Nathan Goldman and Nathan Connolly. He was Nathan Goldman Connolly, just as his birth certificate proclaimed. A man with a past, a present, and with his future stretching wide open before him.

As he headed toward the beach Saturday morning, he

turned onto the sharp drive down to Ocean Breeze with an eagerness and motivation he hadn't known in a while.

It was like he'd gone back thirteen years and said the official goodbye that he should have been man enough to stick around and proclaim that long-ago night in New York.

Instead of tensing as he made his way to his first stop—Harper's place—he parked and hopped out, without concern. If the homeowner came out, he'd welcome the conversation. Turned out, he liked the woman when he didn't have to be always conscious of the threat of walls tumbling down and suffocating him.

And if she didn't appear, the sooner he could get down to his investment property and dig in.

As he was beginning to expect with Harper, neither happened. She didn't come out, because she was already sitting outside on the beach, to the left of what would soon be her deck, in tights and a leotard, a water jug in hand.

Sweaty, and with her hair up in a twisted mess confined by elastic bands, she frowned as he rounded the corner. "What's wrong? Where's the crew?" she asked.

"You did your barre and came out to stretch with the ocean for company," he said the first thing that came to mind. And then answered her question. "I gave them time off. Saturdays are only half days and setting the fireplace is the next thing on the agenda. Something I want to do myself. We've never done one quite like this and I want to make sure that it lies like I want it to."

He'd have to start by building cement blocks up to the height of the deck, cutting them to shape as he went. The rock he'd purchased at her behest would go on later, each rock being set as color and shape dictated so that they fit together in the most aesthetically pleasing way.

Shooting her legs out to either side of her, so far out she

could roll forward and be in the splits, she arched her torso over one knee. And then, slowly, her gaze briefly touching him as she came up and then, all in one smooth movement, arched over the other.

"You want to join me?" Her words, though somewhat muffled from her head facing the sand position, made it to him loud and clear. "There's plenty of room."

She'd caught him watching her.

Taking her point, Nathan jumped down from the deck's framing to the area marked off for the fireplace. Studied the space, waiting for shape to take form in his mind.

"The sand is a little cold, but all in all, not a bad way to start your morning." The voice came from just a few feet behind him.

He couldn't help it that she'd chosen a spot so close to his workspace for her workout space. "Already done, an hour and a half ago," he said, trying his best to focus. To let his mind's eye show him the way.

"Starting your morning?" she asked, obviously not taking his cue that, though he was just standing there, he was working. Or trying to.

"With stretching," he told her. Only just realizing what he'd admitted to after the words were out. And smiling as he realized there was no reason to pretend otherwise.

"You still stretch every morning?"

Resisting the temptation to turn and face her—a total focus thing was all—he said, "All those years of twisting, turning, leaping, landing, wouldn't treat me at all well if I didn't." He pointed out the obvious.

"Once a dancer always a dancer." She said the words softly.

He heard them. "In that sense, yes." There was no defensiveness in his tone. She knew.

Who he'd been.

That he'd walked away without the least desire to ever go back.

And the freedom to just be felt good.

He still did his stretches. As a dancer was trained to do. Knew to do. Did by rote. To give longevity to a body that was put through physical challenges day in and out, yes. But also to keep the body in shape for movement.

He'd been moved by the emotional ending of a number the day before.

But had snuck away.

As though he couldn't bear to step into the room, onto the floor. To be face-to-face with a man who was living the life he'd left behind.

Harper didn't kid herself that Nathan had a secret longing to be back onstage. Performing. There'd been something so peacefully final about their conversation the night before.

But perhaps she'd been wrong to completely dismiss the artistically spiritual connection between the two of them. To fear that she'd imagined the whole thing simply because of who he'd once been to her.

Maybe there was a reason he'd been the contractor Gray had chosen, out of the many he'd interviewed, to do his deck. Beyond the talent. And because of it.

Fate had a way of bringing things together in the right place and time.

Nathan didn't want the life. But did he still have a dance left in him?

Standing as she saw Aggie running back up the beach from her sojourn with Morgan and Angel in the distance, Harper approached Nathan. Stopping just short of the roped-off deck area. "I'm not a bricklayer, nor do I want to interrupt what I suspect is talent in progress, however, there's nothing in your quote for your own on-site labor."

He glanced over at her and started to wave a hand. She interrupted the silent communication with, "So, I was thinking, when you're done here, if you're heading down to your place, give me a knock and I'll head down with you. Depending on timing, I'll provide lunch. And then give you the hours you spend here, down there, cleaning."

Looking more relaxed than she'd ever seen him, at ease, even, Nathan watched her. His face an expression of consideration. "A trade-off," he said.

"I know it's not glamourous, but I really do like to clean," she told him. "Making order out of chaos, brightness out of darkness…it's like creating without needing to think at all. No mental or emotional energy required…"

He nodded. Half smiled. Turned back to his work.

And Harper went inside to shower.

Thinking about the man just outside her bathroom wall as she stripped down and stood beneath the hot spray.

Getting hotter inside by the moment.

She'd never been one for sex without commitment. Without a possibility of the relationship going somewhere.

And there was absolutely no chance of anything going anyplace between her and the contractor. He'd made his life plan very clear. Words that had almost trembled with the depth of their truth.

He wanted, probably needed, something he'd never had. Mom, Dad and the kids.

Something she'd had in abundance and never wanted to even contemplate bringing into her life again.

He wanted dinners every night.

She thrived on being backstage, preparing, while a theater buzzed with those who'd just had their dinner. Or dancing so hard in studio that the sun set, the moon rose and she didn't even notice. As had happened Thursday night.

Besides, Nathan said he wanted the wife, the family, but that didn't mean he wanted or was even capable of monogamy.

He'd been a heartbreaker. She'd witnessed his prowess there, too. Had to hand it to the guy. He did everything full-out.

He'd turned down the Realtor the other night, but that didn't mean he hadn't arranged a Saturday night rendezvous. Or that he didn't have other women already lined up to spend his evenings with that weekend. The way the man exuded…

She couldn't be blamed for falling prey a little bit herself.

She wasn't a kid anymore…watching him from afar.

Nor was she going to become part of his trail of tears.

She'd draw him out about his weekend plans, instead. Get him to talk about the current women in his life. As a friend, teasing him. That's all it would take to calm down any traitorous yearnings her body might make.

In the meantime, turning the water to cool, and then cold, she stood until all thoughts of the man's body had washed down the drain, and then, turning it back to hot, concentrated on soothing the muscles she'd worked hard over the past week.

Because she'd just obligated them to a different kind of work that afternoon.

And if Nathan knocked, she was going to answer.

Nathan knocked.

He didn't enjoy cleaning. In the least. And there was a load of it to do. Before Monday when his regular service could get out to Ocean Breeze.

Besides, with his graduation the night before from life student, to living life, he was kind of enjoying his time with Harper Michaels. The idea of being himself was starting to grow on him.

Right up until they took a break, midafternoon, to have the lunch she'd had him drive down with him, while she and Aggie made their way via the beach.

She'd packed a blanket for them to sit on. Tuna sandwiches. Assorted veggies. Which was all fine. And then, in her leggings and short-sleeved T-shirt, she sat down with him. There. Close enough for him to catch the somewhat lavender scent of the cleaning solution she'd most recently used. To see the incredibly taut muscles in her calves and thighs as she shot one leg straight out to the side to make room for him opposite her.

Every time he looked up, her curves were right there. Directly in front of him. Close enough to touch.

And it had been so long…

She talked about the woodwork in the bedroom she'd been in. Figured he might want to replace the baseboards. They were coming clean, would probably be fine for a while, but they were pretty dinged up. Years' worth of wealthy visitors on vacation, of moved furniture, of cleaning machines…

He heard all of it. Just kept getting lost in her smile every time he looked up.

While he'd been throwing up barriers to keep her away from him, preventing any chance that his present would implode into his past, he'd managed to also avoid any deep awareness of her natural beauty. The grace with which she bit and chewed.

Lifted a carrot to her lips.

And tossed one to Aggie.

The confirmation that he hadn't stymied his ability to respond physically to a woman was good. Not that he'd really had serious doubt on that score.

"You haven't heard a thing I've said, have you?" she asked.

Not wanting her to have any hint of an inkling where his mind had been, he said, "Every word." Repeated the gist of it. Ending with, "I'll take a look. I was already thinking the baseboards are grossly understated compared to the crown moldings, but back in the day, they didn't have the choices we do now. I haven't yet decided if I'll stick with preservation of the era or allow a more modern baseboard to complement the cornices." Proud of himself, he mentioned a couple of high-end baseboard manufacturers he'd look up that evening.

Thinking he'd managed to be a regular guy with regular reactions without spewing a come-on—he helped himself to another half of tuna sandwich. Something else he hadn't come in contact with since he'd changed his life. Tuna, filled with nonsaturated fat that helped heal muscles and also protein, had been a staple in his life since he was old enough to chew. Probably before then.

"This is good," he told her. "It's been a long time since I've had tuna." Another thing associated with his old life that he'd crossed off his list. Needlessly? What else was there?

What was his true self, and what had been created out of his mother's undying need for him to be a part of the world of ballet?

Thoughts for another day. Maybe. Finishing his sandwich, looking over to see Harper smiling at him—the woman was constantly smiling—he stood. Picked up the blanket as she vacated with the picnic basket. "Time to call it a day," he said.

He no longer felt like he needed to escape the dancer because of an association to a world he'd run from, but the temptation to touch her, man to woman, was growing by the look. Too many more and he was going to embarrass himself.

"Got a hot date tonight?"

His gaze shot to her…back…she'd turned toward the kitchen. Had he really heard a saucy tone? Was she mocking him?

"Not unless you consider trolling the internet for period moldings, fixtures, sinks, showers and tubs a date."

That last had her turning around. She was frowning as she said, "I thought you were going to keep the tub. It's lovely…"

"Not that one. There's a jack and jill bathroom between the back two bedrooms. I did enough of a wipe up last night to see that it's not in nearly as good shape as the others."

The subject had changed, but the date comment was still there. Rankling. The second she'd made it aloud.

Because she knew of him as he'd been.

Her opinion didn't need to matter. She was one person he'd likely never see again once her deck was complete, and he got the cottage done and up for sale.

"And for the record," he started a little more strongly than was like him, "I haven't been on a date in…two weeks short of a year."

Two more weeks and he'd have completed his last mandate. Would free himself to officially start over.

Harper's mouth parted. No sound came. Her expression changed as she looked at him, though. Went from shock to something softer. But not a lot better. Was she feeling sorry for him?

Her brows came together as she set the basket down. "You're counting?"

His business was his own. And if he felt like he wanted to throw it out into the room, to prove a point, he was free to do so. "I am," he said, tossing her folded blanket on top of her basket. She watched it fall, looking kind of surprised. As though she'd forgotten it was hers. Would have walked out without it.

He didn't back up. Instead, he folded his arms across his chest and stood there. She could go. He'd thank her for her work, and see her around.

Of course, life wasn't that easy. Or clean.

Her brown eyes held no accusation—or otherwise negative emotion—as, chin lifted, she looked him in the eye and asked, "Why?"

Why. Why did you leave?

Why are you counting?

Why haven't you dated?

The damned word seemed to be the cross he had to bear to be in the gorgeous woman's company. While he learned how to be around a beautiful woman knowing that sex could never happen between them.

Because he was all done with sex for pleasure only. With brief associations. For sex that didn't have the possibility of leading to something lasting.

Losing interest in the conversation, Nathan opted to just cut to the chase. "Because I made a vow to myself that I would not have sex, or date, for one year," he answered the first. Why he was counting. And then, without giving her a chance to respond, replied to the second one, too. "I want more than sex. But found myself going out with the same kinds of women, doing the same things, because they were always there. Offering. And I responded naturally, in the way I'd learned far too young. The year off was to break the cycle. To retrain myself."

"And when the year is up?"

He had the plan for that, too. "I find a woman whose company interests me. One who doesn't throw herself at me. I ask her out…" He shrugged. The rest…he didn't have that down yet.

"You don't know how to date." Her words were kind, not accusing. As though she was just figuring out something. He didn't have long to wait for her to enlighten him. "You had no male role model growing up," she continued. "And I'm guessing your mother looked the other way when it came to sex. She let you have what you wanted. Like bribing a toddler with a tablet so he'll be quiet in the car…"

Shaking his head, immediately rejecting her words, Nathan stopped short of voicing his opinion of her armchair analysis. And the conclusions she'd drawn, too. She'd known *of* him, then. She hadn't *known* him. Or his mother.

How dare she…

Be a little bit right?

Maybe right on the money?

"I can see you need some time with that, so just let me say…" He glanced at her as she paused, caught the soft smile. Felt it all the way to his groin.

When she saw him looking at her, she finished with, "I think what you're doing is remarkable." With that she spun, picked up her basket, made a clicking sound to Aggie and let herself out.

Chapter Ten

Harper went home. Did some laundry. Caught up on bills. Spent some time at the barre…germinating a new piece while she ran through exercises.

And had a head filled with flashes of Goldman, as a young man, pulling at her heart and soul with his movements.

He'd been gifted onstage. And a jerk off it.

He'd loved the dance. Not what came with it. Not the man it made him?

His current choices pointed that way, and she couldn't find any other explanation. Not that any of it was her business.

Still…he called to her. A soul on a quest.

The source of all artistic expression.

By five that Saturday evening, with the sun getting closer to the horizon but not yet setting, she took Aggie out for a walk, just far enough down the beach to see if Nathan's truck was still at the cottage.

Checking up on him…maybe.

But she headed home with purpose when she saw that his vehicle was there. She was at loose ends. His quest called to her.

She pulled out chicken breasts and quickly oiled them,

sprinkling on some spices and parmesan cheese before putting them in a baking pan and covering them with foil. Grabbed a couple of sweet potatoes. Rolled them in foil, too. Adding some greens and blueberries to the mix, she refilled the picnic basket she'd emptied earlier. "Come on, girl. Let's go be neighborly," she told Aggie as she held the basket on one arm and opened the front passenger side door for her girl.

She had no second thoughts as she drove down Ocean Breeze. Just a feeling of anticipation in her stomach. And a rationale to present to the man she'd once thought she'd want to meet more than any other.

Standing at his door, in the same leggings and shirt she'd had on all day, second thoughts crept in. Maybe she'd just leave him the basket...

Aggie barked.

The door opened.

Pasting on her usual smile, Harper held up the basket. "I remembered you saying that you'd be setting the rock around the block frame, which means I owe you more time, too, and since I'm no good at the construction stuff that's coming, I figured I should get my hours in now. At the cleaning stage."

Not at all what she'd been telling herself while preparing the meal. "And I brought dinner," she added. "Assuming the oven works and is safe to use."

Aggie pushed past Nathan to head inside. Harper watched the hundred-pound being turn around behind the man and look at Harper. Showing her how to gain the entrance she'd obviously sought?

Nathan, looking completely unconcerned, leaned a shoulder against the doorjamb. Which was better than closing it in her face. Or ordering her to retrieve her recalcitrant family member.

He left her holding the somewhat heavy basket, though. "What if the oven doesn't work?"

The answer seemed obvious to her. "I go home, put it in the oven, and then have to take a break and go back to get it."

He nodded. And remained in position. Watching her.

Driving her up the wall.

And making her sassy, and kind of wanting to laugh, too.

"You're not that great at cleaning," she said then. "You need me." And maybe she needed him, too. To remember things she'd started to forget.

The reason her entire life was consumed by dance.

How much it mattered.

Things she'd started to take for granted, which would eventually make her stale.

He glanced downward. "That thing heavy?"

Her arm was aching. "A little bit, yeah."

He reached for it. She lifted her arm to let him slide it off.

And then, when he turned his back and headed toward the kitchen, she followed him inside.

It was another test. His association with the woman was all one big test. One he hadn't yet completed. The first day they'd met. At the studio the day before. The way he'd dumped his sad, sorry past on her.

The gorgeous, impossible-to-miss grace with which she moved.

Not to mention the muscles and curves that were perfectly conditioned…

His assumption that he'd passed his final exam, and graduated, had been premature.

He'd lost his virginity to a dancer—one older enough than him that she should have known better. Not enough to make it illegal.

He'd grown up on dancers. And with them.

Not something he was proud of.

But it made sense that in order to know that he'd fully redeemed himself—that he was no longer the man who took what was offered and walked away when he was done—he'd have to face temptation and not give in.

And she was right. He could use the help. He was emptying the picnic basket when she joined him in the kitchen. He didn't look up from the foil-covered baking dish he was setting down the one counter that was disinfectant clean. "I'm hoping to get enough done by tomorrow to be able to assess the job, have a list of what I'm going to need, and how much, so I can get some kind of an idea of cost. And labor hours."

Shop talk. Something he could rely on.

While another part of him ran off with pleasure at the kindness, generosity and timeliness of her unplanned presence.

"The chicken cooks uncovered at 350 for an hour. Potatoes, at that temperature, an hour and fifteen or so. The blueberries and greens will be fine in the basket."

"Or we could put them in the mini fridge in the laundry room. I set it up today. Stocked it with water."

He lifted the thin wooden partition halfway down in the basket upon which the pan had been sitting to get to the blueberries. And pulled out a bottle of wine, too. With two plastic glasses.

"It's locally grown and made," she told him. "I allow myself a glass of wine on Saturday nights."

Wine. Made the evening more…interesting.

"And lest you think I'm hoping you take some kind of

interest in me, I'm not. I don't fit the criteria for your future. And you don't fit mine."

The words should have put a halt to any attraction he'd been feeling. If anything, they made him more aware of her.

"And I really do admire what you're doing. Consciously going for what you most want."

Great. He was noticing her body. And she admired him.

Looking over at her, Nathan felt the same strange sense that gripped him the night before. As though he could trust her with...truth. "I want a wife. One whose person I love, not just who has a body I want. And kids." He'd already told her as much. No reason to belabor the point. But doing so steadied him. He set the wine on the counter, with the glasses and corkscrew.

"And you want dinner at home," she said softly, smiling. "Which is something I almost never have."

She'd brought it to him, though. Dinner at home.

And the gesture touched him.

Harper had been working for an hour—in the Jack and Jill bath she hadn't known was there—when she heard Nathan call out that he'd put dinner in the oven.

Gave herself the time it would take the potatoes to cook to finish with the room. Concurring with Nathan's assessment of the tub—there were chips in it and stains that even she couldn't seem to lighten—she wasn't so sure about the fixtures. She'd run home for vinegar, had let it soak, and was seeing some signs of hope. Was hoping to be done, with full success, by the time they ate.

He wanted all assessments done by the next day and there were still a lot of rooms to get through.

She soaked. Scrubbed at the floor and walls for quarter of an hour, and then went back to the fixtures. Clearing away what she could. Then resoaking. Had just passed the hour when Aggie appeared in the doorway. The girl had been checking in but hadn't stuck around. Aggie wasn't fond of vinegar vapors.

"Almost done here," she said in the higher voice she reserved for reassuring her housemate, without moving from her position leaning over the tub. "Just this one last bit of grit and we can show Nathan that he judged too quickly."

The cough that came as an immediate response was not canine.

Her head twisting to the side, Harper looked over her shoulder. Saw Nathan and Aggie standing side by side. And caught the man looking at her butt.

She almost wiggled it at him. To make sure he had no attention for the comment she'd just made.

Not even sure why she'd made it.

What did Nathan Connolly's judgment matter to her? If he thought cutting off a part of himself was better than living with the repercussions of not doing so, what was it to her? How could she possibly know what was best for him…

Thoughts flew through her mind as he raised his gaze to hers. Looking as though he was about to put her in place. "Dinner's ready," was all he said. And then he turned away.

Letting her off the hook. Relieved, Harper called out, "Nathan? Come look."

He'd judged too quickly about the fixtures in the bathroom. That was all. She'd show him. Make sure it was clear that that was all she'd meant.

And pay more attention to minding her own business about everything else.

Dinner was good. Wine was good.

Nathan had run home after lunch and picked up a card

table and a couple of chairs, along with a few other essentials, like toilet paper, and as he sat in the eating nook with Harper, listening to her talk about how the house would look when it was done, he felt a sense of happiness he wasn't sure he'd ever known.

Until he reminded himself that he wasn't going to be living in the cottage.

Nor would she be sitting across his dinner table from him in the home he did buy.

Life was a series of choices and changes. If a man was lucky, those choices created changes that took him to a better place than he'd left.

He was much happier at Connolly Construction than he'd been onstage. He was good with that.

Harper had been talking about music. She thought they should have some as they worked. Offered to bring her portable Bluetooth speaker down the next day.

Having already established that she'd be back to help again for a while on Sunday.

"I've got a track I need to listen to," she said then. "I've been asked to choreograph a series of modern pieces set to it."

Her eyes lit up anytime she talked about her work. He'd noticed that first day. Hadn't realized how much—they lit and he noticed—until right then. Sitting with her, sipping wine and munching on the blueberries she'd brought for dessert.

And he was curious. "Do you always accept without knowing what you'll be working with?" He'd have thought differently.

"I never do," she told him. "The request came in last week. I told them I'd have an answer for them on Monday. Hence, my need to listen by tomorrow."

She'd be helping him clean his property. And working, too.

While he'd be...working on the cottage...and listening while he worked.

"Did they tell you anything about the music?"

"Just that it's an older work, by an Australian group. Very few lyrics. Haunting..." She shrugged.

"And the company it's for?"

She named a modern dance company that had been around since he was a kid. Changing dancers in and out regularly, of course. Age wasn't kind, that way.

And...he was impressed. "Have you worked with them before?"

She threw up a hand. Leaned forward to reach for the plastic container of berries they were sharing. She said, "For the past few years," sounding as though they were talking about a vacation spot she'd visited over and over. Not a big deal. But still really enjoyable.

"Any of the same dancers?" He was dwelling. Needed to get off it.

She knew the life she'd chosen. And it clearly suited her.

"I have no idea who I'll be working with this time, but I hope so. There's this one woman, Amanda...she's such a natural. You don't ever see her counting, even when she's first learning. It's like she has control of weight and space without even trying. She's got an instinct unlike anything I've seen before..."

Harper's eyes were glowing again. And Nathan said, "How old is she?"

A normal enough question. If you weren't already heading someplace with the answer. And the place you were going wasn't any of your business.

"I didn't ask." Harper's lack of concern was a surprise

to Nathan. As though counting the years wasn't a critical part of what she did.

He didn't get it.

It wasn't for him to get.

But he took another sip of wine and said, "Having me ended my mother's stage career." Whether he was merely sharing another part of his past—a continuation from the night before—or reminding himself of why any attraction to Harper Cecilia was a mistake, Nathan didn't know. "Whether consciously, or not, she blamed me. Which I think allowed her to justify using my life to supplement her own."

"Are you sure she didn't just choose to retire because of having you? Maybe you were her excuse, not something she blamed."

Nathan shook his head. Needing to get the point clear. Maybe because, in her dedication to her art, Harper resembled his mother. And he needed to not lose sight of that fact for even a second. "Dance is her only true love. It drives every waking moment of her day. Her hip alignment wasn't the same after giving birth. Which shifted her balance, her movement. Not enough that someone walking in off the street would notice. But the professionals did. When, before, she'd been a shoo-in for any part she desired, she was suddenly being asked to audition, and then not getting the jobs."

"That happens to all ballerinas, if they hang on too long," Harper said. "Thirty is the pinnacle for many of them. Forty is a lucky max."

Right. He glanced over at her. "And then what?" If one was only happiest onstage, what happens for the next forty to fifty years?

"Teaching. Performing locally, in smaller productions.

Directing. Producing. Choreographing." Her list was ready. Full. She had that smile on her face.

And he knew. Harper and dance were cojoined for life.

Which meant, just as he'd already established, there would never be a place for her in his future.

Except...maybe as a friend?

Chapter Eleven

She needed to get home. Get to bed. The week ahead was full, with four late nights, and she wanted to be able to give her all to it, and to enjoy every minute of doing so. Which meant her body had to be rested, hydrated, her muscles regenerated.

And she'd already promised cleaning duties for Sunday. While somewhat physically taxing, the cleaning wasn't tiring her out. She was using muscles in different ways. Not breaking them down but rather exercising them.

She still had half a glass of wine. And hadn't felt so alive, so energized, off a dance floor in…as long as she could remember.

"I get what you're saying," she told Nathan, still mulling over what he'd been sharing about his mother. "I've known women who fall into depression when their performing careers are over, but it doesn't have to be that way. For a lot of dancers, it isn't. Dance is so much more than that hour or two a night when the lights are bright and clapping comes at the end of every song…"

Was she out to convince him that he was missing out? Or reassure him that she'd be fine when she turned thirty the following year. And then forty. In case he'd been trying to warn her.

She wasn't defending her profession. Didn't feel the least bit threatened by his words. She felt sad for him. And for the world of dance, for having lost the heart and soul of his talent far too soon.

"What about your parents?" His question hit from out of the blue. She didn't talk about her personal life—other than what those on Ocean Breeze saw on Ocean Breeze, and what those at dance saw at dance. It was all very clean. Comfortable. The way she wanted it.

She was happy that way.

Complete. Fulfilled. Peaceful.

And never alone. She had her cottage on the ocean that was always awake—no matter what time of the day or night she might need sustenance. A seemingly lifetime supply of audiences with which to share her expression. And she had Aggie.

Drinking from her glass, she set it down. Poured a little more on top of the few sips she had left. "What about them?"

"Are they local? Do you see them?"

"Yep."

Sitting back, his glass in hand, Nathan smiled at her. "I'm guessing they still come to all your performances? Whether to see something you choreographed, or to see you dance?"

One of them at a time. "Yep."

"Do you have siblings?"

While she wasn't overly fond of the questions, Harper realized that turnabout was fair play. And said, "Nope." Something else they had in common.

With another grin, Nathan asked, "I'm guessing the three of you were really close, then? And life revolved around your dance?"

She smiled back at him. Set her glass down. Maintained her expression. And when, as she strove for an answer that was both true, and nonrevealing, her grin faltered, she picked her wine back up and sipped. Held the wine in her mouth as she drew in a deep breath through her nose before swallowing. And slowly let the air out of her mouth.

In through the nose. Out through the mouth. A second time.

Trained to the core, Harper relaxed. Met the gaze of the man across from her. The light brown orbs seemed to have a ring of gold around them before fading into the whites of his eyes. She was studying them that closely. Remembering how they'd looked to her the night before as he'd trusted her with his truth.

Lifting her chin, she said, "Dance was my escape from them." She paused, breathed normally, then added, "And, ultimately, my salvation."

She watched Nathan's expression change. The gaze that never dropped from hers even as he sipped his wine. And when he said, "Tell me about it," his voice so soft, so warm, she did.

Nathan's smile faded—the pleasure he'd been taking in imagining her upbringing so different from his disappeared—as he listened to Harper describe the war zone that had been her homelife until she was ten.

"That's when they finally divorced," she told him.

"And then it got better?"

With a shake of her head, she said, "If anything, it got worse. Instead of fighting around me, they conducted their battles through me. And about me. No matter whose house I was at, I was grilled about the other, heard negative talk about the other. They both tried to get me on their side to talk to the judge about the other, fighting for complete custody. Or more time in the summer. Promising me how great it would be. Thing is, I always felt like it was more of a competition between the two of them—another way to fight, to win—not any real need to change custody agreements. They didn't so much want me as they wanted the other not to have me." She paused, and he saw the deep breath she took. Mouth closed, her chest rose slowly. And then, mouth open, just as slowly fell. In through the nose, out through the mouth. He knew the drill.

As she set her wineglass down, he waited, needing to hear what came next. "They got pregnant with me the month after they were married. No one told me I was a mistake, but I long-ago figured out that's what happened. If not for that, they'd probably have divorced within the year."

She sounded like he'd felt for those first few years after his walkout. Like she'd never understood it all. Had long since given up trying. Accepting that some things just didn't make sense.

"Truthfully, I think they put me in dance so that they could ignore each other, and just have lives. Without me there, there was nothing to fight over. Or about. I was the pawn, the one thing that could get to both of them..."

It was sick. Twisted.

She just shook her head. Took another sip of wine.

And he had to make it better. "It sounds like they were both jealous of the other's affection for you."

She seemed to ponder his words, as though she found merit in them. "I've never actually thought of it that way," she said. "I always saw it as more like I'd been a way for them to get power over each other. But you could be right."

When he tuned in, he saw things, felt things, beyond the surface. She'd watched him dance. She'd know.

He cocked his head at her. "So, was it that you loved dance, or just loved the escape it gave you?"

And she smiled again. "I loved dance," she told him. "From my first memory of it. I love the music and the movement." She stopped, then looked at him and said, "And when I first saw you dance, I knew why medium spoke to me. I was going through puberty. With my parents' constant drama, my emotions were spiraling out of control. And those minutes, watching you, it all came together for me. From that day on, I understood that dancing was what I was born to do. I had my purpose. I was to pour my heart and soul into what I loved. That I could use the angst to bring beauty, understanding, joy to the world. And I could leave the rest, all the things that were out of my control, behind."

He swallowed. Couldn't continue to connect with the things her eyes were seeming to tell him. He'd been no savior. Hadn't even known she existed.

Wasn't sure he'd have taken the time to tune in enough to care.

Nathan looked down at his glass. Decided a big sip was a good idea. Poured more wine in his glass, just ensuring there'd be enough.

Made himself sip slowly. No gulps. He'd used up all his forgiveness for lack of self-control in his youth.

Still wasn't completely convinced that there'd ever be enough forgiveness to cover his debts.

"You know, the truly perplexing part is…" Her words drew his gaze back to her. The smile on her face. And a reprieve from the intensity that had been glistening in her eyes, too.

"Neither of them ever remarried or had other kids. I kept waiting. Thinking that once they found other partners, had other little ones, the animosity would fade, things would settle into place, and I'd just be another teenager with divorced parents."

She made it all sound so…okay.

With a shrug, she continued, "I've wondered sometimes if it's because they still love each other. You know, just weren't meant to have a kid. Or maybe to get married at all."

And that he got. The kid blaming themself for choices the parent made before said kid was born.

"Or their first attempt at marriage just turned them both off from the institution," he jumped in. "Showed them they weren't good at it." Putting the blame where it lay.

Something that had taken him a long time to sort out. Parts of his past were most definitely on him. Not all of it.

"It sure turned me off from it," Harper said then. "No way I'm risking my homelife, my sanity, on the hope that the love doesn't turn into hate down the road."

He couldn't just sit there with that. "There are a lot of great, healthy marriages. Partnerships wrapped in love… that last a lifetime. Kids who grow up in loving homes. You're going to let your parents' mistakes rob you of the chance to find your own happily-ever-after?"

She didn't even hesitate before she said, "Are you going to let your mother's obsession rob you of a chance to find your own place in the world of dance? One where you don't have to perform on stage in front of audiences, but, maybe, just let yourself fly on a dance floor for the pure joy of doing so?"

Right. He got it.

"We pursue our own paths toward that which makes us happy," he said.

"And ours happen to be diametrically opposed," she added, pushing her wineglass away. But she was smiling as she added, "Which makes us candidates for a pretty decent friendship, wouldn't you say?"

Nathan couldn't look away. He smiled. He nodded.

And said, "I would."

Harper was still flying pretty high when she presented herself on Nathan's doorstep midmorning on Sunday. He'd texted to say he had a few things to do before heading to Ocean Breeze. And to let her know that he'd be providing lunch that day.

She was glad he hadn't said dinner. She'd had a call from a well-known director, Johan Redmond, she'd worked with several times over the years, to choreograph several pieces for a black-tie affair later in the month, all proceeds to benefit several children's charities in the state. A portion of the planned entertainment had had to cancel, and the director had thought of Harper.

As booked as she already was, no way she was turning him down. She'd arranged a video call for that evening, to discuss details.

Life was gloriously unexpected, and she loved it. She'd thought having the chance to meet Goldman had been great. Had never imagined that he'd become a friend. That she'd even want him to be one.

And work opportunities…she filled with the same excitement every single time a new challenge presented itself.

Whether taking his cue from her, or from his own rightness with the world, Nathan was smiling as he opened the door to her and Aggie. Taking the speaker from her he set it up on a new little table in the living room so the music could be heard all over the cottage.

"Did you bring that table just for this?" she asked, bending over to cue the music.

"And for this." He held up his phone. "Figured I could use some music in my life, too, when I'm here alone."

Whether that was a breakthrough for him or not, his choice to bring song into his world, Harper wanted to believe that it was. That she'd helped him open himself up to something he'd once enjoyed.

She was still smiling as she picked up cleaning supplies and headed to the third bedroom to remove grime while she got lost in the evocative sounds permeating the air all around them.

She didn't ask Nathan if he minded if she started the forty-minute piece over when it ended. She just did it. He'd understand. Had known she'd be working. Same for the third time the melody rang through the cottage.

He'd been in the kitchen the first time she'd come out. Was in the main bedroom the third time. Aggie was moving between the two of them as she had the day before. Harper had brought the girl a blanket to lie on, had left it in the living room, but had yet to see Aggie use it.

By lunchtime, Harper had a pretty good sense of the piece. Had already collected mental visions of where it was taking her. Moves she saw within the powerfully atmospheric sound.

And set the music to shuffle through her library as they sat down to eat. He'd brought chef salads. Huge ones. Way too big for her to eat in one sitting. But they were fresh. The turkey thick, the cheese not overpowering, eggs crumbled across the top. All her favorite vegetables.

No bacon. Nothing that would saturate her with fat. A lightly seasoned oil-based dressing on the side.

"Where'd you get this?" she asked, always on the lookout for places to grab quick but healthy food.

"From Rockcliff," he said, naming the elegant restaurant, bar and private event place at the top of the drive that led down to Ocean Breeze. All that was left of the luxury hotel that used to sit up there.

"I've never seen a chef salad on their menu," she said, crunching another bite as soon as the last word was out.

"Special order."

She stopped, fork midair, to look over at him. His attention was on his salad. And she smiled again.

She most definitely had found herself a friend.

Nathan was busy running mental lists as he ate. Adding to the calculations he'd done the night before. As an investment, he shouldn't go top-end on things that weren't going to matter. They'd dig into his profit.

But he also couldn't sell the place short—not with historic places being such a minority in the area. To do that felt like sacrilege...

A phrase interrupted his thought. Musical. Coming from Harper's unit. He'd been half listening, half tuning out all morning. Hearing more than he'd known, he'd realized as certain parts of the score replayed mentally inside him as it played live for the umpteenth time.

But the current one... He stopped eating, and glanced over at Harper. She'd been mostly quiet during lunch. Working on the piece she'd been listening to all morning, he'd figured. Hadn't wanted to interrupt her. As the music played...mostly strings in the background to complement the female voice... Harper was feeding Aggie a carrot from her salad.

For a second, he closed his eyes, feeling first, and then, remembering, he opened them again. To see Harper watching him, her brows raised.

Because he'd appeared to be falling asleep over lunch?

His first instinct, to shrug off the moment, was quickly lost to the realization that he didn't have to keep to himself. Not with her. "This song…'Angels Come to Visit'…" He said the title aloud as it came back to him. Looked up to see her interest, and said, "I remember it."

More and more as the music continued to play. The artist, he couldn't remember her name, singing about a soul that got lost, was ready to give up, and then angels came to visit. Different verses. Same theme. Always with a young girl forgetting she wasn't alone. Ready to give up. And then angels came to visit.

He closed his eyes again. Had to find the rest. To remember.

And it came to him. Opening his eyes, he looked over to see Harper still watching him. Not with concern, but more like she was engaged in his process.

Was waiting.

And so he said, "I remember a dance on the competition circuit." There was no threat in the telling. She knew his past. And his future. Didn't hate him for the former. And was not a threat to the latter. She was…a friend.

"The girl was young. Junior category. But she moved with the grace of an old soul…" As he spoke more came to him. "I didn't watch the other dancers much. I was always…involved…" Either with his own performance requirements. Running through moves. Stretching.

Or with the girls surrounding him. Each vying for her own special moment with him.

"But that day… I'd finished my last number and just wanted…to be alone," he remembered. Feeling that young man's yearning as he sat there so many years later. "I went out to the auditorium, sat in a corner in the way back. It was dark…" He'd been…alone. Unwatched. Tired.

He looked Harper in the eye then. Got a bit lost in her understanding.

"And there she was. At first I was kind of wondering about her costume. It was a lyrical number, and she was wearing a beige full-body leotard with short purple streamers down the arms and legs. And purple lyrical shoes. I remember sitting forward to watch. Couldn't take my eyes away. And it wasn't like there were any incredible moves in and of themselves. A few nice double pirouettes." He remembered noting the lines, the point of the toe. "But it was like she knew something I didn't. Felt something I'd never felt. And I just had to watch."

He finished. Had no other memories of that day. Of that particular season, even. Except, "I looked for her at other competitions that season," he said. "Never saw her again."

Harper's gaze had deepened. She had tears in her eyes. Something he had absolutely not meant to draw from her. "That was in San Francisco," she said, and he nodded. Verifying that he'd been competing on his home turf.

"It was the year my parents brought their battle down to San Diego. Mom moved, couldn't take me out of state, but could head south. And so Dad followed. And petitioned the court for full custody since Mom hadn't petitioned for the right to move me. They had attorneys who argued in court about how much mileage constituted breaking their custodial agreements. About how I had better dance opportunities in San Diego. Both asking me to testify on their behalf that they were acting in my best interests. I had to see two psychologists, one for each side, who testified…"

Feeling awful for her, Nathan took it all in. Forgot what had even started the conversation, until Harper said, "That's why you didn't see that dance again."

He shook his head. Didn't get it.

"That was me, Nathan. 'Angels Come to Visit,' the purple streamers, purple lyrical shoes. It was the first time I ever took first place in my division…"

Her? Harper Cecilia? He gave his head another shake. But…

His mouth opened. Nothing came out. He just stared, bouncing mentally from past to present, memory to current sight.

She held his gaze, steadily, and something settled over him. Within him.

They'd known each other then, on a level that had worked, and they'd met again.

Two loners meant to be friends.

Sometimes life really did hand you a gift.

Chapter Twelve

Harper had been given a gift at birth. She'd been blessed with the ability, the vision, and she earned the right to spend her days doing what she loved. And if she didn't do the work, her talent would lay stagnant in a pool of wastefulness. A knowledge that drove her through that next week, landing her in many perfect moments.

Thursday night was opening night for a San Diego Ballet production, and she was guest choreographer for the final number. In addition to maintaining her hours of personal training, and other duties, she attended rehearsals all week, preparing for that first performance. Dancers were tense, excited, serious and giddy in turns. Some thought they were ready, others were sure they were not. A critical pair of toe shoes was lost.

A couple of costumes needed last-minute alterations.

Hair spray permeated the air an hour before the curtain rose, as Harper entered the dressing room for last-minute conferrals with her dancers.

She stood in the wings, on side stage, hands to her chest, smiling and nodding at her dancers as they entered for the last number. Reveling in the heightened atmosphere as energy levels ran off the charts. And counted every beat with them during a stunning performance.

Still flying high as she drove home half an hour later, Harper knew she wasn't going to get any sleep without a walk on the beach. Scott and Iris had been on Aggie duty most of the week, which meant Aggie had had ample exercise and good time with her four-legged pals, but the girl was always up for late-night sojourns with her Mama.

The one disappointment in her week had been not seeing Nathan much. A quick, impromptu morning cup of tea on Tuesday, when he came by before his crew arrived for an inspection of the fireplace brick that would line the inside of the chimney. And a wave on Wednesday as she'd passed him coming down to Ocean Breeze as she'd been heading out.

She'd texted him a few times. Wanting to know about choices he was making for his cottage orders, mainly. He'd texted back, telling her about them.

And just that evening, he'd texted to wish her a good opening night. The glow those words had brought her hadn't even begun to wear off.

Goldman had shared a real-time, conscious and deliberate dance moment with her.

Aggie was more clingy than usual, keeping her body pressed right up to Harper's side a lot of the time as they took a slow walk down to the water, and then down beach. In the leggings she had on all day, with a hastily thrown sweatshirt over her top half to ward off the ocean's April chill, Harper lifted her face to the sky. Focusing on the soft grainy feel of the sand between her bare toes. Taking deep breaths of salty ocean air.

Coming down from a high that never got old.

She was heading down to Nathan's place. It'd be dark. Deserted. Based on his texts, he'd been leaving by seven most evenings. But she'd been walking that far, anyway.

That night, the venture down was solely driven from within. He'd texted about the show. Had been in the moment with her, at least for the seconds it had taken to think about the text, type it and send it.

And that awareness had been feeding an idea that had been growing in her since her video conversation on Sunday night.

If she could get Redmond involved…

That's where she stopped herself, every time. The ramifications were too far-reaching, and fantastical, for her to allow herself to imagine.

He wasn't going to change his life. She fully understood that.

And after listening to him over the course of the previous weekend—both what he'd said and what he hadn't—she didn't want him to do so. The man had the gift of inner sight, of artistic expression…and dance hadn't been the best outlet for his life's journey. Instead, he worked hard to express that beauty in woodworking that enhanced the lives of families all over San Diego.

Different venue. Same result.

Bringing beauty into the world for others to enjoy, which bettered lives.

And oh…those movements onstage that night…the music crescendoing. The principal executing an exquisite leap, landing into a triple pirouette…chills spread through Harper again, as she relived the moment.

Aggie startled her out of it, bumping into Harper's leg, causing her to stumble, at which point one of Aggie's paws came down on her bare foot, as the dog headed in front of Harper toward the cottages.

Nathan's cottage.

Aggie had made the walk enough times to think that's

where they were going, Harper surmised, holding her foot for the few seconds it took for the stinging to subside, and then glancing toward the girl. And the cottage beyond.

It wasn't dark.

And if she wasn't mistaken, the kitchen light was casting a shadow on a human being in a chair on the sand in front of the rickety back deck.

Nathan was still there?

Heart leaping, Harper headed up without a second's thought. He'd been on her mind all week—and with that night's text…and he was still on Ocean Breeze…fate was practically pushing her on him.

He was wearing long pants, dark. Looked like tennis shoes. A long-sleeved shirt. His dark blond hair looked tousled. From a hat? His fingers? No tool belt.

Harper made the observations as she approached. Just couldn't get a read on his expression. The moon was trying to help, shining down on him, but shadows were there, too.

There's a shadow side to everything, Harper remembered her father saying to her one time when she asked him why he was always fighting over her if he loved her as much as he said he did.

His answer had done nothing but frustrate her at the time. But she'd learned through years of living that he'd been right in his assessment. As he'd been about a lot of things.

Just not about her mother.

Nathan was facing her. She figured watching her approach. He didn't get up.

She hadn't expected him to do so.

Had he been watching for her? A shard of pleasure shot through her at the thought.

"How come you're still here?" She asked the question

as she approached. Would he admit if he'd been waiting to see if she made it down?

The question was quickly followed by another. Did she really want him to?

"Didn't make much sense to keep going back and forth over the next month," he said, as though they'd been meeting regularly on the beach at night. "I moved a mattress in last night after work."

He'd texted her the night before, telling her about the tub he'd found for the jack and jill bathroom. Almost an exact match to the pristine tub in the hall bath. Listed on an antique mall's website in Arizona. He'd already purchased it and was having it shipped.

All those details…but not the important one pertaining to him.

She'd walked down the previous night, too. Hadn't known he was there. His place had been dark.

Had he been out? Seen her? She wanted to know. Didn't ask. She wasn't ready to hear that he'd watched her walk down and head back, but hadn't bothered to join her.

Or text and let her know.

Whoa. Harper's thoughts skidded to a halt as soon as she realized that they were out of control. Aggie sat down. So she did, too. In the sand. A few feet from Nathan's beach chair.

It looked new.

"You're living here already?" she asked then, with common neighborly interest, she hoped.

His shrug was familiar. Said so much. And not enough.

"Camping out?" she guessed, thinking of the small fridge in the laundry room.

When she'd texted Tuesday night to ask how the cleaning was coming, he'd sent back that he'd had a professional cleaning crew in on Tuesday. That all the dust, grime and removable stains were gone. Effectively ending any need for Harper down there.

"More or less. Nothing official."

An odd choice of words, she thought. He owned the place. It didn't get any more official than that.

She waited for him to ask how the night's performance went. To show any interest in her work. Her week.

A sign that she should segue into the possibility she'd been mulling regarding the charity function that would take up most of her working and waking hours in another week.

She didn't want to push him.

But if she could help him find a piece of himself, bring him closure and an opening at the same time...the idea hadn't let go of her all week.

He still did his daily stretches. She couldn't let go of that fact.

But was distracted from it when he said, "I had an interesting talk with Cynthia earlier tonight."

The beautiful young widow who lived in a cottage midway between Scott and Iris and Nathan and owned an upscale salon in San Diego. She'd purchased the place after her husband's death in a boating accident the year before. News reports had said his girlfriend had died with him.

Harper sat silently, her knees pulled up to her chest, her arms wrapped around them, as she waited to see if Nathan had more to say. For the first time in hours, the night's glory seemed to fade. She wasn't jealous. Exactly. Had no ownership whatsoever over Nathan Connolly. Had absolutely no thoughts about them ever being an item.

Not with his life plan being the complete antithesis of her own.

But...they'd just become friends. She wanted more of

his time. Didn't have much of her own to spare…and if he had someone else occupying him on the beach…

Giving herself a mental slap against the side of her head to stop the untoward thought process, Harper concentrated, instead, on what she knew about Cynthia. And came up with…not much.

She was blonde. Gorgeous, of course, given her business. She'd been kind, and not at all afraid, the time Aggie had been charging straight in her direction her while bounding up the beach toward Morgan.

"I'd been telling her about the work I was doing on your place." Nathan's voice was a blessing, interrupting Harper's mental battles, a byproduct of emotions heightened by the night's performance. She didn't get to specify good from bad where the emotional cortex was concerned.

Heightened was heightened. Meaning, what came its way came on steroids for a time.

"That I saw this cottage when I was here to meet with you…"

Not getting any better. Now the two of them were getting together because of her? Aggie glanced her way and Harper took note. Laid a hand on the girl's huge back. Aggie might not read minds, but she could sense when Harper wasn't calm.

"She said she doesn't know you well."

What, had the whole conversation been about her? Had there been any good in it?

A flash of a moment she'd interrupted earlier that day hit. Two dancers at odds, trying to one-up the other. They'd both tried out for the same part. Had both had callbacks.

One had to outshine the other to get what she needed.

A fact of life.

"She said the couple of times she's been present for a

beach bonfire, that you were there, but you were mostly talking with the guys."

The words felt like a direct hit. Harper's silence wasn't for lack of words at that point. It was for lack of wanting to engage in the conversation.

"Sage and Iris agreed."

What the hell! Backstabbing had arrived on Ocean Breeze? She hadn't taken a single thing from anyone there. Except maybe a chicken leg, or piece of watermelon, when it was offered. And she'd always done what she could to be of service, when she'd known someone needed something. Which wasn't often. She wasn't out enough to know much.

Sue her for being a loner.

And what a crappy night it was turning out to be.

"They feel badly that you're always on the outside of things," Nathan's words just kept on coming. "They're out on the beach all the time after work, and so, naturally, they're involved in a lot of the gatherings, and they don't think to knock on your door and let you know when something's going on."

It was word of mouth on the beach. Key words being *on the beach*. "No one knocks on doors," she said then. Just those five words. Said in an even tone.

"That's what they said. But Iris mentioned how much help you were to her after Scott's surfing accident, and they all decided that sometimes people need to know that they're wanted."

Okay, great. They were armchair psychologists.

"They're planning to descend on you, en masse, this weekend. I just thought you'd like a heads-up."

Open-mouthed, she stared over at him with a small note of panic.

She'd been the subject of conversation, but it hadn't been negative.

And Nathan was being a friend. Letting her know what was coming. That last part felt safe.

"I'm not great at the girl friendship thing," she told him. And more came pouring out. "Cynthia was right, I do gravitate toward the guys' conversation. It's easier. If anyone were to hit on me—which no one ever has down here—I know exactly how to handle it. And the rest… I'm not a threat. I listen. I smile. I learn some things. And I go home."

He nodded. Watched her. Seconds passed, and he said, "You're not a threat. But… the women in your life, since you were what, about ten, have always seen you as one. The shining star in dance class. A total danger to anyone who also wanted to be a star. And as your classes got more advanced, pretty much everyone in them wanted to grow up to be a dancer. Or were already studying seriously with that goal in mind."

And as she reached adulthood, and actually did take away others' chances…the situation had intensified accordingly.

He got it. He'd been there. He'd seen it happening to other girls. Among other ballerinas.

She felt…known.

Giving her shins a squeeze, Harper smiled.

He could have texted. Had planned to do so.

The last thing Nathan needed was to be out late at night, in the darkness, with the moon shining and waves lapping in the distance with Harper Michaels.

All week long, he hadn't been able to get the woman out of him. In his dreams…well, guys did that. Most particularly ones who'd been on a physical sabbatical as long as he'd been. Made more prominent as said time off was nearing an end.

It wasn't the dreams, or even the obvious physical attraction he felt when something or another brought to mind something she'd said or done the previous weekend, that was bothering him so much. Physical crap he could deal with.

But the way Harper was creeping into his sense of self… that was a problem. She wasn't a part of him. Nor he her. They were new friends, not lifelong ones.

And yet…he'd known, bone-deep felt, that a group maneuver such as the women on the beach were planning—no matter how genuinely kind and friendly the motive—would be difficult for Harper. The woman's life cried out for feminine companionship she could trust.

Trust wasn't built in an afternoon.

Or during an ambush.

And so he'd brought a chair out to the beach to wait for her to get home. She'd said she walked the beach late at night, to wind down. The woman was predictable. He'd give her that.

In a way that he found…to his liking.

She was dependable.

Not a characteristic he'd thought about much in a woman. But one that he noted for the future. He wanted his wife to be dependable.

Such a simple thing. And yet, huge to Nathan.

"I wanted to talk to you about something." Harper's tone wasn't anything Nathan had heard before. Unsure. Maybe worried about his reaction.

Whatever, it was knocking him off guard.

Right when he'd been sitting there knowing her so well.

Tension tightening inside him, he said, "What?"

Maybe she just hated her deck—what was done of it. It was definitely taking a permanent shape. One that she hadn't envisioned? She wanted her money back?

"Before I say anything more, I need your word that you'll hear me out before you say anything."

No problem there. He was fine to listen and give nothing back. To prove so, he didn't answer. Just nodded.

"And before you rush to judgment."

He couldn't help how his mind processed, or when it came to conclusions. "I'll sit here and listen until you're done," he replied, giving her what he could.

With her arms wrapped around herself, Harper rocked back and forth on her butt in the sand. As though she needed the calming that movement gave her.

Something he also knew from experience. Not that he'd sit on his ass and rock. Ever.

But he was known to tap a heel in rhythm now and then.

Currently. Gentle taps. Soundless. Muffled by the sand.

"You know Johan Redmond?"

His foot stilled. "The director?"

She nodded, the motion of her head in slow beat with her body's.

And, remembering that he'd said he wouldn't say anything until she was done, he nodded. Then said, "And to clarify, if you want me to stay silent, don't ask direct questions." He should've smiled. Didn't.

She did. "Point taken. Abraham's in charge of a black-tie affair at the Ambrosio in LA at the end of the month." She named a well-known producer who'd hired the man. "They're raising money for several notable statewide children's charities." She named them, too. All of which he'd heard of. One in particular, a program designed to keep kids off drugs, was the recipient of his company's yearly charitable donation.

Of course, he couldn't share that information. He'd been commanded to muteness.

"The guest list is filled with a who's who of Beverly Hills and surrounding areas."

He imagined it would be. Figured he'd be familiar with many of the names. His foot was also keeping a more distinct, harder beat.

"There's no set price for the dinner and entertainment event," she continued, making him more uneasy with every word she uttered. He could feel the wall she was building.

Not around him, though, like he figured she thought.

It was shooting up between them. Block by block. Quickest one he'd ever erected.

And no matter what kind of rules she'd set on the conversation, no matter what agreement she'd pulled from him before he'd known where she was going.

No matter how long he held his tongue.

He'd already passed judgment.

And the answer was no way in hell.

Chapter Thirteen

"Attendees are given lists of entertainers as people sign on, and they bid for one of the 450 seats as names appear."

Nathan's chin was so taut his jaw hurt. The muscles in his throat were tight. How could she…

"I was asked to choreograph several pieces." Her words were like a death knell, and a confirmation of his good judgment at the same time. He wasn't doing it.

"Two of them are going to be youth numbers. One a duet. The other, I haven't decided yet. But with the money being raised for children, and so many talented children in the world of dance who are never seen outside competitions and recitals, I can't not have them there."

He almost nodded. The taut set of his neck reminded him that he was not in any way a part of what she was trying to involve him in. As a side note, he remembered that he'd said he wouldn't respond until she was through.

Hopefully that would be soon. The one word he had to give her was pushing up out of him with a force that was getting harder and harder to contain.

"I already have dancers in mind for two others. One is a modern group I worked with last month, out of Arizona. They're only moderately known, and won't bring in high bids, but their performance will be unforgettable. And pledges are taken during the performance as well."

Great. He wished them well. Was sure they'd do great.

Get on with it.

Then I will.

And we can be done.

For the night.

Maybe the weekend, too. Depending on how well she understood that no meant no with a caveat to not ever come to him with such a request again. Understood that to do so could mean that their friendship would be short-lived.

"And the last one, I'm going to do," she said, rocking the same as she had been since the nightmare conversation had begun. "Redmond's request to me, but put to him by Winslow." The producer. He wasn't surprised. He'd googled Harper Cecilia the first day he'd met her.

He'd had to, to work with her. Had to know, so he could avoid falling into the trap of his past.

She undersold herself when she talked about her career.

"I want to do a duet that's been playing with me for a couple of years." She named a tune he'd never heard of. And he didn't really hear it then through the roaring in his ears.

A duet. No.

Holding her onstage...catching her...

His foot thumped.

Blood thrummed through his veins.

Absolutely not.

Blinking hard, he stared at the ocean, wiped out the vision that had jumped into his head at her words.

"I've chosen the male dancer, and he's agreed to dance with me. You might have heard of him. Jamie Oppenstott." The words were muffled, but they managed to reach him through his own inner turmoil.

She'd chosen the male dancer. He'd agreed to dance with her.

But she'd said she had something to ask *him*.

Completely sharp again, foot slowed and mind open, Nathan thought back to the conversation's beginning. She hadn't actually said she had a question for him.

She'd said she had something to talk to him about. And then had asked that he withhold judgment and comment until she'd finished...

She didn't want him to dance. She'd already asked some other guy to do it.

Relief flashed by.

Knocked out when ego crashed into his mental train wreck. Setting it on fire.

She didn't want him.

How in the hell could she not want him?

No way he'd do it. Wasn't even a little bit tempted.

Where dance was concerned, temptation wasn't an issue.

But *jealousy* was?

I'll be... Yeah, he knew full well what he'd be. What he'd been. What he was.

And was thankful that Harper had stifled him, preventing him from ruining a perfectly good friendship.

"Jamie's name drew bids when it posted to the list." Harper was stalling. The way Nathan's foot had been tapping when she'd been talking about the show...she didn't want to cause him tension or stress.

But if she could help him find joy in a vital part of himself that he'd felt he had to completely abandon...and take her own vision to an even deeper level...plus earn a lot more money for the kids...

"The thing is, he's on a supertight schedule and can only show up two nights before the show, to learn the piece, and then for dress rehearsal the day of..."

She watched Nathan's heel. No tapping.

She'd stopped rocking, too. The movement would have helped. But if his foot was a tell to her…she could assume that hers might be to him, too.

The man had quit dancing—he hadn't lost his ability to see things others missed. He was as astute as they came.

And…she wasn't her best, her strongest, around him. He'd brought that vulnerable, loner kid out of hiding.

"And this piece… I'm in a different position than normal…because I'm not just setting it on someone else. I'm choreographing a piece for me to dance."

He opened his mouth. Met her gaze. Closed it. Tapped his fingertips together.

"I need your help, Goldman. Nathan!" she quickly corrected. And then said, looking down as she flexed her shoulders, raised her eyes again to look straight at him. "Goldman," she said.

His lips pursed. She'd run out of time. "I promise, nothing that would put you in the position you hate—no stage, no lights, no audience. Just…if you could join me in my private studio…where you were the other day. Run through moves with me. Dance Oppenstott's part so that I can see it come together with mine, revise as necessary. I'll lock the door. Won't let anyone watch. Won't film any rehearsals." Which was a big one for her. She always filmed. It was the way to give every second a minute, an hour, of introspection, as needed. To learn. To perfect.

He sat there. Staring at her. Saying nothing.

"I'm done now," she said after several excruciating seconds of silence. Preparing for his rejection, even knowing that there was no way to prevent the disappointment that would follow.

With his brows drawn together, he drew a breath. While she held hers, he said one word. "Why?"

"Why?"

"Why?"

"Why what?"

"Why me?"

Right. There were other male dancers. Good ones. Ones who knew her well. Who'd jump at the chance to work with her.

"Because they're not you," she said aloud. And then, hearing herself, quickly explained. "Others know me, know of me, have danced with me, but when it comes to dance we're not all equals…"

He nodded. An acknowledgment?

She heard a silent instant replay of her rambling. Thought she sounded conceited. Blurted, "I'm well-known in the performing arts world." Making things worse. "But not so much in the Hollywood circle. These people have seen the best of the best all over the world, Nathan. And my performance can mean thousands, maybe hundreds of thousands, more dollars if I wow them."

"You're nervous." He was assessing her.

Oddly enough, she took her first easy breath in a while. He hadn't immediately rejected her, turned his back, and walked in the cottage. Which was what she'd been afraid might happen. "Not so much nervous as needing to do better than I've ever done before. Better than my best."

"You open to suggestion?" Aggie moved over to him as he asked the question. Nathan reached out, laying his hand on the top of the girl's head. Not so much petting, but slightly moving his fingers in her thick fur.

He was going to suggest someone else to help her. The

disappointment she expected came. But not as fiercely as it would have done if he'd just given her a cold walk away.

"What kind of suggestion?" The question was put up to buy her time. To look for some way to convince him to give her idea a chance. Not just for her, but for him, too, though she was pretty sure he wasn't ready to be open to that part.

He might never be. But if he wasn't given a chance, he'd never know for sure.

His shrug confused her. And then he said, "Whatever comes up. Do you envision me as your puppet, or are you open to suggestion as we work?"

Eyes wide, she stared. Felt her lips trembling. Had no words at first. And then, pressed by powers from within said, "Always."

"And no one, not even Oppenstott, is present when I am. This is just between me and you."

"On my life," she promised, her hands shaking.

"Then, I'm willing to give it a try. One session. Which might last one minute. And go from there. No guarantees."

Tears flooded Harper's eyes, embarrassing her. She blinked, sniffed, and sat there smiling like a schoolgirl.

She was going to get to dance with Nathan Goldman.

And he...was going to dance again.

Nathan spent a good bit of time on Friday in the office. Tending to important but not timely details that had been sitting on his desk waiting for him to get to them. Filings due at the end of the month. Some vendor invitations. A trade show he'd been invited to attend. He also looked over the week's financials, signed off on them. Met with each of his three full-time office employees to go over workload, productivity and, mostly, any concerns they had. Everyone was busy, but no one felt the workload was too much for them, everyone was handling their responsibilities as he would, and the only concern anyone had was him.

His office manager, Hannah, a woman twenty years older than him who'd been with him from the beginning, thought he should be hiring someone to handle the work for the investment on Ocean Breeze.

He didn't mention to her that he needed to clear his desk to prepare for a little time off for something else. Didn't intend to do so. Ever.

But he *was* preparing. No way he was going to just walk away from his life, from Connolly Construction, without plans in place to keep things running smoothly. Even for a couple of afternoons. He'd still spend at least an hour a day at the office, as he'd been doing five days a week since he'd opened shop.

And he'd make all his inspection runs.

Sitting behind his desk, he stopped his flow of thoughts. He was planning a couple of afternoons? Harper had never said when she'd need him. He'd offered one session, for possibly one minute.

How had he jumped to giving her a couple of sessions for hours?

Keeping himself in check, or checking in, had become a mandatory part of life for him. Something he figured most people had been raised to do. A part of upbringing he'd missed. As long as he'd danced, there'd been no learning or disciplining for him, outside of dance. No life lessons.

And…he knew what learning and rehearsing a piece entailed. No way was he going to step into a studio without the intention of being there full-out. Whether or not he stayed…he couldn't say. If the atmosphere sent him backward, he'd walk out. If not, he needed to be able to focus and contribute to the best of Nathan Goldman's ability.

To that end, he dialed Harper from behind his closed office door, sitting in the office chair that had been with him from the beginning, behind a newer desk.

"Nathan?" She answered with the one word, on a mostly breathless note, symphony music in the background.

"This a bad time?"

"No." She breathed as though she'd been running.

And he knew. "You're dancing." His mind filled with the peek of the studio he'd seen. Her in a leotard and tights, spinning across the floor. Her form...

He shook his head. Looked out the window at the gravel drive that led to his warehouse. And a couple of his guys loading materials into a truck.

"Choreographing," she said then, "so, yes."

The music cut off midstream. She'd stopped it. Wouldn't have answered if she'd had anyone in the room with her. No way Harper would be that unprofessional for a phone call from a neighbor. Even one she'd just talked into helping her out.

Talked into. Who was he kidding? She'd asked. He'd accepted.

"We didn't discuss time, day," he said. Keeping both in the singular. One minute, one day.

"I've got a couple of weeks. You tell me. I'll build my schedule around you."

He nodded. Was used to such treatment.

The thought stopped him. No, he wasn't going back to that.

Except...he was the owner of an ultrabusy company who was doing her a favor. So...okay...but... "I can be flexible to a point," he told her. And then asked, "How would you like to play it?"

"Ideally, I'd like for my duet to go week after next. I'd

like to get everything choreographed first, and then start bringing people in. Working all weekend, and evenings, I should be ready to go by Wednesday, bring in the kids first, I've already got one piece done for them. An idea I've been playing with for a while. Their teacher will be there, learn the piece, can work with them after that, and I'll get them again the day before the show. And one of the group pieces is close. I'd done some phrases for a master class I'm teaching at the end of the month and want to incorporate them into a full number. So, then the Arizona-based modern group, in town on Thursday and Friday…how about next weekend?" she asked. "A week from tomorrow."

He was grinning. Hadn't even realized it. It was like he was there…not in her head…but…almost.

"The weekend's actually best for me," he said. He was never in the office on weekends. Was planning most of them for work on the cottage, and there was no deadline there. No one but him waiting for the work to be complete.

Except an overly attentive Realtor who he did not plan to call back.

Women who threw themselves at him, even after he'd made it clear he had no interest, were no longer a part of his life. He hadn't even had to think twice about that one.

And felt zero regret at missing the chance.

"Really?" She sounded surprised. And not at all like the professional he'd been speaking to.

Did she really think him as entitled as he'd once been? He'd assumed she knew him better.

Because…what…she'd spent a couple of days with him? Helped him with his cottage cleanup? Texted a few times. Walked down the beach at night as she'd been doing, so he'd been told, for years?

He didn't call her on the slight. Her lack of trust that he'd be aware of all that she had on her plate. "Yes."

"Oh! Well, then, yay! And…just… I'm glad."

What the hell! "You thought I was going to demand that you be ready to fit my schedule?" he blurted, getting his dander up in spite of himself.

"Oh! No. Not at all." Her tone had softened, sounding like the woman he'd spent so much time with the previous weekend. The one he'd told things he'd never even consciously told himself, let alone anyone else. The one who was his final challenge, who was bringing him full circle…

"I was afraid you were calling to tell me you'd changed your mind." Her words cut his thoughts off at the quick. "I'm just…glad. And…thank you."

Was that why she'd taken off the night before? Jumping up as soon as he'd agreed to help her and saying she had an early morning and had to get back? So he didn't back up on her?

"One session, one minute." He needed that clear.

"I know." Her voice had dropped in volume. But not intensity. "Trust me."

And Nathan's system settled into a reliable calm as he said, "I do."

And hung up.

Chapter Fourteen

I do.

I do.

Music on, an emotionally evocative strings and piano piece, Harper did a string of pirouettes, expertly thrown, across the sprung wood floor of her studio.

I do. The famous verbal duo was known as a deal sealer on a lifetime partnership promise. A promise that had never meant anything to her.

And still didn't.

But the words...for the first time, she felt power in them.

Nathan trusted her to have his back. Personally. Just as he'd trusted her with his truth.

I do. She'd never received such a gift from another human being.

Maybe she'd never asked for it. Expected it.

She'd earned trust in the professional world through her own actions. Had proven herself, shown people what they could expect from her. So it was a no-brainer when she received that trust.

But with Goldman...she felt the weight of what he'd just given her...and at the same time, flew across the room a second time. Light as air.

He'd entrusted her with a huge undertaking. Giving him

a chance to express himself through movement, to let the emotional knowledge within him have a big voice.

Without strings attached.

And as much as her heart cried for him to be onstage again, to find the same fulfillment she did just being a part of the dance world, she knew that it wasn't meant to be.

Had accepted the truth the first night they'd talked.

And because of that, she didn't want for him what she wanted for herself. Didn't want for him what she needed him to be for her.

The realization threw her into a state of confusion. Of nonmovement for a moment. And then she was on the floor, one leg folded beneath her, one straight out in front of her, toes pointed. Her back ramrod straight, and bent at the waist, her nose to her knee.

She wept for where she and Goldman would never again meet. In her world. Tears seeped from her eyes, wetting the knee of her tights, as the music continued to flow through her. A piano riff started, and she lifted her head. Sharply. Listening. Her bent knee straightened, lifting her entire body up until her weight was held by the toes of one foot. And she spun. Once slowly. Then, on the other foot, again. More quickly. And again and again. Switching feet with each new piano chord, spotting one point in the mirror, seeing nothing else.

Aware of the instruments' call, the despair coursing through her…and the joy.

She tried to leap. To plié. Bourrée en couru—tiny steps that made her appear as though she was gliding. But it all fell flat. And then she threw a battement jeté—pulling one foot up her leg, and then extending the leg to throw it out, leap and land on the thrown foot. Her arms were thrown wide as well. Hitting out against the pain. Leaving her open for the joy.

And then she stopped. Just stood in the middle of the floor. Coming back to herself. Took a couple of deep breaths as she walked calmly over to her music system. Turned off the sound. Grabbed her towel to wipe her face and chest. And then her water bottle, drinking a gulp at a time. Letting the water hydrate her, not drown her.

She was who she was.

Nathan was who he was.

She loved her life.

He'd deliberately and consciously shaped his. Seemed truly happy in it, and with himself.

She saw her future, clearly.

He had his all mapped out.

The two really were diametrically different.

And yet...she was thrilled to have met him.

And was deeply honored to have the chance to be his friend.

Nathan stayed in town Friday night. Because of a desire to sit on the beach after dark and watch for Harper and Aggie.

Not only was he not ever going to be that guy—if he wanted to spend time with a woman, he was going to ask—but he wasn't going to ever be more than a friend to Harper, so giving in to longings where she was concerned wasn't healthy.

The man that he'd been—prior to starting his self-imposed sabbatical the year before—had let his longings, his sexual desires for willing women, have free rein. The man he'd become would not do so.

He also would not kid himself about their presence. He had the hots for Harper.

But he valued her as a friend more.

Which meant he had to learn how to be with a woman, enjoy her company, without letting sex enter the equation.

Another test.

Shouldn't come as any surprise. Clearly Harper was the challenge of all challenges. He'd chosen to become a better man, a better human being. He had to like himself before he could find real happiness. And until he'd proven to himself that he'd succeeded, he'd never be able to reach for the ultimate goal. Being more than just satisfied. He wanted complete fulfillment.

So thinking, he was waiting for her when she got home on Saturday night. There'd been a bonfire on the beach. Aggie had been there with Morgan and Angel. Was being watched over by Scott and Iris. Dale and Cynthia were there. A petless veterinarian who lived on the beach, Kara, had come down. Nathan was introduced. And Cassie, the pediatrician, and her husband, Dennis, a teacher, joined them. A few other residents out enjoying the beach stopped to chat throughout the evening. Nathan saw them from across the circle that had formed around the fire, wasn't introduced.

Sage and Gray, with little Leigh, were the first to leave. Sage's pregnancy was clearly pronounced and, while she glowed, she was also wanting to get Leigh to bed so she could relax. Or, as Nathan surmised to himself, she wanted some quiet time alone with her husband.

Shocked at the envy that shot through him—he'd never been the guy who'd coveted what others had—Nathan watched them go. And was interrupted when Aggie approached and nudged his arm with her great big head.

The beast had somehow gotten the idea that Nathan was free game. She didn't seem to get that he was a guy who'd never had a pet in his life.

Guessing she'd figure it out soon enough on her own, he let her sit there. Using her as an armrest, warming his fingers in the cool ocean air by running them back and forth through her massively thick fur.

And when the gathering broke up, Aggie stood with him. While Iris and Scott made plans with another couple to watch some video they'd been talking about, Nathan offered to take Aggie home. Everyone knew his company had been doing the work on Harper's place for the past couple of weeks. And Aggie was clearly happy to go with him.

He didn't have a key to the place, but didn't bother saying so.

Instead, he stopped by his investment place to pick up the nutrition he'd left in the refrigerator and walked down the beach to wait for Harper to arrive.

His men had finished the deck that morning. Four days early. He'd paid for the extra crew to come in both of the past two days so that Harper would have the peace she'd need when she got home over the next week, after working from daybreak until after nightfall.

It felt good, doing good for a friend. Not like giving to charity, or paying for catering for Hannah's family when she'd been sick. Those needs were obvious.

But Harper's needs... He'd been invited inside, to a place not many people saw. Just as she'd been with him. She hadn't asked for the work to be completed sooner...he'd just known that it would benefit her to have it so. Figuring that out, and then acting on it...felt good.

From what he'd gathered, Harper offered to do for others, but, as far as he could see, no one offered to do for her. He guessed it was because she didn't open herself up to the opportunity. She'd never let anyone know if she had a need with which they could help.

She hadn't been home to receive the friendship ambush that afternoon, either.

He'd casually let drop into the night's conversation that she'd said something about a special project on her plate... would be working really long hours.

And from there...he was out of it.

Meddling had never been his thing. He wouldn't be good at it.

His mother, yeah, she'd been a pro, but... No. He wasn't going there. Except to ponder a realization that hit him as he grabbed the handle of his cooler and headed toward the door, waiting for the giant to precede him out.

Harper and his mother were from the same mold. Dance was life. And the only road to happiness. But beyond that...

Harper wasn't obsessed. Or in constant need of the spotlight. It was more about the dance than it was about Harper herself.

Not that it mattered a whole lot, he quickly conceded as Aggie walked silently beside him, keeping perfect pace with him.

Harper's life was dance.

Nathan's would never be again.

Not even for her could he reenter that world. He'd be no good to her, or anyone, without his soul.

Iris had texted Harper while they were still on the beach, getting her thumbs-up on Nathan taking responsibility for Aggie. He left it at that. If Harper assumed that Scott and Iris had given him the key...then she did.

He hadn't wanted it that way. If ever he'd have a key to

his friend's house, to help her out as needed, that key would come from her.

So thinking, when they reached Harper's deck and he saw the dark cottage, Nathan put down his cooler, turned on the fire and admired the rockwork his men had done after he'd set the stage. Checking out the workings of the propane apparatus, the ease with which he could adjust flames, both at the source and with the remote he'd carried over in his pocket to leave with Harper, he considered building a fireplace at his investment property as well.

Standing there with the ocean breeze, the beach two steps away, and the glimpses of the moon on the water in the distance, he determined the addition would make a great selling point.

Aggie, who'd been standing by the back door, seemed to tire of waiting for him to let her in, and lay down in front of it instead. Head down on her front paws, her soulful eyes were open, watching the flames.

Taking his cue from her, he sat close by, leaning back against the cottage. Running his hands along the wood beneath him, he felt good. Took pleasure in the moment. And was still sitting there, engaged with the night, the flames, the experience, when Harper opened the back door to the cottage half an hour later.

She'd texted to let him know she was on her way.

He hadn't bothered to move.

Nor did he do so as he eavesdropped on the greeting between housemates. Aggie's wagging tail slapped the door. Her paws moving rapidly on the floor, based on the claw sounds he was hearing. He couldn't make out everything Harper was saying, but he recognized the higher tone of voice she reserved for her pet.

And then she actually stepped outside.

"Oh my gosh, Nathan! I can't...you didn't tell me."

He'd wanted to surprise her.

"It's all done and...oh...it's gorgeous! Perfect!" She stepped to the middle of the deck, lit only by the light coming through the opened door and kitchen window, the moon and the fire's flames, and turned a circle. Then walked to the fireplace. "I was so tired last night I didn't even come out to check on progress. And I've been letting Aggie out front in the mornings."

Holding her hand out to the flame, she stood for a second, her shoulders and spine in perfect alignment, even with the fatigue she had to be feeling. He just wanted to sit there and look at her.

But he had more.

Grabbing his soft-sided cooler, he pulled the blanket out of the underneath zipper portion, opened it and tossed it down on the deck, aware when she turned around.

"I know you're tired, but sustenance after dance, to rebuild for tomorrow, is important," he said, feeling kind of foolish all of a sudden as he pulled the container he'd dropped into the cooler.

It had meant a lot to him when she'd brought food down to his place. His attempt to reciprocate wasn't giving the same vibe. "I brought turkey rolls with avocado and egg," he told her. "My mother used to have them at night after shows."

When she danced, and when he did.

It had been a thing. A quiet time between the two of them. Usually backstage before they went home—because there'd been some aftershow to attend, or a stop at her studio to do. But sometimes she'd waited until they'd arrived home. "Those little picnics are one of the few good memories..." He stopped when he heard the words aloud.

Hadn't even been aware of the memory until that afternoon, when he'd been thinking of a way to celebrate the christening of Harper's new deck.

Avocado and egg, with a little bit of oil, wrapped up in a slice of turkey. He didn't do a lot of cooking, ever, but he'd perfected the rolls so long before, it had been muscle memory remaking them.

She'd glanced at him with his butt on the edge of the blanket, his legs out in front of him—the turkey rolls in their opened container beside him, leaving most of the blanket, and closest to the fire, to her. And then, without a word, she walked into the cottage.

Aggie had been inside since Harper had come home.

Nathan waited to hear the door close behind her. Didn't really expect it to, but he wasn't all that great on reading women. Except in the bedroom.

There he excelled.

Had never once had a woman walk out on him.

And for a second, he wondered if he'd been living on a pipe dream. Setting himself up for abject failure. A leopard couldn't change his spots.

He should stick to the sex.

After one week short of a year without it, his body was ready to rise in celebration of that idea. While his mind lingered somewhere in an abyss.

The door opened beside him. Aggie came out.

He took the win.

Figured Harper wouldn't just leave without a thank-you and good-night. She wasn't rude.

But he'd put her in a damned awkward situation. Forcing her to socialize after a gruelingly long day. As though he was too insensitive to care.

Too bad he'd only gotten that after he'd littered her deck with his sad little picnic.

He heard her coming out before she reappeared. Expected that she'd changed into the sweats and T-shirt he'd seen her in more often than leotard and leggings she'd had when she'd first come out.

He'd been right on that score. Recognized both the sweats and the T-shirt. What he hadn't seen before was the tray she was also carrying.

With a bottle of wine and two glasses.

And it hit him. Saturday night. The one evening a week she allowed herself a glass of wine. More local brew, he noticed as he reached up to take the tray and lower it to the blanket for her.

In the jeans, button-down shirt and tennis shoes he'd worn out to the bonfire, he felt decidedly overdressed for the intimate scene.

Figured that for the best, too. He'd failed to acknowledge the danger inherent in his plan for the late-night snack by the fire. Their previous meals had been shared in a filthy, dilapidated cottage, in the midst of work. And a very public restaurant.

Without a word, Harper settled on the blanket, poured the wine, and handed a glass to him, before raising hers and saying, "Thank you. I can't imagine a moment more perfect with which to end a hugely productive and exhausting day."

He met her glistening gaze in the shadows. Smiled. And sipped when she did.

Maybe his friend skills where women were concerned weren't so bad after all.

Chapter Fifteen

Nathan hadn't ever stepped foot in her house, but Harper felt as though he filled every inch of the space that next week. He'd never even touched her, other than a handshake, and yet his spiritual essence floated inside her.

She told herself it was because she was choreographing her piece for the charity event. And while he wouldn't be dancing that night, the piece was for him.

A part of him.

Every piece she'd danced since she'd seen him on stage had been, at least partially, inspired by him.

But she knew it was more than that. In a couple of short weeks, he'd become the best friend she'd ever had. Anticipating her needs.

From the picnic Saturday night, that lasted only until she'd had her one glass of wine and had eaten two turkey roll ups, before he'd stood and said he'd leave her to get her rest. To the text he'd sent the one night she'd been home before dark, inviting her to stop in and see his progress on his cottage.

She'd been out on the beach with Aggie when the text had come in. Standing alone, staring out to sea, wondering if she'd bitten off more than she could chew with the charity show. She'd had to reschedule a couple of other choreography jobs, had skipped class twice that week, was in beginning rehearsals for a show she'd be doing later in the spring, and she wasn't happy with the duet.

He'd shown her the moldings that had come in. The new bathtub. The drywall work that had been completed in one bedroom.

Not the primary.

But the one with the mattress on a cheap metal bed rail where he'd obviously been sleeping when he stayed over.

She loved what he was doing with the place. Could see the former beauty starting to appear already.

And he'd looked at her and said, "So, when you get drained, if you have any doubts, just remember that, like this cottage, a little TLC is all you need."

He'd seen her out on the beach. He hadn't told her so, but she'd known.

And had gone home to have a hot soak, followed by bed just after the sun set.

That had been Tuesday—the night before she'd worked with the kids. They'd been her tender loving care, far more than the hot bath and sleep had been.

Still, she was more nervous than ready on Saturday morning when she locked the inner door leading from her studio to the bathrooms and small break room that came with her lease. They were off from a hallway shared with a couple of other suites. With an entryway on the other side of the building.

She'd blocked out the entire weekend. No one was scheduled to be there. And she was taking no chances that someone might see her car in the lot and stop by. With so many balls in the air, she couldn't predict who might need what and hope to catch her in a quiet moment.

And walk in on Goldman.

Locking that inner door sent the tension inside her escalating. Rapidly. What had she been thinking? Inviting Goldman to rehearse with her. Yeah, as a kid she'd fantasized about dancing with him. But she'd been too young then to know better.

And had never really believed it would happen.

That was the nice thing about fantasies. You could experience something in your imagination, and be in complete control of the outcome.

Which meant they always went your way.

In reality...she wasn't ready to test her skills against his.

Or, more accurately, to have him there, assessing her. Finding her less than he'd imagined. Being disappointed in her.

Other than a lyrical dance when she'd been a kid, he'd never even seen her dance. Unless he'd searched for her on the internet, and with his battle to keep himself separate from her world, she doubted he'd done that.

Nor would he have seen any of her choreography. What if he didn't like her style?

Would he just politely take his one minute and leave? Letting her think he was going because of his own need to get out?

How had she ever thought that she could be instrumental in bringing one of the greatest male dancers ever to dance, back to the dance floor? Like she was some guru whose work would speak to him. Would bring out the dancer in him.

What if it didn't? What if, instead, the next half hour brought back all the trauma that had caused him to walk out of the only life he'd ever known, to turn his back on his mother, on everyone he knew, just to save himself?

What kind of friend was she to put him in that position? To ask him to take that risk?

In through the nose out through the mouth. Standing in the middle of the floor, facing the mirror, she dropped her hands to first position, arms rounded, fingertips together at her pelvis. Raised them to her belly button as she drew in air. Slowly let them drop in time with the air's release.

And repeat.

On the third draw, she raised her hands to second, arms still rounded, hands together facing her breasts. And, heels together, toes pointing outward, slowly rose up. She started to move. Driven by sensation, not thought. First with a small jeté to the side. To the other. And then the dance took over. With music playing in her mind, she floated and flew, back and forth across the floor. Feeling the battle between forces inside her. The wants. The needs. The despair. Moments of ultimate joy.

Ending on the floor, one leg folded beneath her, the other straight out in front, toes pointed, with her back and neck straight, her torso bent slowly at the waist until her nose was to her knee.

She'd barely taken a breath when her bubble was shattered by the sound of applause. One set of hands. Clapping slowly. And coming closer.

She'd left the door open for Goldman. If someone else was there, ten minutes before he was due to arrive…

Heart pounding, she shot up. Turned. And faced…

Nathan. Sort of.

In black leggings and a dance tank top, exposing muscles she'd known had to be there, the man was centerfold material. Twice over.

Mouth open, partially because of her post-dance breathing, she stared. And then caught herself. Shook her head.

Hurried over to the outer door to lock it.

Telling herself to get a grip.

Afraid to turn around.

He'd seen her dance. Not at her best.

More like, witnessed a very private moment of expression.

Embarrassed, getting off on such a wrong foot she wasn't sure she could recover, Harper walked to the front of the mirrored room, heading for the sound system.

Trying to look professional, to take control of the moment that was happening at her behest in her own space, she cued the music they'd be using. Said, "Welcome."

She wasn't looking in the mirror. Needed a good, solid take-control-of-herself moment before looking at that body again.

Ridiculous. She worked with male dancers all the time. Had never once noticed a body in any way but professional.

"Was that part of the piece we'll be working on?"

His voice sounded…beneath her.

With a quick glance in the mirror, she found him on the floor behind her. Stretching.

"Sort of," she told him. "Parts of it are." She'd been building the dance all week. Movements coming to her randomly. During a rehearsal. In class the one day she'd attended. Even waking up in the middle of the night.

Always filled with an intensity that was almost over-the-top. Even for her.

Would he see that? Call her on it?

He'd requested carte blanche in terms of creativity critiques. She'd awarded it. Wished she hadn't.

Felt professionaly insecure, for the first time in her adult life, as she turned around, then turned back, lifting her leg to the ballet bar attached to the wall. Then, on one leg, and with one arm extended, with fingers slightly split, leaned over until her nose was just above her upraised knee.

And felt exposed. She should have worn a ballet skirt over her tights and leotard. And better ballet shoes. Her oldest pair were her favorite for studio time.

But under-impressive looking.

And her hair…he'd never seen it any way but bunched up on top of her head in a messy scrunchy. But for a work session with Nathan Goldman? It should be in the tight bun she wore when appearing professionally anywhere but her studio.

He'd finished on the floor. Was at the same barre she stood along, several feet down. Facing her as he ran through ballet positions. "You don't need me."

She'd been focused on breathing. Making her stretches look as though she knew what she was doing. And was really trying to get benefit from them, rather than just hiding. With her foot back on the floor, she let go of the barre. Faced him. "What?"

"Based on what I just saw, you don't need me."

"I'm not following."

"You said you needed to be sure that you were better than your best. You wanted someone who wasn't your peer to help you be better."

She'd said that, yes. And had meant it. But there was so much more.

"Well, I can tell you, after having watched several of your performances online last night in preparation for today, that what I just saw exceeded every one of them."

Mouth dry, she reached for her water bottle. Took a sip. Swallowed, then, took another. "What did you watch?"

Could have been from a few years before.

He named three of her most recent appearances.

And she stood there, gathering her composure. He'd watched films to prepare. Was taking her seriously.

He deserved to have the professionalism she gave to everyone else. More than she gave to others.

And the honesty that had become a staple between them. "I'm concerned about choreographing myself into a duet that might make me stand out too much. Or not show me at my best. When I choreograph for others, I see strengths and weaknesses and choose moves accordingly. I know my own, but one never judges oneself fairly. Beyond that, for my own confidence I need time to work the piece with a partner, more time than Oppenstott has to give."

She stopped there. Looked over at him, and said, "I'm dancing my life. The feelings I've known personally on my dancer's journey. They start with you. Dancing the piece with you, even just here, will bring the fullness of it out of me. Bringing me full circle. And that sense is what will be with me when I'm onstage."

Too much…

But there it was.

He'd given her his truth, and she'd given him hers.

His minute was up. Had been for at least five more of them.

Having done what he'd said he was going to do, Nathan looked toward the door. Pressure mounted in him. A far too familiar sense of personal unease.

A need to get out before the cage closing around him locked him in forever.

"And I was hoping…" Harper's voice reached him, pulling his gaze in her direction. She was so beautiful standing there.

In control. And vulnerable, too. Staring at her, he waited for her to finish her sentence.

"I was hoping that maybe, just maybe, I could help you find joy in movement again, without any strings attached."

Strings. More like ropes. That were binding him from the inside out.

Her gaze bore into his. Holding him there. But not captive.

"Just do something for me, real quick," she said then, turning to push a button on the sound system. Then, when a piano concerto sounded, clicked again, leaving them in silence.

"I'm seeing a lift," she said. "I've got the music cued to it." She was walking toward him as she talked, her tone completely professional, serious, drawing his focus. "It's a deadweight," she said, and his body, his mind, were completely there with her. Running through various deadweight lifts he'd done during his short-lived career. "But until I can try it, feel it, I won't know if it's right for the piece. And what comes after... I've got it there, but if the lift doesn't fit..."

She'd have to make changes. Not something anyone would want to do two days before a big show. "Tell me about it," he said, moving to the far corner of the room where he'd seen mats. Pulling one out.

"I'm coming from the floor, full crouch. He's done a turning jeté to get to me. Reaches down and lifts me. I arch back, turn away, but he spins me around, has me by one hand in the middle of my back and lifts me above his head, my legs fully extended and split, in front of him, extending me even higher as he slowly raises up on his toes..."

Not an easy lift. Or one anyone but an accomplished dancer should even try.

But Nathan had no doubt he could do it. His lifts had brought him national fame. Though…it had been a while.

Laying out a couple of mats, he stood in the middle of them, hands on his hips, and, glancing down toward the safety padding beneath his feet, said, "It's been a while."

"I was thinking we'd do an hour of class to get you warmed up."

"I've been up an hour early every day this week, running through class work. And, as I've already said, I've kept up with barre stretches and basics all along. Followed by weight machines." He was who he was, and his body needed what it needed. No business of anyone, but him.

And now, her.

"The discipline of dance is a part of me. And it suits me," he elaborated. Not wanting her to take what he was telling her the wrong way. He was not—ever—planning to dance again. Was not holding on to the exercise for a just-in-case scenario. "Barre work not only helps stretch muscles and keeps them limber, but it's a mental exercise that helps me focus. As does the daily discipline."

He'd gained some things of great value during his youth.

One of which was a strong, healthy body trained for hard work. He'd never walked away from that part.

"How long has it been since you've thrown a jeté on a dance floor?" Harper had her hands on her hips again. Hadn't come anywhere near the mat.

He hadn't planned on throwing the jeté.

She'd asked for help with the lift. Had drawn him in with the one request. He hadn't responded to the rest.

His mind flashed back to the first second he'd entered the room. Had been hit by the scene unfolding before him. She was not only technically as close to perfect as he'd ever seen, the woman—without costume, hair done, and stage makeup—had captivated him. Taken him to a place inside himself where emotions roiled with reality.

She felt the lift.

Would have to drop it from the piece if she couldn't work with it before Oppenstott could get to rehearsal.

Comfortable with the logic hitting him, Nathan stepped off the mats. Pushed them far back. And, stepping like a dancer onstage, lightly, heel barely touching the floor, took himself to the far corner of the room and looked at Harper. "Okay, teach. An hour of floor work," he said, straightening his spine.

He was in position.

Ready to begin.

But not at her mercy.

The door was still right behind him.

Chapter Sixteen

Standing at the front of the room, as she did with every class she taught, Harper called out the exercise, turned on the music, prepared to watch carefully, every body part involved in the move. Point, turn out, lines and curves, spine and limb placement.

So much of dance, of ballet, was muscle memory. With a lifetime's worth of regular dance classes, most particularly from a young age, the brain adapted, accepted. And the body just knew.

Nathan's first three steps took Harper's breath away. She couldn't take her eyes off him as he completed the exercise across the floor, and then turned to do the same for his return journey. She tried to find someplace, anyplace, she could be of constructive help to him.

Instead, she walked over to the corner by the door, stood behind him, and said, "You choose, I'll follow." And then did.

For the next hour, she met every challenge Goldman gave her. Following him down the floor with one technique after another, growing more difficult in performability as the hour moved along. More and more moves added to each pass. Until they weren't exercising, they were taking turns dancing phrases.

When they stopped for a water break, each retreating to their own side of the room—him by the door where he'd set a small duffel when he'd come in, and her up front by the sound system—Harper was a little out of breath. But smiling from her soul to the heavens.

Happier than she could ever remember being.

Filled with a sense of fun, of the greatness of the moment, with confidence, she stepped in front of Goldman as they rejoined each other in the corner of the room. And with a few short words of instruction, she started on the floor first, dancing the phrase that would bring Oppenstott onstage at the beginning of the number.

And then stood and watched as Goldman brought the moves down to her.

Feeling them more deeply than she had when they'd first appeared to her. And wanting a change, too. Needing the technical difficulty, just not as many moves thrown together, and more show of strength.

Moving to the front of the room, she called out a change as Nathan turned to head back. Elation burst briefly inside her as he immediately switched gears and moved exactly as she'd directed. His body not only exuded brilliantly executed, breathtaking technique, but filled her with a sense of wellness. A knowledge that good triumphed over evil. That beauty could heal.

And that the male body was a work of art.

She had it.

Nathan Goldman Connolly had just given her the perfect opening phrase.

She turned off the music, and disappointment filled Nathan. He'd been in the middle of a huge high, nailing challenge after challenge. Exhibiting a talent that few in the world could master.

In front of a woman he wanted to impress.

But it was more than that. Far more.

He'd taken the floor. Freed his body to fly.

It had felt…damned good. Truthful.

And it was done.

The silence that filled the room left far too much space for reality to intrude. He had a talent few could master, and zero desire to put it on display.

Once the music stopped, there was…nothing. No drive to get out and show himself.

And then there was something—the possibility that Harper thought she'd turned him. That she'd been playing him. That he'd fallen for her ruse. That the next card she laid on the table would have his name on the marquee.

Grabbing a towel out of his bag, he wiped the sweat he could reach, maintaining a stance by his bag. And the door.

Up by the sound system, she was wiping her neck and shoulders. Sipping from her water bottle. Giving him the impression that she was buying time before laying her next move on him.

He already had one foot mentally out the door.

"Thank you," she said, smiling as she turned to face him. And then started toward him before stopping midroom. "That was not only the best hour of dance I can ever remember spending, but you gave me my opening to the number." She stopped, looked from him to the door. "Are we out of time?" she asked him.

Yes was right there, waiting for him. He had to hear her spiel first so he could put an end to it once and for all. He wasn't going to have his attraction to the woman—her sometimes infuriating person as much as her body—hijack his common sense. Or let what felt good in the moment ruin the future.

And he wasn't going to have the matter hanging over him, either. Ready to attack anytime he saw her on the beach.

During the six weeks or so he figured he had left before he was ready to put his investment on the market.

A piece of information they hadn't talked about. He'd told Sage and Gray, with no caveat to keep the information silent. Someone might have a friend with interest in the place.

It was likely the whole beach knew.

"Nathan, do we need to call it quits for the day?" She'd taken another step closer, her smile overshadowed by the frown on her brow.

She'd asked if they were out of time. He hadn't answered. "I bought the place on the beach as an investment," he told her. Words coming out of him from deeper within than he wanted to go. "My plan is to fix it up and put it back on the market."

The words hadn't helped. He felt as though different parts of himself were starting to wage battle within him. Had sworn to himself that he'd never go back to that place in his life. Where his peace of mind was at risk.

Harper gave a start, but didn't seem all that affected by his news. "Okay, so you're telling me you need to go get to work on the place? That my favor is costing you money?"

"No." He wanted to say yes and get the hell out. He couldn't lie to her. "I'm telling you that I am as certain, right this second, as I was before I walked in here, that I can't reenter this world as a way of life." He had to add the last disclaimer since he'd already entered the world, gloriously enough that he'd never fool her into believing otherwise, over the past hour.

What the cottage on the beach had to do with that, he wasn't sure. Other than the fact that the remodel, building, contracting, construction were his livelihood and he would not let her pretend otherwise.

"I know." She'd come closer. Was smiling fully again, but the expression was softer than he'd ever seen it. Her eyes glistened as she laid a hand on his arm. "I swear to you, Nathan, I'm not asking for anything more than more of what we did today."

He wished he could believe that.

She'd taken her hand away. But not the smile. "I'm not your mother."

God no. "I know that." No way he looked at Harper and saw anything mother-like. At all. Which was part of the problem.

The feelings that were coming back to him, burying him in their avalanche...were they part of the test? A part of him?

Something he had to deal with before he could find his wife and have his children with her? Would he ever find a woman who moved him as much as Harper had in the past couple of weeks?

He couldn't marry someone he didn't love, who didn't captivate him more than any other woman on earth.

Was his family plan a pipe dream?

"So...you need to be done for the day, or do you have time to continue?"

"You've got the afternoon," he told her. Beyond that, he was making no promises.

Not to dance with her.

Or to be her friend, either.

Because no matter how much change she was bringing to him, springing him forward to reaching the goals he'd set himself, helping him grow into the man he ultimately wanted to be—she was also starting to pose his biggest threat to reaching them.

Harper's heart lurched as she watched the struggle going on within Nathan. He'd opened himself up to the most intense expression, and so doing, had seemingly unleashed far more than she'd known would be there.

Reminding her of a documentary she'd watched about the changes in many soldiers when they came home from war.

Psyches were fluid and changing...and hung to things the conscious mind sometimes couldn't even remember.

Nathan hadn't been at war...his physical safety hadn't been at constant risk...but his inner peace had been. His sense of self had been stripped away, possibly since birth.

She couldn't be responsible for sending him back to a private hell. No matter how much sacred joy she'd seen on his face as he'd whipped across her floor.

While she stood there castigating herself, he'd moved. Was pulling the mats back out. "Let's get to this lift," he said. "You said it's key to the piece and since it's the first one I've done in a while—lifting a human being, not lifting weight in general—I want to be full energy and focus."

Watching him, she saw purpose. Confidence. No hint of the man who'd seemed ready to run out the door of her studio moments before.

Was she giving up on him too soon? Seeing failure where success might be starting to peek through the window? Could he be ultimately comfortable with the dancer in him, welcoming his spirit, and still live the life he needed to be happy? As a professional contractor, creating lovely spaces for people to relax—not onstage.

Why her heart kept pulling her in that direction, Harper had no idea. It wasn't like she had any right or business involving herself in the man's life or his choices.

So thinking, she moved to the mat, discussed various aspects of the lift she'd already described to Nathan. Was slightly in awe of the way he not only grasped her vision, but explained to her in minute detail the way it would work. From muscle use to distances in half-inch increments, and angles at which weight was the heaviest.

She was great at what she did. He was far better. The fact was just there. Clear.

Solidifying for her the realization she'd come to as a kid the first time he'd seen her dance. She was meant to be a dancer. He'd shown her then.

And was showing her again.

Her life was dance. Just as she'd seen clearly, by his struggle to relax anywhere in her world, his words, his love of building unique spaces, that his was not.

The irony in that was hitting her hard when he said, "Ready?"

A student, instead of the teacher, Harper succumbed to Nathan's direction eagerly. Needing not only a confirmation that the lift worked with the piece, but whatever he could teach her about her art.

She started when he first reached a hand down and touched her shoulder as she crouched. Embarrassed, she apologized, and resumed her position, prepared for the feel of the warmth of his palm against her skin.

That time, when his touch came, she was in the move, in the dance. His hand slid down her back, stopping at her lower spine, her arch, and holding there, he reached for her arm with his other hand. Sliding his fingers down the flesh until they'd joined with hers. One beat to the next, he gave a tug and, pushing with well-toned muscles, she rose from crossed feet onto her toes, made as though to pull away from him, allowing him to swing her back, and lift her deeply arched body with one hand on her back. With her head hanging backward, over his, her legs spread out and around him, toes pointed. Nothing touching between them except his palm to the small of her back.

His arm extended fully, suspending her nearly seven feet above the ground, and he slowly rose another couple of inches as he lifted to his toes.

The stance lasted only seconds, and they seemed like a full lifetime, too, as Harper's entire being hung as an ethereal part of something out of body. Something much larger than humanity.

And then, still holding her straight above him, Nathan bent at the knee and lowered himself until her feet touched the ground, and she spun out. And stopped.

In the dance, she'd be doing a series of turns, but turned immediately to face Nathan, eager for his take on what they'd just done.

He was staring at her—as though he'd seen a ghost.

Nathan had had spontaneous erections before. More times than he could count. Onstage, and off. In rehearsals, even in barre class.

He'd been wearing a dance belt since puberty. Not only to protect his tender areas from injury during movements— another dancer's kick misplaced by an inch could be catastrophic without one—but also to smooth the anatomy while onstage. And to cover the natural male growth that happened on occasion.

He'd never been so turned on he'd felt like he'd explode if he didn't have immediate sex. Loathe to move, lest he embarrass himself irreparably, he stood completely still. Trying to think of something gross.

Awareness of Harper, of the feat they'd just accomplished, together, blinded everything else he tried to bring into focus. Overrode his rational brain.

She took a step closer. He didn't dare move.

"Are you okay?" Her concern got through to him. The furrow in her brow, the straight line of her mouth.

He shook his head. "Fine." And then words came barreling forth. "Just…it's a lot…so much time has passed and it was right there," he said, then, without taking a breath, continued on with, "Wow, that was…something."

"Good something or bad something?"

"Great something!" He grinned. Sobered. Shook his head again. In control enough that he could turn, walk to the corner of the room where his water bottle sat alone in the corner. He reached for it. Swallowed. Needing to pour the whole damned thing down his front.

"You got a muscle cramp? Need to stop?"

His muscle discomfort most definitely was cramping him. Not at all in the way she feared. "Absolutely not," he blurted. He wasn't going to have her thinking he was out of shape. Less strong, less capable than he'd been.

In the first place, because it simply wasn't true. But also, because he had a sudden need for her to see Nathan Goldman. Just for a little while longer.

An hour.

A day or two.

He had to pass his personal test. Or fate's test. He was no longer sure who was in charge. But his resolve to get to the life he wanted—finding a woman with whom he wanted to share the rest of his life, a woman who wanted what he wanted, who was going where he was going—had not wavered even a little bit.

Nor had his certainty that Harper wasn't that woman. No matter what his overactive emotions were saying at the moment. He'd die before he'd watch her leave behind the world in which she thrived. And he'd suffocate if he was back in that world, too.

A hell of a lot was changing. Not his certainty on those two facts.

Other than asking him if he needed to stop, she'd left him alone in his corner to wipe off and hydrate. Assumed she was doing the same.

He squirted some sips into his mouth. He wiped. Mostly he waited while he deflated. Giving his emotional output some downtime. Allowing his self-control time to kick in.

And turned back to see Harper facing the mirror, staring at her phone, blinking back tears. Clearly not realizing that he was watching her.

Just as he had the thought, she glanced up. Caught his gaze in the mirror. Her face immediately shaping into a lovely smile, she put her phone down on the cabinet that held her sound system and approached him.

"Ready to go again?" She looked, sounded, perfectly normal.

And it hit him…she was putting on a show. No one went from being upset to the point of tears to being eager and in a good mood that quickly.

But someone whose life revolved around being onstage, around putting on shows, would be able to *pretend* as though everything was fine.

Stood to reason that as gifted as Harper was, as dedicated as she was to the life she'd chosen, she'd perfected her art to the point of being able to perform at a second's notice.

The show must go on.

His mother's words came to him. How many times over the years had he heard them? Too many to count, for sure.

He'd been approaching Harper, but stopped, mid-room. "No, I'm not ready," he told her, chin jutting. She was challenging him to be open to aspects of himself that he'd refused to acknowledge for years—and yet she was going to stand there and hide in plain sight?

Why the idea infuriated him so much, he didn't know, but there was no way he was going to just stand there and take it.

Frowning, seeming honestly perplexed, she was slowly approaching him as she asked, "What's up?"

The soft concern in her tone just riled him up more.

Had it all been an act, then?

He'd thought they'd connected. Had let down a guard he'd thought would never lower at all when he'd shared the ending of his dance career with her.

Trusted like he'd never trusted anyone.

And she'd been…putting on a show?

Standing there, watching her, something else hit him between the brows. Hard.

The way he felt right then—betrayed…even…hurt—was that how he'd left the trail of women in his tracks feeling? Younger women, even, eighteen-year-olds who'd just been testing out their femininity on the seventeen-year-old dance superstar…

He felt sick.

And angry.

Ready to walk out on Harper Cecilia and never look

back. Her deck was done. He had no reason to ever see her again.

But first, "Why were you crying?" The question was as much challenge as it was a query. She thought he didn't see through the show? Hell, he'd mastered the ability to put on the fake smile that looked real before he'd reached double digits.

And he'd still been hoodwinked by her.

Pursing her lips she looked away, then back, and said, "Someone just forwarded a copy of a text exchange that took place this morning," she said with a shrug. "It was nothing."

Eyes narrowing, Nathan felt his anger dissipate. "You often cry over nothing?"

He hadn't known her long, but he knew she was the strongest woman he'd ever known. One who'd survived the battleground of her childhood and fought to have adult relationships with both sides of the war.

Another thought occurred to him on the heel of that. Skidding right up into it. She hadn't been giving him a show the night she'd told him about her childhood.

Nor on the morning he'd met her. When she'd recognized him.

Or the night he'd told her about walking offstage and out into the dark, leaving all his earthly possessions behind, and never looking back.

And... Aggie. A flash of the giant's soulful eyes flashed before his mind's eye, and everything inside Nathan settled.

Aggie knew the real Harper. And she'd accepted Nathan's presence, too.

Harper hadn't answered his question. She'd walked away. Over to the cabinet. Was returning, phone in hand.

She held it out to him.

Taking the cell, he read what she'd left open on the screen.

Elle: The princess is pulling the high and mighty again.

Sara: What'd she do this time?

Elle: Canceled last minute. Put off my company, my piece, for another two weeks. I had my dancers ready, excited, and, no…my stuff isn't as important as hers. As she just, by action, let my dancers know. She'd take them from me, too, if she had time for them.

Sara: I guess be glad she doesn't have time…

He glanced up. Burning hot. "Who sent this?"

"A third woman, June, who'd been included on the text. She's got a reputable ballet studio in LA. I do master classes for her and quite a bit of choreography, too. Sara works for her. June wanted to make sure that if I got wind of grumblings, I didn't think she was in agreement with the two of them. What she doesn't know is that Elle sent a similar chain to me a couple of months ago, again the three of them, where June told the other two to watch out because I'd auditioned for a part a couple of their students were also up for. She made some pretty nasty comments about my age. Suggesting that I should realize that I was done, and let others have their chance."

The words were all nonchalant. Harper stood straight in front of him. Looking him in the eye without a hint of emotion. And he got it.

She wasn't putting on a show for him. She'd been living her life as she'd learned to live it. Most likely starting with her parents. Push away the hurt. Don't let it affect daily life. Because there was no way you were going to be able to stop it from coming at you.

A lesson he'd learned before kindergarten. As long as he did as he was asked and didn't throw tantrums or get mad, he got to have whatever he wanted, and do whatever he wanted in his free time.

Her learning had been much more painful. And lifelong.

He lifted Harper's chin, running his thumb along her lips. It wasn't meant to be a sexual move, but when her eyes met his, it became one.

He couldn't let the fire catch. Remembering her pain, his reason for reaching out, he took his hand back but held her gaze. "Don't push the pain so deeply inside that you lose you," he said softly. Seeing the truth in himself. "I know it's hard, dealing with that kind of crap, but think of how much satisfaction you get out of the life you've chosen. The way you effervesce when you're dancing, the sense of quiet joy you exude when you're not…don't let them steal that from you."

She smiled. Her eyes brimmed with tears again, but they shone, too.

"Come to me instead," he said then, figuring that he was beginning to understand things a little bit better. "We met for a reason. Maybe this is it. To be the friend that we're both lacking. The one who doesn't want, need or expect more than we can give, but who can take the intensity inside. The one who's just happy to be present, a part of our lives, and ready to support in time of need. The one who really does understand."

In any other room, with any other person, the words would have embarrassed him. They'd have never been said. With Harper, they were just right.

Holding his gaze, she whispered, "You want to dance?"

And in that moment, with her, he actually did.

Chapter Seventeen

Harper made it home first that night. Nathan had left the studio before she did, but he'd had a couple of work stops to make. They hadn't made any plans to see each other outside the studio. Just a casual 'Tomorrow, same time?' before he stepped out the door.

But she made enough cold salmon salad for two, packed it up with crackers, and her Saturday night bottle of wine, and slung the canvas bag over her shoulder as she took Aggie out for a walk down the beach.

If he was out, great. If not, that was fine, too. She'd enjoy the meal and some quiet time on her lovely new deck, with a fire going.

Maybe he'd already eaten. But assuming he wanted company, he wouldn't take offense if she ate in front of him.

She didn't need him to be outside.

They'd spent some pretty intense hours together that afternoon, getting through half the piece before she'd finally called it quits.

But she liked his company. And if he wanted to share it, she wanted to be there to partake.

As she caught her first glimpse of his place in the far distance, and didn't see him out, her spirits dimmed a little. So maybe she wasn't quite fine. Maybe, after the day they'd spent, she really did want him to be there.

Even knowing that he specifically wasn't open to women who came on to him anymore. Ever again. Maybe because of that, she'd had to be the one who made the move.

Establishing, for both of them, that she wasn't ever going to be more than a friend to him.

Or maybe, understanding him as she did, she knew that she didn't have to worry that he'd think her appearance meant that she was coming on to him. Any other man probably would have. Nathan wouldn't take it that way.

Trying not to be disappointed as she drew close enough to see his place in the distance and didn't notice movement on the beach up by his cottage, Harper reminded herself that Nathan Connolly was a very busy man. He ran a successful business that supported a lot of people.

For all she knew, he wasn't even going to be at the cottage that night. Though he'd been staying there most nights, he didn't actually live there yet. And according to what he'd told her, didn't plan to ever do so.

And…it was Saturday night.

That was when it hit her. He'd said he had two weeks left of a yearlong, no dating sabbatical. Two weeks ago.

And it was Saturday night. The thought hit again. With increased force.

Was he on his first real date? One that he'd instigated? With a woman whose company he enjoyed, but who hadn't thrown herself at him? That's how he'd described his future wife to her.

Was she one of his clients, maybe?

Or…someone on the beach? Cynthia?

Embarrassed, feeling foolish, Harper kept walking. No one but her and Aggie knew what was in her bag. No one would ever need to know.

She loved the beach. And after the day she'd had, she needed the calm it brought her.

So thinking, she didn't stare as she drew closer to Nathan's place. She glanced, but spent as much time gazing out to sea. Letting the vastness of the universe fill her up some.

Which was why, as it turned out, Aggie was the one who noticed the man sitting out on the sand in a chair, just off Nathan's broken-down deck. The girl turned, headed up the beach, grabbing Harper's immediate attention.

And drawing her gaze to Aggie's intended destination.

He waved.

Harper waved back.

Noticed he was alone.

And decided to walk up and say hello.

Nathan had been pretty sure she'd come down. He hadn't asked. Couldn't.

He was off sabbatical as of the day before and was only going to ask out women with whom he saw the possibility of a future.

No way he was risking everything, including his friendship with Harper, by giving any hint of the desire for a date between the two of them.

But because his mandate included specifically *not* dating women who came to him…there was no way her visit could turn into more. Not unless he let himself down.

Which he was confident he was not going to do.

Didn't stop him from admiring the way she moved up the sand, though. Or from appreciating the slender form that he now knew firsthand was impressively strong.

As was the woman inside that fine-tuned body.

Strong enough to allow the intense sensitivity inside her to live. Rather than shutting it down. As he'd done.

She'd walled herself off from people, who were imperfect, from close relationships, which were fallible, but not from the pure emotional bounty with which she'd been born. The spirit and soul that gave her a level of understanding, a connection, beyond what most people saw. An emotional well so deep and so full that without words, she could speak to the hearts of people, even when their minds didn't fully comprehend the message.

In a few short weeks, she'd taught him a lot about herself. And himself, too.

His strengths.

And his weaknesses.

Like the fact that even while he revered her talent, knew that she'd been gifted, his body was still growing hard, just from watching her approach.

The humanity in him.

Which, at that moment, was making him leave the most powerful, spiritually pure thoughts behind, to wonder if Harper was turned on by him, too.

Like Harper, he might have a gift that set him apart, but he was also weak. Human in the basest sense.

"Have you eaten?" she asked as she approached. As though their coming together had been planned.

A fast-food sandwich as soon as he'd left her studio. He'd been planning all full-out rebellion as he'd driven off the lot, but instead of the greasy burger and fries he'd envisioned, he'd ended up with the grilled, not fried, chicken breast. With lettuce and tomato, only. No saturated fat–filled dressing.

"Just a snack after rehearsal," he said. Rehearsal. He hadn't been rehearsing. But she had. And he'd been helping her.

That's when he saw the bag slung over her shoulder, resting on her back.

"I've got salmon salad with crackers, and wine, if you'd like some."

She'd packed another picnic. Letting him know that she'd been hoping he'd be out, too. Which made him smile as he got up to grab another beach chair and set it out for her. And when he saw the towel hanging over a rail of the deck—one he'd rinsed out and left to dry—he grabbed that, too. Threw it down for Aggie. No point in the beast getting more sand than necessary all over herself.

"I didn't expect to see you tonight," she said as she pulled out two plastic wineglasses before opening the bottle.

His spirits drifted down for the second it took him to register what he was seeing, right in front of him. "Then why two glasses?"

With a grin, she handed him one. "I hoped. It was a good day today. I'm still coming down from it. It's nice to be able to do that with someone I trust." She held up her glass, as though in toast, and took a sip.

"Hear! Hear!" he said, and took his first drink of the dry white liquid as well. Enjoying the taste of fermented grape without all the sweetness. The feel of it sliding down his throat.

The way Harper was looking at him. As though she was happy just to sit there and sip wine. In the same leggings she'd had on when he'd left her at the studio. With a long-sleeved T-shirt he'd never seen before. It was purple. Tie-dyed. He liked it.

He'd gone home after the snack stop, parking in the garage before getting out and changing from the sweats he'd pulled on over his dance attire into jeans and a button-down denim shirt. Work boots instead of ballet shoes.

He had planned to get some more work done on the cottage that night after he'd made his other stops. Had ended up out on the beach instead.

In work boots.

He'd rather be barefoot.

As Harper was.

Why did the woman always seem to have one up on him?

And yet…give the sense that just being around him was a joy to her?

She opened the container of salmon salad. Offered him his own pack of crackers. Took a pack for herself and dipped into the bowl, then handed the salad to him.

One bite and he was sunk. Using crackers as his utensil, he continued helping himself, passing the bowl back and forth as necessary, until the mixture was completely gone.

She'd put her crackers away long before he had.

Neither had spoken.

Pouring himself a little more wine, he held the bottle up, and when she offered her glass, topped hers off, too. The silence between them was nice.

Companionship to enjoy the ocean air, the vastness in the distance. Darkness had fallen completely while they ate, and the moon's glow over the water spoke to him of secrets.

He'd promised himself no more of those. At least not from himself. No more bottling things up until he bolted.

"Why are you here?" He didn't want to ask the question. Didn't want it between them. But he had to know. If she was…

"I wanted to be."

He got it. He wanted to be there, too. With her.

But…no more leading a woman on.

He was not going to leave another broken heart behind.

He had to be sure…most particularly since he was having a bit of an issue himself… "I mean…where do you see this going?" He groaned inwardly at the words. Had he transported himself back to high school?

Except…back then, he'd never have thought to ask. Never would have considered a possibility that anyone could see any relationship with him going anywhere but to bed.

The women he'd left in tears…back then, he'd figured those broken hearts hadn't been his fault. He'd never even hinted at pretending, not even once, that he was open to any kind of relationship with anyone. Never had a single conversation about feelings—other than sexual.

As fast as his life had been moving during those years, mostly out of his control, he hadn't been sure where *he'd* be month to month, let alone being able to keep track of anyone else.

But he'd always made sure that the woman he was with was getting as much pleasure as he was from the encounter.

And was sitting there, holding his glass of wine, without an answer to his immaturely posed question forthcoming from the woman he'd posed it to.

Where do you see this going…?

At that point, he hoped the words would just float away on the salty air, head out to sea, and never be heard again.

Of course, life didn't work that way. At least not for him.

"I'm not seeing into the future." Harper's voice wasn't loud. Or soft, either. He heard no undertones. Just words.

"Why?" she asked.

The question tacked on at the end. He should have seen it coming.

He put his foot in something, he had to find his way out of it. That's how life worked.

"I just want to make sure you aren't going to get hurt."

"You expect me to make sure you don't get hurt?"

"Of course not."

"Then how can you expect yourself to make sure of something—that's completely out of your ability to control, by the way—when you know others can't make sure of it?"

She was talking in riddles. Trying to confuse him?

Right, like the way she'd been playing him earlier? Meaning not at all.

"I've hurt a lot of women in my time. I can't have you be one of them."

He heard her hiss of breath. Saw her shoving her empty container back in the canvas bag. Saw her reach for the wine bottle, and grabbed it himself, exactly when she did. Holding it with her. Equally.

She didn't try to take it from him. He didn't pull it toward himself, either. He just looked at her. Eventually, she looked back. "You think I'm coming on to you," she said then. He'd swear there were tears in her voice.

When there should have been anger.

"Because I came down here. I'm chasing you. Just like every other woman in your life."

He wanted to deny the accusation. Couldn't honestly do that. He wasn't sure what he thought. Except, "I wanted to see you tonight. I couldn't ask. I came out. In case I had a chance to see you. You didn't just take a walk. You brought a picnic." Which he'd devoured.

While she'd been sitting several feet away, sipping wine, obviously coming down. Asking nothing of him. Promising nothing. Needing nothing, but that. Just to be with him.

Knowing that the afternoon in her studio had to have left him with mixed emotions. Ones she alone understood. Since no one else knew what he was doing for her.

She'd come down as a friend.

And he'd been fighting a hard-on ever since.
That was the problem.
He was the problem.
Not her.

Harper held her grip steady on the wine bottle. Refusing to look away first. To let him see her pain.

You brought a picnic.

He'd just gone outside to sit for a bit. Hadn't even set out a second chair. She'd planned a romantic event for two.

He didn't look away, either. Even when he started to talk. "If you'd had any other dance friend to hang out with, you'd have done the same, just like I brought you turkey rolls."

Maybe. "That's a fairly big 'if,'" she said, as relief flooded through her. He'd found a way to make it okay.

He let go of the wine bottle, too. Didn't give up his glass. "You wanted to hang out with the dancer you'd just spent a pretty intense day with," he said. "Nutrition is a given part of a dancer's life. And most important after spending several hours full-out as we did today."

Setting the bottle and the canvas bag back down, Harper held her glass between shaking hands and nodded. But couldn't let the moment turn into a lie. "I don't see this going anywhere, Nathan," she said quietly. "If we're careful, maybe a friendship that lasts awhile. I'd love that. But I'm not looking to you for anything more than that. It wouldn't work. One of us would have to give up on our mental and emotional health and I'm not ever going to be okay with either of us doing that."

His gaze narrowed, but he didn't look away. Not that she could see much more than glints in the moonlight. "I'm attracted to you," he said.

She saw his lips move. The words bounced off her. But

they lingered in the air. Settling over her slowly as she tried to figure out what to do with them without allowing herself to take them inside. She couldn't let herself do that.

And couldn't figure out where to go next, either. "Why are you telling me?"

Did he want a fling? The whole purpose of his sabbatical from sex had been to rid his life of sex that couldn't lead to a lifetime.

Was he telling her they couldn't be friends as it would lead to his ultimate destruction?

"Because friends are honest with each other."

Oh. *Ohhhhh*.

He was working toward a friendship, not ending one.

Gooey warmth coated her stomach as tendrils of sweet promises blossomed lower. In spite of knowing she'd made a mistake with the salad and wine. "You need me to stop being quite so friendly," she translated.

"No." Sitting forward, elbows on his knees, Nathan's focus seemed to be on the wine in his glass. Until he glanced up and caught her watching him. "I don't honestly know what I need right now," he told her. "Except this. Right here."

She smiled, didn't bother to blink away the tears that sprang to her eyes. "Me, too," she told him.

Took a sip of her wine.

And looked out to sea.

Where the not knowing was okay.

Chapter Eighteen

Nathan made an appointment to see a new client for late Sunday afternoon. Partially because he was overloaded with work. But also so that he had a reason to just help Harper rehearse and then get out. He needn't have worried. She was all business from the time he'd arrived until she'd dismissed him an hour earlier than he'd planned to go. She had the local ballet group she'd chosen for the gala's last piece coming in for the evening so she could teach them their dance.

Which precluded any chance of them sharing another picnic that night as well. Instead, he brought a couple of power lights out to the beach, shone them on his investment, and worked off excess energy tearing up the dilapidated deck. He'd planned to just leave the space bare, figuring he'd offer, as part of the purchase price, to design the new deck to owner specification and have one of his crews build it before closing.

Instead, he spent the evening sitting in the space, lights on and lights off, chair in various places, having a beer, listening to the ocean, and contemplating life. After a second beer, he had no answers to questions he hadn't asked, but figured he'd spend the night so he could have a third. Then later, inside on his mattress and leaning up against the wall, he mapped out exactly how the deck would go. Down to specifics he hadn't consciously thought about.

Every space on the deck would have its own unique view. Its own special gift to give its occupant. There'd be areas of sun and shade morning until night. The fireplace would be a drop-in, built up in the middle of the space. With a table built around the edge of it to prevent anyone or anything from getting too close to the fire. Judging from a photo he had on his phone of Sage and Gray's little Leigh on their new deck, he calculated the length of a four-year-old arm, added another foot and called it good. The propane would be loaded from underneath. The starter in a childproof electrical outlet door mounted to the base of the pit.

By midnight, he was tired. But felt good. Productive, and satisfied, too. The deck would be a perfect complement to the life he wanted. Which meant it would likely be a draw for any other professional couple in their thirties with plans for a family.

Unlike Harper's deck, which was mainly suitable for adults.

And really big dogs.

He'd kind of thought she'd text when she got home that night. Had checked his phone a time or two. Figured midnight was too late to text her.

To fall asleep, he tried to picture himself a year into the future. If not married yet, at least dating seriously. And then a few years hence, a little one on the way. Or toddling toward the firepit, standing up to the table around it. Reaching, but unable to touch the flames.

And instead of sleeping, he lay awake wondering what Harper's life would look like in a few more years. If she'd still be alone. Needing a friend because Nathan's free time was consumed by his wife and kids.

Or maybe she'd be married to someone in her field. A benefactor, maybe. Much younger than Nathan's father had been. Someone who loved the theater. Who thrived on stage lights and applause. Who didn't want routine. A schedule by which he could make plans more than a month into the future. Or family time at home. Who didn't want kids of his own.

And he fell asleep shortly after realizing that he'd done a great job visualizing what his friend's life would look like, but had failed to connect with his own.

Nathan had the hots for her. Did she pretend she didn't know, act as usual, even though they both knew she did? Did she avoid him until he found a woman to date and had a chance to dispel a year's worth of pent-up hormones?

Did she tell him that she wanted him, too? More desperately as each hour of the next two days passed and she didn't know if he'd found his first potential future wife yet.

It was that last very dangerous and equally potent sense of time running out that kept her from doing more than texting him a time or two on Monday and Tuesday. She'd purposely kept her walks with Aggie in the opposite direction on the beach from Nathan's new place. Didn't sit out on her deck at all. And kept her food strictly to herself.

As she sat up in bed on Tuesday evening, having turned in early, she felt like a terrible friend.

She had to admit, she didn't have a lot to go on.

But knew that she missed Nathan's companionship. A lot.

It could have been a coincidence that at just that moment she got a text from Oppenstott, telling her that he had an appointment the next day and wouldn't be able to meet with her as planned on Wednesday afternoon to rehearse with her. He had an appointment he couldn't miss.

And with the show that next Saturday night, her professionalism, her confidence, couldn't miss a single scheduled rehearsal.

On Monday, she'd sent a tape of Oppenstott's part in the duet, other than the lifts, having danced it herself for him, along with complete written dance notation, so she wasn't as concerned about his ability to learn the piece in time. But her own dancing...

She was twenty-nine, not nineteen. She needed to know that she had every single nuance down to perfection. It wasn't that she doubted herself, her ability. She'd know when it was time to retire from the spotlight, and that wasn't yet. But she'd been growing more and more paranoid about others watching for signs of her professional demise.

And couldn't let them see any.

The dance was only a small part in a huge night of entertainment. In an auditorium consisting of as many nondance enthusiasts, as those who'd know if she and Oppenstott missed a cue. But...

She texted Nathan anyway. You got a second for a pep talk?

Her phone rang before her text alert.

One look at the screen and she was smiling big when she answered, "Thank you. Case of nerves."

"What's up?"

She started in about the show. The bids that had already come in. The media that was attending. Things she'd been trying not to think about. They all came pouring out. In one fell swoop. Giving him no time to respond. Ending with, "I know that with our skills, Jamie and I could go out there and adlib the entire piece, skip all the lifts, and no one would know any differently, but I don't want that, Nathan. I want to be as perfect on Saturday night as I was as the principal at the Met in New York."

"How are rehearsals going?"

"That's just it. They haven't gone yet. He was supposed to be in tomorrow and Thursday. And actually just agreed yesterday to come in Friday, too. But then I get a text from him tonight, canceling for tomorrow. He has some appointment that just came up that he can't miss."

"You still have the two days you originally planned on." He sounded so…calm. Yet like he was engaged with her problem. Understanding it, even. Maybe.

"Right, but when it was tomorrow and Thursday, I still had Friday to work out any kinks before dress rehearsal on Saturday morning… I still haven't done a complete run-through, start to finish, with a partner."

"You want me to come to the studio tomorrow." The words were a statement. Not a question.

Her heart leaped. Of course she did! And then she crashed. Was upset all over again. "That's not why I called, Nathan. I'm not asking you to give up your valuable work time to pander to my little hissy fit." And with that, she hung up.

She sat there, shaking. Feeling like a total loser. An over-the-top emotional child who was having a tantrum.

Which, she'd sort of just had.

Her phone rang. She knew who it was before she picked her phone back up off the mattress where she'd just dropped it. She tapped to answer and said, "I'm sorry. I never should have reached out. I'm exhausted. I know I'll feel better tomorrow. It just…it hurt my feelings when you thought I was just calling because I wanted something from you. And…

can we please just forget this ever happened?" Was their friendship strong enough to allow major fails?

"I'm completely booked tomorrow, but I can spare an hour or two early evening. Around six?"

She smiled. And felt tears pushing, too. "No," she told him, able to pull up and hold emotion inside. "That is not why I called."

"Point taken, but you have a situation. I can help. Isn't that what friends are for?" He started to hum the very famous song with the words as a title, which had been a constant on the competition circuit.

She did start to cry then. Since she was alone in her room with no one but Aggie to see, she let the tears fall and with a huge smile on her face said, "Thank you. I owe you one."

"Buy me dinner," he told her. "I was always starving after I danced." And hung up.

It didn't occur to her until after the conversation was through that she didn't even know where he was. At the cottage. At home? Out somewhere?

But knew that it was just as well.

What he did, and with whom, apart from her, was none of her business.

Even if, in her weakest moments, she wished it could be.

Nathan threw a duffel bearing his dance stuff in the back of his truck Wednesday morning, heading out of his gated community with a growing desire to never have to go back there.

He'd outstayed his contentment with the place.

And hadn't taken the time to contact another Realtor to find him the perfect beach house someplace within the San Diego area. Had been toying with the idea of waiting for the Ocean Breeze place to sell so that he'd have more to invest in his new place.

But that didn't mean he had to wait to put his current house up for sale. If it went quickly, he could put the bulk of his stuff in a storage facility and take what little he needed to the investment cottage for the duration. Enough of the work had been completed that he could manage. The master suite was done. And the rest…while the oven worked, the stove did not. He had a camping cookstove out in the garage someplace that would suffice along with the little refrigerator at the cottage in the laundry room.

And the deck on Ocean Breeze was already underway. Once it was complete, he could cook out there, over the fire. Something he'd always wanted to do as a kid, camping out, cooking hotdogs over an open flame, roasting marshmallows.

One of the few things he'd missed out on that he hadn't already done as an adult. He'd conquered the fishing. Learning to shoot a gun. He'd been up on skis—something that had not been allowed in his former life due to the risk of leg injury. He was a halfway decent surfer. Had snorkeled, gone skydiving and had owned a motorcycle for a while. He'd played for a season in an adult softball league. Spent three months on a men's basketball team at the local gym. Had mastered the skills of both so quickly other guys had talked about it.

But hadn't enjoyed either sport enough to want to invest the time on a regular basis. Neither were as physically all-consuming, as challenging to both mind and body—using every muscle and taking up total mental focus—as dance had been.

During lunch at his desk, he found a Realtor, and by midafternoon, had his house officially on the market. He'd also been by four jobsites, and signed with a new-build upscale strip of condominiums going up on a beach south of San Diego to design and build custom decks for all twenty-five units. Half with fireplaces.

Because his investment cottage was closer to his last appointment of the day than his house was, he stopped there to change into his dance clothes, pulling his truck into the garage and closing the door so he could get back in, in sweats and a Lycra tank without being seen.

A conscious choice. Made to take care of himself.

While he'd kind of been looking forward to the night's activity, he most certainly did not, ever, want anyone to see Nathan Goldman in Nathan Connolly's life.

Some things he just knew.

Dancing, as a sport, an activity, felt good. The life of a dancer did not. If nothing else, his time with Harper was showing him just how right he'd been to walk away from his past. He probably could have handled how he went about it a little better.

But then there were a lot of things about that young man's life that he wished he'd done differently. And perhaps, if he hadn't been in such a pressure cooker, he might have done.

As he pulled into the parking lot of the complex where Harper had her studio, and was consciously glad that he was only there to help out, Nathan figured maybe he'd been lucky after all. He'd learned young the importance of paying attention to personal choice, and his life's direction. He'd been pushed into realizing that he had the right to be in charge of himself. That he alone owned his life. That he had to guide his present to give him the future he wanted.

And that he had to know what he wanted.

In that moment, he wanted to spend a couple of hours

doing something he was really good at. Getting in a workout that would leave him feeling replete. Knowing that he was able to do so because of Harper. That she'd be doing it with him.

Most of all, he was eager to get in there and help her. To at least partially ease the tension that he'd sensed building inside her the night before.

The exact tension he'd left in his dust.

And going through it with her, even peripherally, he knew that the life she chose to live was one he would not ever take on for himself again.

Harper was eager and ready to dance like the wind when Nathan walked into the studio on Wednesday evening. Class that morning had reminded her that she was technically prepared to handle whatever challenge Saturday night's show brought her. Rehearsals had lifted her even higher as she worked with talented dancers who were bringing her choreography to beautiful life. Professionals who'd given their all, adapting to changes on the spot, eager to make her piece the best it could be, and by so doing, be the best they could be, too.

And all day long…there'd been an awareness riding on her shoulder. She had another dance session with Goldman that night.

It didn't get any better than that.

His first look at her as he dropped his bag inside the door was assessing. "How you doing?"

"Good." She smiled, warming under his awareness. "It's been a great day."

Made more so by the knowledge that he was at the end of it. The man was magic. Whether dancing with Goldman or cleaning with Connolly, she felt more alive being around him.

Was that what friends were for, too?

Putting on music, she dropped down for some stretches, and, in the back of the room, he did the same. Then stood and ran through some bar work.

At the front of the room, she watched him. Mesmerized. Not just by his technical perfection. Or even his natural movement. But by the man she knew.

He'd said he was attracted to her.

She'd been trying not to think about that ever since.

Because there was nowhere for that to go. Not if they were to remain friends. He couldn't do a fling. Or casual sex. She wouldn't ask him to.

Didn't want it for herself.

But, God, she wanted that body on top of hers.

The thought choked her. She turned away. Distracted herself by straightening the days' worth of notes on the top of the sound system cabinet. Reached inside it for the new box of tissue she'd meant to put out in place of the empty one.

Pushing back against an emotion that would not serve her, or her talent, well. She was good at it. Had been mastering the art since she was a kid in dance class and got chosen for the solo in the recital piece.

She just didn't have a lot of practice trying to get rid of something that felt so…compelling. And…wonderful.

He'd stopped working out to take a squirt from his water bottle.

"You ready?" she asked, reaching for the music she'd cued. Dance was the answer. Had always been the answer. As soon as she let the music, the movement, take her, she'd be centered again.

Without a word, he took his position at the side of the room, and, starting the music for his entrance, Harper took hers. With her body poised, her mind sinking into the chords, she watched Goldman's technique as he started to move. Her spirit moved with him, feeling the music, and her body started to dance the exact second it was meant to do so.

She was with him. And apart. "Onstage" with him, and alone. She balanced. And she flew in a series of turns that sent adrenaline racing through her as only dance could.

In motion, preparing for a lift, she caught sight of his face, the fierce concentration, and her own focus melded with his. Her trust in him that complete. With his hands at her waist, she tipped off from the floor, centering as he lifted her up like a swan, and then, over his head, to set her back down again behind him. Without pause her legs passed in quick succession, then moving only inches at a time, as she lifted a foot to her knee and turned, then, on the other leg did the same, as though she was running away from him.

She turned, ready to jeté back with growing intensity, needing him. And her phone rang. She heard it as if from a distance. Kept moving.

In what seemed like an eternity, the ringing stopped.

Nathan grabbed the tips of her fingers, she lifted on her toes and spun in place, over and over, as he turned his hand within hers.

The garish peal of the phone's ring started again. She danced through it. Didn't meet Nathan's gaze as they parted and connected again.

Cell quieted. She moved in for the arch lift above Nathan's head.

And the phone's sound interrupted for a third time.

Harper stopped. "I apologize," she said, slightly breathless. "I turned it on after everyone left, in case you needed to reach me." In case he'd changed his mind about dancing one more time. "I can't risk going into that lift with a distraction…"

She'd reached the phone. Hadn't looked at Goldman. He wasn't speaking.

Oppenstott's number was on the screen.

The man knew she was rehearsing. Was the epitome of professionalism. And he'd called three times in a row.

Until that second it hadn't even dawned on her that the continued calls signaled someone needing to speak with her urgently.

And hoped to God that Oppenstott wasn't about to cancel the next day's rehearsal, too. A swell of the same panic she'd sat through the night before raced through her veins as she picked up the phone and pushed to take the call.

A minute later, ashen, she hung up.

And stared blankly at the man who'd approached silently.

Who was standing right in front of her, ready to help.

A man who couldn't help her anymore.

Chapter Nineteen

Staring at Harper's pinch-lipped expression, Nathan could only imagine what she'd just heard on the phone. Something to do with her parents? Had one of them been hurt?

He wanted to help.

"What is it?" he asked softly, close enough to catch her if she started to fall.

She shook her head. Turned away. Set the phone down on her music cabinet.

Shutting him out.

He needed to be in. To be a true friend.

As she'd been to him, setting him free, from her very first calling out of his stage name on the beach.

"Harper?" She turned. Smiled. That smile he was beginning not to like very much at all. As gracious and kind and well-meaning as it was, that smile was Harper's way of shutting the world out. Or locking herself in.

"I'm sorry, Nathan. It's…just work. I'm going to need to call it a night, in terms of rehearsal, though. Even though we didn't get all the way through the piece, you being here is exactly what I needed. I can't thank you enough…"

I can't thank you enough? Like he was some kind of costume designer who'd just delivered a tutu? Or some…some director who'd offered her a part she'd coveted?

While a part of him told him to go, he wasn't going to just let her brush him off like that.

Crossing his arms, he stood there. Staring at her. "What's going on?"

She shook her head. A muscle in her jaw started to twitch. He wasn't making things easier on her. He got that. It felt like more than "easy" was at stake.

For him or for her? It mattered.

If he was in the middle of a selfish twit, he had to get the hell out and never come back.

He couldn't walk out on her while she was in distress. Not without knowing if there was something he could do.

"Friends don't walk out on friends," he told her, pulling from his very small repertoire of comfort moves. And then added, "At least this friend doesn't." And knew he spoke the truth.

Hands at her sides, she studied him. Lifted her chin. He saw an argument coming his way, and prepared to deflect it. He would do whatever it took to help her.

Fate had brought them together. Others might scoff, but he knew the fact to be true. As many years as he'd put in, as hard as he'd worked, he'd never have succeeded in his new life if he hadn't found a way to accept his past. To be at peace with it.

Crossing her arms over her chest with a harrumph, Harper tilted her head and said, "That was Jamie Oppenstott." She sounded almost…snotty. Clearly giving up the information against her will. And daring him to really want it.

He'd pushed. She was pissed. Which was better than shutting him out.

He was a man. He could take it. Would prove it to her. Stood there and waited her out.

"His appointment tonight was with an orthopedic surgeon. He has a stress fracture in two of the metatarsal bones on his left foot. If he wants to continue to dance professionally, he has to stay off from them for a minimum of two weeks. Could be as much as six. His entire year is booked. His understudy can cover him for the show he's currently in, but he can't afford to do a charity event, and risk everything."

Oh, God.

Hell.

She'd been right to shut him out. Her professional woes were none of his business.

He held her gaze because he had to. He'd started the whole thing. The challenge in her eyes, telling him quite clearly that he was going to bolt before she did…she was going to make him eat crow. To admit that he should have respected her right to her privacy.

Unless he simply turned around and walked out.

With one quick twist of his feet, Nathan was facing the door. And then, spotting it, keeping his eye glued to it, he walked toward his bag. Quietly. At least making his exit without challenge.

She didn't call him on it. Or call him back.

He reached his bag. Bent over and grabbed the handles. Slinging it over his shoulder. Didn't need to change his shoes. Didn't matter that ballet shoes couldn't be worn outdoors and then on the dance floor ever again.

He wouldn't be needing them.

Hand on the door, he stopped. Could feel Harper behind him. Waiting for him to go.

So she could…what?

And then what after that?

What was she going to do about the show?

She'd worked so hard. Her piece was one of the most evocative he'd ever danced.

She'd poured her heart and soul into it.

She was his friend. Had saved him from himself.

"Just go, Nathan. It's okay." The anger had left her voice. "Really." Her sincerity washed over him. Freeing him one more time. Sort of.

He'd turned his back. But couldn't stop seeing the stricken look on her face. She was dealing with a professional disaster.

And he was walking out on her.

"Please. Go. I really have to get to work."

Rechoreographing the number into a solo piece for herself. Telling a different story than the masterpiece she'd created. In two days' time. Create it. Learn it. Then show up at dress rehearsal…

"And I'm sorry about dinner. You'll have to settle for a rain check."

Because she was settling for being alone.

Friendless.

"What if I do the thing with you?" The words were out of his mouth before he'd fully considered them. Given them license.

He hated them the second he heard them. Knew they weren't right for him.

But sometimes being a friend meant sacrificing oneself for another.

He turned enough to look at her over his shoulder.

Eyes wide, she had her hands over her mouth and was shaking her head. Then, dropping her hands, said, "No. I can't let you do that." Her voice was shaking.

Dropping his bag, he moved slowly toward her. "It's not up to you to *allow* me to make that choice."

"But you hate being onstage."

He continued advancing slowly, gaining more and more conviction as he did so. "Yep."

"You don't want an audience. Or to ever go back. Being a dancer makes you miserable."

He nodded. "All true," he told her, not budging from the facts one bit. "But if I can help out the closest person I've ever had to a real friend, someone I trust with my life... what kind of man am I if I walk out on that just because I'll be uncomfortable for a few hours?"

"Or days," she told him. "The look in your eyes...you're like a scared rabbit."

He shrugged. Didn't deny that he felt a bit of anxiety kicking in. "You don't grow in life if you don't face your fears." A lesson that had just in the moment come home to him.

If he could get himself back up on a stage, he'd be helping her, but he'd be helping himself, too. The next time he walked off a dance stage forever, he'd do it the right way.

He wouldn't run and hide.

He'd walk. Openly. With a genuine smile on his face.

With gratitude for the dance.

And with the calm realization that it didn't own him.

He'd walk off knowing that he was finally, irrevocably, free.

And, if he pulled it all off successfully for Harper, giving her what she needed, he might just end up feeling like a decent human being, too.

She loved the man.

Standing in her studio, in the middle of a potentially horrible moment, Harper watched Nathan approaching, prepared to take on his demons for her, and the truth smacked into her. Hard.

In all her life, there was nothing she'd been surer of.

She'd known him less than a month and she loved the man. Felt as though she'd always known him. Had just been waiting for him to appear in the flesh in her life.

And…

It was all wrong for her.

For both of them.

Her life made him feel as though he needed to bolt.

And his…consciously not being a part of the dance world in any way…she'd shrivel up. Lose joy.

No matter how much you loved someone, you still had to be yourself.

"I want to do this, Harper." Nathan had stopped walking seconds before. Was right there in front of her, offering her one of her heart's greatest desires. To be onstage with Goldman.

One time. Just one time.

Could she actually turn her back on that chance?

What if she could help him face his fears? Help him let go of the past and get on with the rest of his life? His sabbatical was over. He was ready to reach out and grasp that for which he yearned. A future, a family, with another woman. There was pain in there. Possibly mind-numbing pain.

But if she loved him, she had to want what was best for him. To help him get there, if she could.

That much she knew.

If she accepted his offer, and he backed out at the last minute, she'd have no time to create a piece for herself to do instead.

He wouldn't do that to her. The surety settled over her.

Nathan was a man of his word. Even back then. He'd

spared himself nothing in the telling. But what had been clear to her was that he'd completed his current obligation. And had run the very next second. Before being pressured into another one.

"And I need you to know that if I accept your incredibly generous offer, that's it. I won't see this as a possibility of any kind of future performance with you in it."

Any kind of future, period, her heart told her.

But for one night…she'd have it all.

Which was more than some people ever got.

"It's kind of you to say so," he said, grinning. "But I can rely on myself for that one. I *will* say no, to anyone who tries to make it more than one piece, one time. A favor for a friend."

She nodded. Smiling, too. Filling with the same kind of nervous excitement she'd felt backstage before her first competition solo.

"And one thing I'm very confident about," he added, taking her hand and pulling her out to the dance floor. "Is that in the years since I've left the stage, I've learned how to speak up for myself."

He twirled her then. Taking her to the place they'd left off during rehearsal. And with a distinctly said, "five, six, seven, eight…" took right up into the lift.

The woman was going to be the death of him.

And what an intensely painful and gratifying way to go. Assuming he got through to the dying part without a major fail.

Stopping his thoughts right there, Nathan pulled into the studio complex at Oppenstott's scheduled rehearsal time Thursday afternoon, eager for the hours ahead.

He'd always liked the time alone in studio, even some of

the rehearsal times with others, to dance. Just to give his all to a sport that was also an art. His sport.

He didn't want fame, a stage, lights, an audience, an agent. Hadn't ever yearned for any of that.

Nor had he ever wanted the jibes other guys at school had given him. Right up until his mother had pulled him out and hired someone to homeschool him.

Stopping short, halfway out of his truck, his bag on his shoulder dragging behind him, Nathan froze.

The jibes? Where in the hell had that come from?

Granted, he hadn't fit in all that well at school. He'd been cast in his first full-time professional production at fourteen. Had missed a lot of classes…

Dragging his duffel, he jumped down, slammed the door and headed across the parking lot. With flashes coming to him. Some guy, taller than him, blond, trying to block his way. Calling him a sissy. So what? He shook his head. He'd pushed past the guy.

But there'd been more. He couldn't call back any specifics. Just that sense…his peers had thought him…less of a guy, because he'd been different.

He remembered being angry with his mother for making him that.

Really angry.

He couldn't ever remember having it out with her, though. Or even telling her in passing that she was ruining his life.

He'd just channeled, as she'd taught him to do. Channel everything he felt inside and express it onstage.

Approaching the door of the studio, he gave himself a mental shake. Some memories were bound to surface. He'd opened the door to them, too, by stepping back onto the dance floor.

And going onstage?

He'd be open to the opinions of others again, too.

Fortunately, only for one night. And he could ignore them all. Because he had a full life waiting for him. One he'd built to his own specification.

A life that not only suited him, but in which he thrived.

And when he found a woman to share a life with him, and they had kids…

Pulling open the studio door, Nathan smiled. He was stronger than he'd ever been. Inside and out. Had taken control. He had his plan.

And no one on earth was going to be able to change that.

Harper thrived in the studio on Thursday afternoon. She was more…everything…than she'd ever been before. Her technique was as near perfect as a human being could get. She never missed a beat. She tuned into her dance partner, to her own body, and the two melded perfectly as they danced the piece full-out, from beginning to end.

And after a water break across the studio from each other, they did it again.

Then things got even bigger. Better. Beyond what she'd ever imagined.

"You ready for a suggestion or two?" Nathan asked, pulling out a mat. He was sweaty, smiling, muscles fully visible and bulging, and she suffused with such an intense wave of love for the man that for a second, she was almost lightheaded with glee.

"Of course," she told him, taking a deep breath as she approached. Getting herself fully back into focus.

"Eighth stanza, second count, we…"

"Come together in recognition…" she interrupted, right

there with him. They danced a quick six-beat waltz to stage left. Before he turned his back and walked off.

Leaving her alone, on her own, and because she was forced to do so, she found her wings.

"Instead of just walking off, I'd like to do a send-off."

Excitement swirling within her, she walked closer to him. "Okay, like what?"

"There's this lift I always wanted to try," he said, his gaze bright as it met hers. Alight with pleasure.

Dancing with her.

She'd brought that out in him.

Not because he wanted to be a dancer, and she could get him there. But just because he was enjoying dancing with her.

They'd been meant to meet. Her spirit soared with the knowledge.

Stopping right in front of him on the mat, she said, "I'm game."

"I'm going to bow at the last beat of the waltz, put my hand on the ground. You step on it, both feet fifth position. And I lift you, a statue, not seeing that you're fragile. Until you plié, signaling a break in the marble, and I catch you around the waist. Set you down, and you go into your piece as I walk offstage."

She got it. Wasn't at all sure it was possible. Knew it would be inspired if they pulled it off. She'd wanted to wow her nondance audience, many of whom probably thought ballet was boring, and he'd definitely come up with a way to do it. But...

"I've never seen anything even remotely like this done before, have you?" she asked him.

"Nope. I always wanted to. Suggested it several times. Nobody was willing to try."

For the next three days, she was living at the top of the world. Existed in a fantasy where her wildest dream had actually come true.

She was going onstage with Nathan Goldman. And was going to be dancing with the man she loved, too. Nathan Connolly.

"Let's do it," she told him. For him, she'd try anything. Because, for him, when the show was over, she was going to walk away, too.

He'd told her he was attracted to her. She suspected, given time, his feelings could go deeper than that. And she was absolutely not going to take even a chance that she'd ever let love rob him of his spirit a second time.

Nor would she. Because no matter how much you loved someone, you still had to be yourself. The thought from the day before came back to her.

And as herself, she stepped onto the mat. Into the unknown. Trusting Nathan to keep them both safe.

Chapter Twenty

Adrenaline pumped through Nathan. He knelt on the mat, one knee down, one perpendicular with that foot flat on the mat. "Fifth position," he said. "Palm of my hand."

His focus completely on his body, on the various muscles he'd use to help his hand, his arm, lift the weight it was bearing, he stared at the perfect fifth he held and slowly, using his knee to brace his forearm, lifted.

He shook some. Steadied himself. Got Harper to a foot off the ground, and prepared to take more weight on his supporting leg. The idea being that his arm would hold the weight, but his body would do the major lifting.

He'd practiced the move with weights over and over when he'd been younger.

And through the years, too. Testing himself.

He was not less, he was more.

The thought, the feeling it brought, an unwelcome blast from the past, he started to shake again.

And Harper hopped off.

"You almost had it," she told him, sounding impressed. "You want to try again?"

He glanced up at her, his muscles bulging. "What do you think?"

He knelt again, she stood in fifth. He lifted, got her knee

high off the ground, and she jumped off. They worked on the move for over an hour. Taking breaks. Having a snack to build up muscles they were breaking down. She was ready to keep the dance as it was. He figured more for his sake than for hers.

"One more time," he told her. He was tired. And thirty-three, not nineteen. But he was also strong enough to compete in any lifting competition. Had been since the year after his mother had pulled him out of school.

With a smile, Harper resumed position on the mat. And then on his foot. And with a calming, deep breath, he felt everything click. Him. Her. The day. The dance. His body took over. Executing every detail as he'd envisioned it so many times. He started the lift and all the parts of his body worked in unison, until he was standing, holding Harper with his hand at his shoulder.

He gave a slight push up. She pliéed. And both of his hands were at her waist, sliding her down his body. And, as her pointing toes touched the mat, he let her go.

It was perfect. A blip in time that would be forever engrained. Right up until she didn't go.

His hands vacated her waist.

Her bodyweight didn't leave his.

And then it did. With a giddy laugh, and a couple of quick steps, she was off the mat. "We did it!" She turned, smiling that so welcoming smile of hers—the one he'd seen her on tape gracing her audience with.

He got it. She was a performer. And she'd just done one hell of a performance.

He smiled, too.

Sharing in her celebration, he raised a hand to hers. Felt her clap against his palm.

And came down a bit, too.

He'd been sharing an incredible feat with a friend.
She'd been working.

Harper called it a day as Nathan moved the mats back. He'd already agreed to come in late on Friday afternoon again, in the time slot Oppenstott had agreed to. Prior to that, she had a full day working with the other groups of dancers who'd be appearing onstage before her Saturday night. The kids would be in full costume, both Friday and Saturday. Everyone else was bringing costumes to show her, but would run through pieces without them.

"You owe me dinner," he told her as she hung out by her cabinet, shaking inside. Ostensibly taking sips from the water bottle she listed to her lips periodically.

In truth, she was burning with desire. Her hardened nipples, her belly, below it, were all swirling with a need that was tempting her to just assuage them. Consequences weren't there.

"It'll have to be on the deck at my place," she called out to him, her ability to hide what was inside coming to her aid. One thing she could count on from herself was professionalism to the core. "Aggie's been alone too much these past couple of weeks."

"She's been with Scott and Iris." Nathan was coming toward her as she spoke, wiping his chest and shoulders with the towel he'd had hanging over the back ballet bar.

She grabbed her towel, too. Held it up to her chest. "So maybe I've been without her too much," she said with a grin. She needed to be on Ocean Breeze. Where he was Connolly and she was his friend.

She needed a break from physical contact with him. And didn't trust herself not to sink further into the fantasy if they were in a restaurant where they'd be seen as a couple by others.

They weren't a couple. They were dance partners. She'd had many of them. Had never, ever been turned on by one during a rehearsal.

"I can pick up some crab on the way home," she said. The Rockcliff had a couple of excellent choices. He'd mentioned once that it was his favorite seafood. And since he'd brought up dinner, she wasn't going to turn down the chance to spend the evening with him.

All she had was three days. She'd be responsible. Get her libido under control. But she couldn't deny herself the chance to get the utmost out of the chance she'd been given to experience life at its fullest. She was storing up memories that would be bringing smiles to her heart in old age.

She had no doubt about that.

And she had Aggie. The girl would be her chaperone. Her conscience. Her reminder…

He'd stopped midway across the room. Looking so good with those sweaty muscles in the Lycra tank, completely exposed to her hungry gaze and she was practically drooling. "How about you place the order, and I'll pick up dinner on my way down to the beach," he said.

"I owe you. I pay."

"So pay when you place the order."

It dawned on her then that she'd never said she was going to stop at Rockcliff. Which was the only place on the drive down to the beach. Sticking her tongue out at him, she said, "How do you know I wasn't going to pick up fresh crab and bake or boil it at home?"

His grin melted her. Knees weak, she leaned against the wall.

He'd headed to his corner. Turned to glance over at her.

"I know you," he said, and then, as he grabbed his bag, finished with "Text me the time it'll be ready."

And let himself out.

The adrenaline high slowly dissipated as Nathan drove home to shower and change. He had one more appointment before heading to Ocean Breeze, but before he left, he emptied his bathroom. Throwing everything into a couple of duffels he pulled out of the back of the closet. In a third suitcase he threw enough jeans, boxer briefs, socks and hanging clothes to get through several days and then loaded everything into his truck.

Driving away without looking back.

He was sitting at his desk, alone in his office—in the entire office—when Harper's text came through letting him know when their dinner would be ready for pick up.

Anticipation fueled him during the trip over. Rather than climbing the mountain, he was finally moving forward with his future in sight. Saturday night loomed, but it was like a bruise on a great week, not a bone breaker.

Because of the food he came bearing, he stopped at Harper's as soon as he hit Ocean Breeze, pulling into her drive. But not heading to the front door.

He'd never been inside her place. And didn't want to be. Some things were just off-limits.

Aggie caught on to his arrival first, lumbering around the side of the cottage to greet him and escort him back to the deck.

Where Harper stood in front of the fire, in purple leggings and a flowing colorful gauzy top with flowing sleeves that hung to her thighs. In the darkness, lit only by the moon and the soft lighting his team had installed on the underside of board decks, she was more silhouette than woman.

Taking a hands-off message from that—he could enjoy the spirit of the woman, not the body—he still had to stop and just…look.

He'd had his hands all over Harper that afternoon, and while he'd most definitely been turned on at various interludes, their joining hadn't been about the flesh. Their bodies had mated spiritually, in the art they'd created. While they'd been rehearsing for an onstage performance, they hadn't been performing.

He knew he hadn't been. And would bet his life that she hadn't been, either.

If he could only ever have one moment in time with her, that afternoon of dance or an hour in bed, he'd choose the dance every single time.

Aggie, standing beside Nathan on the beach, wagging her tail, gave a rather quiet *grff* and as Harper turned, Nathan held up the packaged bounty he carried and climbed the three steps to join her.

He was never going to know Harper as some lucky man had or would, but he had a piece of her that no one else would ever have.

And he would cherish it until the day he died.

She'd arranged chairs on either side of the fireplace, with a table between them. He wasn't close enough to touch. And she wouldn't be looking directly into his eyes, either. The fire was there to gaze at.

And still, as they ate, Harper was aware of every breath Nathan took. She could feel his warmth more than the fire's, saw his hand resting on his thigh and knew exactly how that felt. Watched as he leaned forward, reaching to adjust the fire's flame, and remembered how those shirted muscles had looked, bulging and bare, in her studio that afternoon.

It didn't help that all they talked about was the dance. Both critiquing every aspect of the number, looking for any way to improve it, agreeing on parts that worked so well they couldn't change them. What was easier for one of them than the other. Their favorite sections.

She loved those moments with Goldman. And missed Nathan Connolly, too. Was afraid that she might have lost one to the other. Maybe forcing him to choose one or the other to be present with her, since he kept the parts of himself so completely separate.

She understood. She was just sad.

For him. And for her.

She was almost relieved when the food was gone and she could stand, clean up the debris, tend to physical basics. Figuring he'd head out, she took a minute in the kitchen, putting silverware in the dishwasher, rinsing the water glasses they'd used, watching the deck from the kitchen window.

She'd done all she could do, aside from sweeping floors or wiping countertops they hadn't used, and Goldman was still sitting out there, one hand ruffling the fur of Aggie's neck.

The sight pulled her in. Her girl and the man.

And pulled her back out there, too.

Day one of three was almost gone. If she wanted Connolly with her, she had to speak to him. "I realized something today," she said, as she reclaimed her seat, drawing her feet up to the chair with her, hugging her shins to her as she faced the fire.

"That I'm not the dancer you thought I was?" There was a chuckle in his voice. She chose to ignore it.

"Well, yeah, but not in the way you mean. You're far more than I imagined. As a partner on the floor," she quickly elaborated. "But that's not what I was talking about." She needed Connolly back at the table. Not for any clear reason. Just a feeling.

"I was thinking about the fact that no matter how much you love someone, you still have to be yourself." Yep, just throw them right into the fire, why didn't she? The thought pushed her into barreling on. "And you know, my parents… I believe they really loved each other. And probably still do. And what hit me was that it wasn't me that was the problem. I think having me probably was…because I gave them a reason to stay together. To remain tied to a love that wasn't working in day-to-day life."

Okay, she hadn't gotten that far in during rehearsal, but ideas were pouring in like rain, once she gave rein to them.

"Dance has a way of showing you the deeper stuff," Nathan said, drawing her gaze. Was he purposely refusing to leave dance out of it? To separate her from Goldman?

His glance was serious. As though he knew exactly what she was experiencing.

And she continued, "My mom's super outgoing, making friends everywhere she goes. She's a take-charge person. Ran for city council. Was on the state youth dance board. My dad was more of an introvert like me. And… that saying that opposites attract… I think it's true. They do. But just because they attract doesn't mean they're good together. Mom could have gone so much further if Dad had been willing to stand with her. But he wanted no part of local politics. Or being out or noticed at all. His ideal vacation was a cabin in the woods. She'd be climbing the walls within hours. Needing something to do. And when she dragged him to big social functions, or, God forbid, a fundraiser, he'd find a television someplace and sit and watch it. Usually in a room by himself. Then add me to the mix, someone they both adored, with two very different views of what they needed life to be…"

She'd rambled. Hadn't stopped herself. Because she'd been going somewhere specific, a destination she would not announce out loud.

But he did. "You and me," he said. Connolly said.

And all she could do was nod.

He should go. They both had completely booked Fridays ahead of them, followed by their own last studio rehearsal and then on to Saturday's dress and then the show.

He just wasn't sure he'd have another chance to talk to her, just the two of them, person to person, once Saturday night was done.

She'd just made very clear that the two of them wouldn't be good together long term. Even down to the point that having a child would not only be wrong for the two of them, but for the child. Not that either of them had ever talked about getting together. Exactly the opposite.

But neither were irresponsible enough to pretend that there wasn't something powerful between them.

She'd been right to bring their reality out of hiding. To lay it wide-open right there between them.

Her deck was done, his investment cottage would be ready to sell within the month—he might never have a chance to say what was on his mind.

"I've grown a lot, during my association with you," he told her, looking at the fire, but also out at the night. The moonlight over the small sliver of ocean visible from his vantage point.

He wanted her to know. "I've begun to see some things differently. To understand a bit more." He would never have seen himself talking about some things, but suddenly, it seemed pertinent. One of the more important things he might do with his past. If by exposing himself, he could help her trust enough to open her heart up more…to give more of herself than a professional smile all the time…

"I was teased as a kid…about my dancing. Most particularly when I hit puberty. By my peers. Other guys." A few more of the taunts had come to him over the past twenty-four hours, but they'd no longer had the power to hurt him. "I can only guess that my life choices posed some kind of threat to them. Or they were afraid to be around me lest they be labeled, too." He shrugged. "I'll never know, doesn't really matter. *They* don't matter. Not anymore. But back then…it got so bad my mother pulled me out of school. Which also did not sit well with me. I felt as though I was being punished. Ostracized. And… I overcompensated. I worked out relentlessly. Not just in the studio, but in the gym. And the first time a girl made it obvious she found me sexy, I *was* sexy. The girls who threw themselves at me were my way of showing the world how much of a man I really was."

Hearing the words aloud…a truth that had only been dawning on him consciously in the past hours…made him sad for the young man he'd been. For the women who'd been hurt by his thoughtless taking up on their offers. And in the years since, the habit he'd fallen into as a youth—playing the field, taking what was offered—following him. With a difference. As he'd matured, he had the foresight to make certain that women he was with knew that their association was only for the short term. He wasn't a one-woman-settle-down kind of guy.

Until he'd realized he was.

Which brought him full circle back to Harper. He wasn't spewing his guts for himself.

He glanced over at her, to find her watching him, a glisten of tears in her eyes. "I had no idea," she told him. "By the time I knew of you, you were a legend."

He nodded. He knew the kinds of things she'd have heard. Wasn't proud of them.

"The thing is," he continued, "people can be accountable to their faults. They can choose, at any time, to be different from what they once were."

"Nathan." There was a warning in her tone. A get-up-and-go-inside-and-never-speak-to-him-again kind of warning.

And, in light of what she'd just told him and the conversation she might think they were still having, he quickly added, "There are things they can't change, of course. Things they're born with. The way you thrive in the dance world. And I don't, those are things we're likely born with. At any rate, as with your parents, they're things we probably shouldn't try to change. They make us who we are. The lucky ones are people who know what those things are and make their life choices accordingly."

"Like you and me."

"Yes." But he wasn't done. "People aren't born with animosity in their hearts, Harper. Except, perhaps, in very few cases where wires might be crossed, human beings aren't born with a desire to backstab. Or be petty. Or mean. Life teaches them those things, and they choose to walk that path."

He glanced over just as she said, "And your point is?" She was meeting his gaze. And warning him that he was trespassing where he wasn't welcome.

He felt the message. And said, "You take it as your due," with all the caring he had in his heart poured into the words. "The text you got dealing with the bad attitude of a ballet instructor due to your schedule change…you accepted it as your due, and it isn't. It's their choice to walk with ugliness as their guide. But it shuts you down. Away…"

She'd been looking toward the fire but turned back to him. Frowning. "Your self-actualization somehow make you a therapist now?" The tone wasn't quite snotty. But it was close.

He didn't look away. Or think less of her. If anything, he cared more. And might not get another chance to try to help before he was out of her life. "I'm just saying…in the dance world, I get that you have to keep your walls up, but not everywhere. You learned young, at home, to have them there. I get that. A kid does what he has to do to survive." He was proof positive of that. "But you're sweet and kind, wickedly smart, and have a huge heart. I see you here on the beach…the way you walk Aggie after everyone is in for the night, even when you're home earlier. The love you pour all over your companion there, but don't seem to be able to give or accept from others. I just…wish you could hear the way the other women down here talk about you. They're genuine people. With good hearts. They want to know you better, Harper. And if you let them, you'd find a gold mine."

That was it. He'd said what he could. Done what he could to try to make even a tiny bit of the difference in her life that she'd made in his.

To help her heart heal as she'd helped his.

To pave the way to the happiest future possible.

The rest was her right to choose.

Chapter Twenty-One

He'd said she'd find a gold mine. And while that would actually be a very welcome change, she didn't need the mine. She wanted the man. Gold*man*.

He'd left shortly after delivering his epistle the night before. Things had been heading toward awkward—into territory they would not chart together—and, as if on cue, they'd both abruptly stood at the exact same moment, to the point that they'd startled Aggie, who'd barked.

They'd laughed, he'd issued a quick "thanks for dinner" followed by "see ya," and was gone. If she hadn't felt so relieved, she might have become offended by how eager he'd appeared to be to get away.

Still, she'd ended up soaking her muscles in a hot tub, thinking about him the entire time. Closing her eyes and remembering the strength in his hands on different parts of her body, taking control of her safety.

And the trust with which she'd let him.

He wasn't the first man she'd done lifts with. He wasn't even the tenth.

But he was the man who'd shown her how to be happy in life. He'd shown her her life's course. How ironic that it was that very same course that prevented them from ever being more than friends.

And…she feared, they'd be less than that once the weekend was over.

Knowing that she'd fallen in love with him meant that to keep hanging out would be too dangerous. She would not become her parents. She wouldn't do that to him. To any children that could happen. Nor to herself.

Which was probably why she'd woken up Friday morning filled with almost a desperate eagerness to get into the day. The second of the three days in her life that he'd be starring in.

Rehearsals with the kids were a total blessing. They absorbed her completely, taking her outside of herself. And settled her spirit, too. Same with the two adult groups that came in. One ballet, one modern. The pieces, the people, were so different, and yet hit her in the same good places. Bringing her back and healing her inner confusion. Centering her mind and emotions to the point that when Goldman showed up at her door, she greeted him with a completely sincere calm smile.

Which he returned in kind.

He was there to work.

And so was she.

She ran him through warm-ups, as she had with every other act that had been in that day. As she'd do in the morning, with all of them onstage, before dress rehearsal started. And while she knew he was highly proficient at getting through them himself—had probably already done so that morning as well—she was the choreographer. The one in charge.

And, at that point, he was just another number in the show for which she was responsible.

Albeit one with whom she trusted not only her talent, but her heart as well. All day, in the dark recesses that were quieting down inside her, one small portion had remained.

Nathan had been right. She spent her life opening herself to the expression of beauty. Of life at its most intense, joyful level. And building walls against the individual people whom she came in contact with.

All of them.

And what worth did joy carry without the love through which it flowed from person to person?

Somewhere along the day, she'd realized something. And on her first break with Nathan, after a complete cold run-through before breaking things down one last time, she stood at her cabinet and looked over at him in his corner by the door. Taking occasional squirts from his water bottle.

Seemingly in a good mental space.

She went to the middle of the floor, decreasing the space between them by half, to sit down and do some leg stretches. "You were right," she told him, wanting to feel as nonchalant as she was projecting herself to be. "About the way I shut myself off." Admitting it out loud held her accountable. "Once this show is over, I'm going to reach out to Sage. See if she'd like some help with the baby, and dealing with Leigh." She'd only just thought of that last part as she said the words. But added, "I need to start slowly…"

His smile lit her up inside. Again. Just as it had before.

It warmed her.

And she let it.

Just because they weren't meant to be life partners, did not mean that their time together was superfluous.

Nor did it mean that it couldn't be life-changing for both of them.

Feeling empowered by the previous night's successful pointers to Harper, Nathan dropped his water bottle back into his bag and went to pull out the mat while Harper finished her stretches.

She turned when she heard him behind her.

"I know…it's not good practice to change a piece the day before a show, but I've got just one little thing…"

Where he'd half expected a frown, she smiled, stood up and came toward him. "With you, I'm game."

His chest swelled. *With you.*

Not with someone else.

"I'm seeing the new lift with a more engulfing finish," he told her. The move had come to him the night before as he'd practically run from her cottage.

"Instead of me setting you down to move into your section after the plié catch, I need to slide you down to floor. You'll do a roll into a tendu, rise up on those toes and go. I'm on the ground as well, watching you as you leave me, I'll mirror the tendu as though to also rise and give chase, but instead, as I rise, I pirouette once and walk with purpose offstage."

A mirror of them.

Because they both knew it had to be.

"You're right," she said then, frowning, but stepping onto the mat. "It's much more real—and gut-wrenching." Her words were steady enough.

She wasn't looking at him.

Or smiling.

They spoke their strongest truths through physical movement.

He stepped with deliberation to get into position. She owned a part of him forever. He'd realized the truth days before.

His duty was to hold that fact, and still let her fly away.

Because it was what was right. For both of them.

He didn't like it. Not in the moment. Probably not for a

long time. Dancing it would solidify his resolve to follow through, though.

Just as, in his mind, that last piece he'd done in New York all those years ago had been him telling the life goodbye. He hadn't left without saying a word to anyone.

He'd said them all. The entirety of that five-minute number. To anyone who'd have been tuned into him, known him well enough, to get the message.

On one knee, his hand before him, as though he was asking her hand in marriage, he lowered his digits to just above the padding beneath them. Didn't see anything but her feet, perfectly positioned ankles and the bottom edges of her leggings as she stepped onto his palm.

He lifted, she remained steady as marble, just as they'd done during the full run-through minutes before. Standing, with one foot turned out in front of him, the other slightly behind, his hand rose to shoulder height.

She pliéed. He slid his hand out from her feet so quickly, the movement could hardly be noted as both hands sprung to her waist, catching her and, sliding her down his body, lowered her to her toes. Crumpling down over her toes to the mat, she placed one hand by her shoulder, and shot her arched body backward over it, and then, with the other leg straight, toes pointed, she pulled her weight forward, dragging her other leg in full point. A crawl. Not the rise and fly that he'd envisioned.

Described.

He'd seen it happening as he also crumpled, shot around, prepared to watch her jeté away, begin a series of dizzying turns, as he rose and walked away from her.

She hadn't risen up to her feet. She'd landed in a dancer's crawl instead. He could feel her heartbreak reverberating through the air he breathed. Through him.

He couldn't stand, not until she did. The shape would be all wrong. Him looking down on her. His body, his dancer's instinct took over. With one hand, he reached out. Grabbed her ankle, pulled her slowly back down his body on the mat, mirroring the move they'd made standing.

Trusting the dance to show them the way.

Trusting her to do so.

Her thigh brushed his penis. Electrifying him. And then her face was in front of his. Her arms wrapping around him, and her lips were on his.

His hands, pulling her back. Climbing her body. He'd been hard beneath the padding on his dance belt. His mouth… right there.

Her lips on his. She didn't question. Couldn't. Her body was on fire, liquid heat passing through every muscle. Every vein. Igniting her heart. The movement became her director.

Nathan's lips were strong, taking hold of hers, and then his tongue was there. Teaching her a brand-new dance in the midst of the revised one they'd already been doing.

Eyes tightly closed, she focused on sensation. On making perfection.

She groaned, enveloped by the sound of his breathing. His taste. The touch of his hands still on her waist.

Hers had to travel. Movement had to have shape to speak and she had so very much to say. In the only way she knew how. Through the use of her body.

Her hands rose over her head, and she broke off the kiss messily, leaving their lips wet as she slid downward until the hands on her waist were on her breasts. She shifted, rocking her upper torso within his outspread palms, titillating her nipples as she brought a knee up to rub gently against his groin, in beat with the touch on her breasts.

They were in a world of their own. The audience dark. And she was moving like she'd never moved before. Deafened to anything but the sound rushing through her. A melody of desperation.

And of salvation, too.

He'd pulled her back to him. Calling for more physical expression.

The dance couldn't end.

Not yet.

Not without more movement. More exquisite torture until they reached their moment of glory. Were one with the singular power that had introduced them so many years before, and had driven them together again.

Her legs split then, and, opening her eyes, she pulled up to a sitting position, legs straight on either side of her, lining his body where he lay—a virile, hungry man. Reaching for her. Needing her.

With one strong brush down his body, she had his leggings down. And with her last two fingers, took his dance belt with her.

His penis sprang up into the dance. A perfect jeté, while his hands ran up and down the lengths of her legs. She arched back deeply and he lifted her with one arm, stripping her bottom half bare with the other.

Their synchronization was perfect. The harmony haunting. Calling. Forever calling. And then she was on her back, the mat beneath her bare butt, and while he held her legs out in the splits, he spread his legs into splits of his own in front of her. She reached, he did, and they wrapped each other, pulling toward the center, until the tip of him touched an opening that had never been a part of her dance.

They shifted together, completing the initial motion, the entrance, and then, in rhythm that they shared, pulled apart, and then together. Again and again.

Until the music they were making crescendoed so fiercely inside her she cried out.

His yowl followed right after.

The dance was done.

What in God's name had he done?

Pulling out of Harper, he grabbed his dance pants and belt, held them against him as he walked bare butt to the bag by the door. Ears roaring, he couldn't think.

Didn't recognize himself.

Digging in his bag, he pulled out the underwear and jeans he'd had most of the day. Slid into them pretty much simultaneously. Got himself zipped in, preparing to reach for his bag and the door at the same time.

And stopped.

He was thirty-three, not nineteen.

He couldn't just know he was in a bad spot and walk away to a new one.

And neither could he explain or justify the mammoth error he'd just made. Throwing years of self-discipline in the trash as though they'd never been.

And with Harper. The one woman in the world he'd give his life to never hurt.

"It was inevitable."

The voice was hers. In a tone he didn't recognize.

He had to turn, to look at her.

She'd pulled her leggings back on. Her Lycra top in place as though nothing had ever happened. It hadn't. To the top. Neither of them had moved it.

Only against it.

With a shrug, she stood there, meeting his very troubled gaze with one that appeared...completely accepting.

"We were first connected in the midst of our individual personal struggles," she said. The words matter-of-fact. "And we've come together for some closure of them." She'd been walking toward him as she spoke.

He didn't back away. Didn't reach for the door. He couldn't.

Because, though he had no idea what it meant to his future, he knew she was right.

"We had to finish the dance, Goldman." His name had come out in a whisper.

Sounding more like a goodbye prayer.

Raising his brow, he held that gaze coming at him so steadily. "And now?"

She shrugged. "That's up to you."

No way. There were two of them. Two lives. Two plans. Two sets of choices. All of which she knew. "How so?" he asked.

"You choose for this moment to be our goodbye. You walk out that door and don't look back."

Part of him, the youth that would always be a part of him almost took that choice. The man he'd become stood his ground. "Or?"

"You go now. Come to dress rehearsal tomorrow. And we dance our goodbye."

He had the address. Had already purchased the black tights and tank that were to serve as his costume.

And though he'd failed that afternoon's rehearsal, he was going to pass the final exam.

"I'll see you tomorrow," he said while turning, and, bag in hand, headed out the door.

Chapter Twenty-Two

Harper couldn't bear to be on her deck. She craved the warmth of a fire, though, and so she built one. With purchased fire logs. In the sand on her acre of land. Halfway down to the water. And then, in clean leggings and a long-sleeved plain black T-shirt, she sat by it, hugging her shins to her chest.

She cried some. Rocked some.

Talked to Aggie a lot.

And noticed more and more people walking by her place. They stayed down by the water, but they were there.

As much of a family as she'd built for herself.

It was inevitable that at some point Morgan and Angel, who were inseparable since their people Scott and Iris had hooked up a couple of months ago, would know that Aggie was out. And once they knew that, they'd come running. Probably not that far of a stretch to see a visibly pregnant Sage head toward her with Gray beside her, an arm around her back, and holding little Leigh's hand.

She tensed. Had been crying. Didn't know if her face bore evidence. Hoped that the darkness hid whatever might be there. And she pasted on the smile she always had ready for all of them.

Scott lay down on his side in the sand, head propped up

on his hand, and played with all three dogs. Iris snapped photos with the night vision camera she'd had with her. Leigh squealed and posed. And, for a bit, came to sit on Harper's lap, tracing Harper's chin with her finger to ask, "Mommy says I have to ask, not her, but, can you teach me to dance? I want to do circles, too."

"Too?" she asked, near tears again, happy ones, but focusing on the curiosity until she had her emotions more fully in check.

"Like that mean Emily at my school who told me that my house was broken and it wasn't."

Iris, who'd been circling with her camera, bent down then and whispered in Harper's ear, "Because Leigh only had one parent."

Ahhh. Broken home.

Kids could be so mean.

And sometimes, things they said and did changed lives forever.

"Of course I'll teach you to dance," she said then, grinning from ear to ear. "And you can tell this Emily that you're learning from one of the most famous ballet dancers in the state of California."

Leigh's nose scrunched. "What's ballet?"

Laughing, Harper told her, "It's a fancy word for dance," and glanced up to see everyone staring at her.

And she realized her mistake. They knew what she did. Sort of.

They had no idea how well she did it. Or in what form.

"You're a professional ballet dancer?" Sage asked. "I thought you owned a studio. Taught little kids..."

All those eyes on her...open-mouthed, she was a doe caught in the headlights, staring back, unmoving.

Until she saw movement behind them. Grateful for the

distraction, she watched, couldn't distinguish who or what was there until she heard, "She does own a studio, and does teach little kids." Nathan appeared out of the shadows. In shorts down almost to his knees, a sweatshirt and barefoot. Staying at his cottage that night?

She'd been certain he'd have gone home.

"Just like I build decks," he added, as he plopped down in the sand beside her. "But I'm also a one-time famous ballet dancer who graced stages from here to New York City. And tomorrow night, Harper and I are dancing together, a piece she was asked to choreograph, along with several more that she did. Including two dances by kids not all that much older than Leigh."

She stared at him. Had the man lost his mind? More likely been drinking? A ton? He'd not only told on her more fully, he'd outed himself.

What in the hell was he doing?

While she stared around her, focusing mostly on Leigh, who'd lost interest and was laughing and squealing as she played with the dogs, Nathan took every bit of the unwelcome attention he'd just thrown on her, onto himself.

Answering the barrage of questions.

Talking about his mother, growing up in the world of dance. Having his pick of agents.

And she stared. Was he…

Could he possibly be…

Telling her—in his own way of actions speaking louder than words—that he was okay with a life he'd thought he didn't want?

That he'd found that the life he needed to live didn't have to be outside the world of dance?

Sitting there, with little Leigh's question still swirling with good feeling inside, Harper's heart started to soar.

Right up until she heard Scott ask, "So seriously, man, you going to give up Connolly Construction and head to New York?"

She hadn't even considered the option for him.

"Hell no!" Sitting beside her like he was, the words were loud. Reverberating through her with their intensity.

And Harper accepted what had to be.

What a total creep he'd been. The jerk of all jerks. Nathan had come down the beach to have a serious discussion with Harper whether she wanted it or not. Because he was half the problem and had the right to stand up to what he'd done that afternoon.

Had the responsibility to do so.

He'd been shocked to see her little fire on the beach. Bothered that she hadn't used his fireplace—as though the choice was some personal affront against him. And more so, to find her surrounded by the people she'd distanced herself from. That surprise had been a welcome one.

She'd said he'd been right to call her out the night before. Leigh's question about ballet had hit him hard, for her to have to be so unknown on her own home front, that he'd just blurted.

And in so doing, had proven himself even more untrustworthy than he'd thought himself.

He'd have left, if not for the purpose that had originally driven his walk down the beach to her. He'd hoped to find her on the deck.

Hadn't wanted to have to knock on her door.

Most certainly hadn't wanted to be inside her home. Too much. Closer than he could handle.

Instead, he had to sit with her neighbors and be friendly.

Paving the way for the deeper future relationships he hoped she'd have with them.

She loved Ocean Breeze. And if he was right about anything, he'd put his money on her wanting to have those relationships. Most particularly with Sage and Iris. She spoke of those two the most.

Thankfully, folks didn't stay long.

Unfortunately, he didn't leave with them. A sentiment Harper seemed to share as she stood and moved to cover the fire to put it out.

"Wait," he said, holding out a hand toward her leg when she would have shoved a pile of sand toward the flame with her foot. "Can we sit for a minute longer?"

Aggie looked over at him, those big brown eyes seeming to be filled with question. And he had to agree with her. Was what he was doing the right thing?

Was he sure he wanted to do so?

Ultimately, the answer didn't matter. He'd done. So he had to do.

Sitting halfway around the fire from where he'd been, he stretched his legs out in front of him, his toes pointing to the ocean in the distance. Across from him, she was doing the same.

He glanced out toward the water that was, except for a strip of moonlight running across it, mostly just a vast sea of darkness. Trying to form coherent words.

"Let it go, Nathan." Her tone as soft, and filled with caring, as he'd ever heard it, drew his gaze to her.

While he'd been looking into black space for his answers, she'd been turning to him. Her gaze was shadowed, but he saw enough of the intensity shining from them to get hooked.

And be unable to disconnect.

"It happened. Looking back on it, I think it was all part of our separate journeys. A natural way to express how much knowing each other has meant, while being a period at the end of our sentence."

Right. He'd thought so, too.

At the moment, hoped to God that was what it had been. Sort of. If it meant his other concern held no weight.

"We didn't use birth control."

And he'd never, not one time, in his entire, somewhat reckless life, had unprotected sex. The one law his mother had ever laid down for him, outside the dance studio, was that no son of hers was ever going to take a chance on ruining a woman's life.

Like hers had been ruined. By him. He'd heard the sentence she hadn't said. Every single time she'd grilled him about protection.

Until one night when he'd come very late into the hotel suite they'd been sharing and she'd been waiting up for him in the living area, drinking wine, to ask the usual question. He'd been seventeen and had unloaded on her. If she ever asked him the question again, he'd stop using condoms just to get her to shut up.

He hadn't meant the words. Had apologized for them later.

She'd never asked the question again.

And Harper wasn't speaking. Or looking at him, either.

That time it was her looking out into the emptiness.

"Harper?"

"I can't have children, Nathan."

The words weren't a shock. He knew how she felt. But if she was telling him…what? That if she was pregnant she wasn't having it? Her body. His child. Her body. Her right.

"I was born without a uterus."

The night had grown so still the silence hurt. Physically hurt.

"I have ovaries. I make eggs. I just have no way to provide a home to them while they grow."

He choked up. Not for himself.

He'd just gotten what he'd been praying for all the way down the beach. The assurance that there was no way he'd ruined her life that afternoon.

He'd been hoping she was on some form of birth control. Not that...

"Oh, God... Harper, I'm sorry. So sorry." He swallowed hard. Had to blink back a shot of moisture behind his lids.

"Don't be." Her easy tone shot his gaze over to her. She was still looking out at the ocean, but seemed to sense his need for more, because she turned right there to meet his gaze. "Seriously, it's something I've known since I was old enough to understand. And, you know, maybe if I wasn't a dancer, I'd care more. But don't you see...this all fits into the life plan that was supposed to be mine. It became clear to me when I saw you dancing. That dance was my life. Not being a mother."

Her gaze didn't waver. The smile on her face did some. But her voice...as steady and sure as he'd ever heard it.

"But to know you never even had a chance...maybe dance was just your way of making lemonade out of lemons." What the hell? Was he trying to make her hurt?

Or to somehow ease his own?

It wasn't him who couldn't have children.

It hit him then...though he denied the thought as it occurred...it hit again. Had a part of him secretly harbored a small hope that he and Harper *had* made a baby that day? That doing so somehow meant that they were meant to be more than ships passing in the night?

He hoped not.

"With modern medicine, there are ways I could have a child of my own," she said then, in the same tone. "I've known that for a lot of my life as well. My mother's delved into any research known to man on the subject. Because she was the woman in the pair of people who made me, she somehow took my lack of a female organ to be her fault." She paused, shook her head. "In vitro fertilization is a common thing these days. I could have a baby nine months from next week if I wanted one. You go to a clinic, they remove your eggs, put them in a dish with donated sperm, and there are women who get fully vetted by the clinic, and paid by them, with signed legal documents all the way around, who are implanted with the embryo, grow the baby, and then birth it and hand it over."

He'd been watching her as she looked oceanward, the entire time she spoke. He'd also seen the way her hand had been slowly rubbing Aggie's head, hugging the girl against her thigh.

And he realized he was superfluous, sitting there.

Being there.

"You just don't want one," he said, for himself, far more than her.

She nodded.

He quietly apologized for…everything…and excused himself to head home.

Harper had tears rolling down her cheeks before Nathan had even reached the edge of her property. Aggie lay with her, watching him.

The girl knew how to help when the tears came. She just lay there. Pressing her big warm body up against Harper's leg. And looked around.

Aware on any level that mattered.

Present in the moment.

Loving her through that which couldn't be changed.

For the first time in her life, she was shedding tears over the lack of a uterus. Which made no logical sense. She'd been so young when she'd first found out that by the time she'd fully understood the ramifications, she'd already accepted them.

And when she'd reached high school, her mother had already had a list of clinics she'd vetted, showing them to Harper so she'd know that she could have as many children as she wanted.

Though she had them in the same file folder her mother had originally given them to her, she'd never even looked at one of them.

Had no intention of doing so that night, that week or that year, either.

But for the moment, she couldn't stem the sadness that was pouring out of her. Nathan had come down to see her to take responsibility in the event that they'd made a baby that day.

And she wished they had.

When he'd first mentioned the possibility.

The truth was there. Undeniable. She wanted to be pregnant with his child.

Not because she yearned for the life, the family, he wanted. Her life truly was planted right where it needed to be. In the dance world.

But to have been unexpectedly pregnant with his baby… she'd have had the chance to have it all. Dance. Goldman in her life. And a new being that was the two of them together.

It would be unfair to all three of them. Just as her parents giving life to her had been. And yet…there she was, alive, thriving. In a life she loved.

Loving both of them.

She wouldn't rather not have been born.

And while she would never consciously choose to put a child of hers through what she went through, never choose to make the mistake of trying to meld her life with Nathan's—if she'd had no choice…she could have shared a part of life with Nathan permanently.

Could have had a little one to love.

Like Leigh…

Standing, Harper scooped handfuls of sand on the dying fire, making sure all the embers were fully covered so no four-legged friends stepped on them and got burned. And with her hand on Aggie's head, walked up to her cottage, had a hot bath and went to bed.

Comforting herself with the thought that even after the show the next night, she'd still have at least occasional glimpses of Nathan now and then. On the beach. Outside his cottage.

And she'd had the perfect moment. With him. That would always be hers. Theirs.

Something a lot of people never had.

She fell asleep with the firm reminder that she'd eventually see him out with his wife, and then child—the loves of his life—and assured herself that by then, she'd simply be happy for him.

And not at all sad for herself.

Chapter Twenty-Three

Harper didn't look surprised when Nathan showed up backstage as planned at the theater in LA on Saturday. Her smile took on the same light he'd seen the day before, as they'd been dancing.

Before the big fail.

He smiled back. Glad to see her, in spite of the futility of it. And walked with a lighter step knowing that she hadn't doubted he'd be there.

She'd grown to trust him.

And he her.

He nodded at her, letting her know that he'd be ready when called, and then slid into the small private dressing room side stage that she'd assigned to him. She'd emailed a floor plan of the entire backstage area, highlighting his space.

There was a lock on the door. And a bathroom.

She'd had him arrive during the first group rehearsal—the kids who were taking dance, not yet part of the dance world. Kids who'd have no idea who he was.

He knew what she was doing. Giving him time to acclimate before he was face-to-face with someone who knew him. Knew who he'd been.

Hours stretching before him in a dressing room was

not new to him. Hell, he'd grown up that way. Had learned to walk backstage. And rather than driving around in LA traffic looking for something to do, he'd brought the job with him. Computer. Photos of spaces where the condominium decks would go. And, settling into one of the two mismatched chairs at a small scarred wooden table along a white painted brick wall, he got to work.

Focusing on his own artistic expression. Being himself.

Something that was critical in the midst of the chaos that would come that day. Dress rehearsal and showtime always brought heightened sensitivities. Misunderstandings. Self-doubt warring with intense excitement. Nerves on overload.

He'd been at it for about twenty minutes when his phone binged a text. You need anything?

Ready to text back that he was good, instead he typed, Would you rather have the built-in rock fireplace I did for you or a sunken table one? He read. Hit Send.

And was surprised at how quickly the answering bing hit back. You are not changing my fireplace. It's perfect for the space.

And just as quickly, he typed, Doing a series of beach condos.

The response was a little slower in coming, but got there. I prefer the rock. But a sunken table in the middle, rather than one built up might be better in some locations. Depends on the view.

That's how his morning went. He sent a quick note to his crew, telling them he was adding a rock base to the firepit on his deck. And then, stuck in the small room with no distraction, he got more work done than he ever would have at home or in the office.

With occasional input from a woman whose opinion he respected.

Life could be one hell of a lot worse.

All he had to do was consider the day that came after, and a lifetime of days after that. He'd find someone to spend his life with. Sharing honesty, loyalty and respect with her. He'd love her. He was confident of all that. He wouldn't settle for less. Nor would he offer himself to a woman unless he could give all that.

But he was no longer sure she'd be the love of his life.

He might have already found *her*.

They just weren't at all suited to a lifetime partnership.

And that was a snag he most definitely had not seen coming.

The day of the show had always been Harper's favorite. Always. She loved the energy. The anticipation. The people in her world working together for the common good.

Onstage, animosities and jealousies faded away as the dancers had to rely on each other, help each other, to make the piece come together, or they'd all look bad.

And assuming the show went well, the aftermath was the best. Everyone flying on a natural high. Congratulating each other.

That Saturday, though, she was more nervous than excited. Focused on Nathan. On what he might be going through locked alone in his small dressing room. But more, what he'd be facing when he came out.

She'd had to give his name to the director for the program change. And as word had spread through the dance world that Goldman was going to be performing, the amount people had to bid to get one of the 450 seats had skyrocketed. Attendees had been sent links to their phones to enable them to make pledges that night as well. Every act had a link. All they had to do was connect their wallet, and enter amounts as they watched the show.

And she was performing a dance that had had sex in it the day before.

With a man whose baby she could never have. But somehow suddenly wanted?

She'd be touching Nathan Connolly for the last time. Feeling his hands on her body for the last time.

All things she managed not to have on her mind as they ran through dress rehearsal just before lunch. She'd been so focused on Nathan's challenge, walking out among those who revered a man he no longer wanted to be, and then on the lighting and sound system as she danced, on making certain that the right curtains were closed behind them, and they had their marks on the stage—she'd had no time to think about herself.

She'd texted him before their piece, giving him a five-minute warning before he'd be due side stage, and let him know that she thought it best that they skip the new lift landing he'd come up with the day before.

And had received a "100" emoji in response.

She'd expected him to make a beeline for his dressing room as soon as he'd exited stage for the last time. Lunch was being catered, and would be delivered to all the performers, musicians as well as dancers. His went to his dressing room.

Instead, he waited offstage for her to finish and follow him off.

At which applause erupted. Backstage. From the wings. Out front. In the sound booth.

Heart pounding, she looked at Nathan, assessing, saw only his Connolly confidence. Leaning in, head bowed, he said, "We rushed the beginning a bit. There's a slippery spot upstage, a third of the way between middle and left stage. And otherwise it felt good."

Looking at the stage, catching her breath, aware of the bodies starting to form around them, and keeping some distance, too, she said, "I rushed. You covered. I know the exact spot and will see that it's tended to. And not only are there dancers gathering, but I see Winslow and Redmond there, too." In light of the onlookers, she kept her expression schooled. Serious. Working. "Let's walk and talk." She moved as she issued the last bit, keeping her head bowed with his as though they were still in deep discussion.

He shook his head. "It's okay," he said. Then met her gaze full on. "I'm okay."

She searched his eyes. Nodded.

And he added, "I'm not looking forward to tonight, the audience, but the rest... I'm fine."

He sounded fine. And for a second her heart soared. "You don't mind being back?" she asked. Hoping. Could they...?

He shook his head. "That's just it," he told her. "I'm here, doing this today, but I'm not back."

With a slow nod, she watched him, saw the confidence brimming from him, and a tiny hope she'd been secretly holding since he'd first agreed to help her—that the dance would bring him full circle back into his need for the world—died.

"I said no," he told her, as though that explained everything.

She frowned. Aware of the people, the buzz of conversations in the close distance, but seeing only him.

"I'll talk to them all. Be cordial. And if anyone asks for more, I just say no," he added.

She saw the truth in his gaze. It really was that simple.

And clear to her that he'd come full circle, and knew exactly who he was. More than that, he liked himself. Which was a far cry better than how he'd felt about Nathan Goldman.

Any minute chance of a future for them, of him being okay in the world of dance, had been wiped off the table.

He'd just said no.

And she couldn't walk away from the life without leaving her spirit behind.

In between calls that afternoon—stage calls for a short final bow, for individual introductions of the acts, for producer and director instructions—Nathan got six decks designed. He'd been instructed to make sure they all "matched" the look of the overall complex, and so wood choices and styles of railings were made once and incorporated into all of the individual-to-the-unit designs. Which cut his time monumentally.

He'd also been in a couple of semiserious discussions with both the director, Redmond, and Winslow, the show's producer. Both of whom had made several offers to him.

The only one that had even halfway caught his interest had been teaching at a national master class event that Winslow was putting on later in the spring. Serious dancers in both ballet and modern from all over the country would be paying to attend. A portion of which would go to Nathan. The idea of teaching full-time—which meant preparing for competitions and shows, because no dancer could fully learn without them—was a definite no for him.

But a one-time master class would involve nothing but the instruction.

Sharing his vast knowledge of how to dance, one muscle at a time.

But in the end, the no had still won out.

He was back at his computer, drafting an octagonal deck for a corner unit, when Harper texted that she was outside with a snack for him.

And while he wanted to invite her in to share it with him, he didn't. The day had shown him, quite clearly, that he had to say no to her world to be himself. He didn't belong there. And didn't want to. He didn't want the notoriety.

What he did say, as he took the plate of fruit and cheese and crackers—enough only for one—was, "It wasn't just the notoriety, and feeling like I was an object, not a person." He owed her what he knew.

"What was it?" Her gaze was open, warmth in her eyes. Even in their parting, caring was there. Genuine.

"The hero worship," he told her. Something that had come to him as he'd contemplated the master class offer. "I can't live my life knowing that others look at me and try to emulate what I do. Not when kids are involved. And they wouldn't only look to now, they'd look to who I was, what I did, analyze what I ate. How often I worked out. With what weights. Which…fine. But they'd look to the rest, too. And, no."

She nodded. But, for once, didn't smile. "You're a good man, Nathan Goldman Connolly," she said, and turned and walked away.

But he couldn't. Not yet. Watching as one of the professional ballet dancers stopped Harper to speak to her, seeing the concentration she gave to the conversation, he knew there was one more thing he had to do.

Picking up his phone, he dialed.

When the female voice gave him the basic hello he always got on the other end, he said, "I love you, Mom."

And spent the next half hour talking to the woman who'd given him life. Who'd made mistakes along the way. Who hadn't been the best parent in the world. But one who'd kept him. One who'd loved him. And, in her own way, one who'd looked out for him, too.

He had the tough conversation with her he should have had at nineteen, instead of just disappearing.

He apologized.

And then said, "I'm doing a charity show tonight in LA. A one-up. Not a comeback," he quickly inserted when he heard the sharp intake of breath come over the line. "One piece. A duet," he continued, needing to walk away right. "Seating was limited, by bid only, and is sold out. But I'm told the production will be available to watch starting tomorrow…" He gave her the internet address, and let her know that there'd be a small fee to watch. All proceeds going to statewide children's programs.

He'd done what he had to do. Felt…more complete than he had…maybe ever.

Was just hanging up as she said, "Nathan?"

"Yeah?"

"You think you might be able to make a trip home sometime this year? I promise I'll take time away from the studio for you. And…your adopted half brother needs to meet you, son. He needs to see that there are other options in the world besides dance…"

The words brought tears to his eyes. He blinked them away. Gave his mother his word that he'd head upstate before the summer was over.

And for the first time in over a decade, felt like he was ready to take the stage.

For his legitimate last dance.

She wasn't ready. In full costume, burgundy tights, red leotard with a powder puff tutu—no wire, short skirt, made from light fabric, not tulle—and ballet shoes to match, Harper stood side stage, watching the modern number, counting every step along with them. Trying to ignore the tension growing in her muscles, the butterflies in her stomach.

She hadn't had stage nerves in years.

Not like that.

But still knew how to deep breathe her way through them.

Thirty seconds before the piece ended, she raised a hand to check that her bun was tight and secure. And looked to the ground to see the black ballet shoes on side stage, one pulled-curtain over.

Nathan.

He was in place.

The song would begin.

Their dance would happen.

The stage had been treated after the musical entertainers had finished and cleared their equipment. They'd been last to go during dress rehearsal, and had been the first half of the show, so their cumbersome equipment only had to be set up and torn down once.

Dessert had been served during the intermission. And there'd been a string quartet set up on a smaller, temporary side stage set up by a dance floor for patrons on one side of the room.

Hearing the applause out front, she positioned herself, one turned-out foot in front of the other. Running through her first eight count in her mind.

And as the music started, she paid close attention to the beat. Focusing all her conscious thought on the phrase that would carry her onto the stage, to the moves themselves. If she rushed again, no one but she and Nathan would know.

It was their last dance.

She needed it to be perfect.

Watching him enter the stage, seeing his strength, his grace, his perfect technique, her nervousness, her tension, disappeared, and when her cue came, she made a flawless entrance.

As soon as she'd taken her first step, felt the stage beneath her foot, Harper gave herself over to the dance. It took her, holding her body as she centered, spotted and turned, as she leaped and flew into a series of fouettés, whipped throws in tandem with Nathan, whose hands came back to her waist in between each one.

They were on the stage together, and apart, and yet, for five glorious minutes they were together in a realm where earthly needs and aspirations, where life journeys, didn't exist. And where anything was possible.

Where she was one with him and the spirits rejoiced.

All too soon, the finale approached and even as she dreaded reaching the end, Harper threw herself into those eight counts with every ounce of her heart.

She spun in on faultless count to step into fifth position on Nathan's extended hand, seeing his bent knee but only peripherally, for a second, as she found her spot, a blinking light in the back of the auditorium and focused on it, keeping herself centered.

When he lowered her to his shoulder, she pliéed, slid quickly to his hands gripping her waist, then toes to floor. But instead of the rond de jambe that came next, a prelude to her spinning away, she dropped to her knees, and into the dancer's crawl Nathan had choreographed the day before.

Her heart was in anguish. She couldn't feel the spin. Couldn't find it.

And so she crawled, hearing the beats where he'd be leaving the stage, having no idea of her next move.

Then felt a hand graze her foot, fingers at her ankle, and she fell flat to the stage.

Her heart pounded, she had a rushing sound more than music in her ears, as Nathan pulled her slowly down his body, then taking her waist, set her before him.

Her legs opened into faultless straddle splits of their own accord, in line with his. A beat passed. She had no more moves. Nothing left.

Until Nathan, with his back to the audience, winked at her. A quick push off of his hand and he was standing. Extending a hand down to her.

She rolled out of reach and then, legs together, rolled up over her toes into a standing position. The music had reached its crescendo. Nathan, with his neck and back straight, head facing side stage, was making his final dramatic exit, and...

She couldn't let him. With a couple of quick jetés, she reached him three counts out. Grabbed his waist with both hands. Not sure what to do next.

He spun within her grip, took her waist in his hands, and, lifting her over his head as she threw a swan pose, walked offstage with her.

There'd been no rehearsal. No choreography. No counts.

There'd been heart and soul.

Expression that went deeper than words.

And a truth that she couldn't ignore.

She was never going to be as good apart from Nathan as she was when she was with him.

Chapter Twenty-Four

As soon as Nathan set Harper down in the wings, music started for the final bow and performers filled the wings and then the stage, with him and Harper stage center. He smiled. He took his bows. And as soon as the crowd on the stage was released, he made a beeline for his dressing room.

Changed into jeans, a button-down work shirt and tennis shoes, he grabbed the bag he'd already loaded and was out the door.

Looking for Harper. No way was he just going to walk out on her.

Surrounded by dancers, she looked up and saw him, excused herself and walked over to him. Eyeing the bag on his shoulder.

Nodding. Then looked him straight in the eye, gave his hand a squeeze, and said, "Thank you."

He nodded back, emotions confusing the moment, and, as someone called out to them, he left her to her glory, exiting through the same, mostly unknown side door through which he'd entered that morning.

Feeling nothing like that guy.

He'd been so certain that he was solid in life. On staying his course.

Still knew, unequivocally, that he couldn't live in Harper's world.

He just didn't know how he could walk away from her.

The party would be going on until midnight, another three hours, and he couldn't imagine wanting to stay, being swarmed by the crowd.

Just as he understood that Harper thrived on the energy she got from the collective recipients of her life's work.

To take her out of that world would weaken her, in the same way depriving her of food would do.

The two-hour drive back down the coast settled him some. Enough to know that he had to see Harper one more time. And that he wasn't going to sleep until he did.

Scott and Iris were going to be returning Aggie home around eleven, or whenever they decided to go to bed, and as Nathan turned onto Ocean Breeze, he saw their lights still on. Pulling into their drive, he took Aggie off their hands, kind of surprised when the girl just stepped right up into his truck as though she'd been riding in the front passenger seat her entire life.

Continuing down to his temporary residence, he parked the truck in the garage, and then with Aggie at his heels, headed straight out to the beach.

Walking Harper's canine friend home was a given.

Turning on the fireplace on Harper's deck just kind of happened. He didn't think his actions through. Didn't have a plan.

He just knew he had to talk to her. And that it all had to end that night.

That was what the dance had been about.

Saying goodbye to a piece of your heart.

And yet…the way she'd come after him…that ending…

He could hardly think about it. Every time he tried, angst rose within him.

Confusion.

A sense that there was no clarity without finality.

The knowledge that his life plan had changed.

And a lack of a path in front of him.

Once the fire was lit, sitting with it was the only logical choice. He'd brought Aggie home but had no way to let her in the cottage.

And no idea when Harper would be home.

She'd driven up to LA with the director of the local ballet company she'd chosen to do a piece in the show. Perhaps they'd want to stay for the rest of the party.

Maybe they'd want to spend the night, rather than make the two-hour drive so late.

He'd just settled back into his seat when his phone rang.

Blared into the beach's late-night peace was more like it. Grabbing the cell from his shirt pocket, he pushed to answer even as he saw who was calling.

Harper. He settled in some more. He should have known. If his business wasn't done yet, hers wouldn't be, either.

Apparently, that was how they rolled.

"Hey, you on your way home?" he asked.

"Just leaving. Did I wake you?"

"No. I'm—"

"Oh, good." Her tone wasn't peaceful as she cut him off. She was about as het up as he'd ever heard her. "I just had to call and tell you, Nathan...the minute you hit the stage...pledges started to roll in. Our number made twice the amount tonight of any of the other performers. Including the first half as well."

The news made him smile. For the kids that would benefit. For her.

And it was nice to know that the young man he'd once been had carried enough merit within him that even thirteen years later, he brought out good in people.

She rang off then, saying they were just getting on the freeway and she had to pay attention. And, considering that she wasn't in the car alone, he didn't wait a few and call her back.

He just sat and waited.

Harper pulled on to Ocean Breeze just after midnight Saturday night. Still buzzing with the night's emotional overload.

A sense of accomplishment, of success, she'd never get used to knowing.

And foreboding, too.

She'd pushed Nathan with the impromptu and completely unprofessional last-second change in the last sixteen counts of their dance.

Onstage.

Had she been an employee in the show, any show, she'd have been fired for such a move.

His first time onstage in years, in front of a roomful of powerful people, and she'd thrown him to the wolves.

The fact that her moves hadn't been forethought or intentional didn't fly. She was a professional. The show always came first.

He'd been up for the blip. Had handled it like the true great that he was.

And hadn't really looked at her since.

She knew he had Aggie. Iris had texted. Sage had, too, earlier. To wish her a good show.

And for the first time in forever, she'd screwed up onstage.

Shaking her head as she pulled into her garage, figuring she needed the walk on the beach down to his place, she rephrased her previous thought.

Nathan wouldn't explode. Wasn't how he did things. He'd just quietly state his position and walk away.

A trait she appreciated more than he'd ever understand. Unless someone had grown up in a rancorous atmosphere, they couldn't fully appreciate being with one who resolved issues without spewing anger over everything and everyone in sight.

In leggings and the sweatshirt she'd changed into before doing a final check on all her dancers' spaces to make sure nothing had been left behind, Harper didn't bother entering her house. She needed to get to the beach. Breathe some salty air.

And get the rest over with.

Starting with an abject apology. Every time she thought about what she'd done to him—a man who abhorred being onstage, who'd only been there as a favor to her—and she'd sideswiped him.

To make matters worse, she couldn't explain to him why she'd done it. She'd have to know that for herself before she could do that.

Rounding the side of her cottage, she knew that she wasn't going to get her walk on the beach. Aggie warned her, first.

And she saw the glow from the fire.

Burrowing her face in her pet's fur, she wrapped her arms around Aggie's big, solid body and held on, buying herself a few seconds to breathe in support before she climbed up to the deck.

He knew she was there. She'd caught a glimpse over Aggie's shoulder of him watching them.

And she started talking with her foot on the first step. "I'm sorry, Nathan. I don't know what came over me. You have every right to blast me to hell. You trusted me and I blew it. And I can't even tell you why."

"I can." He'd barely moved. Watched as she took the only other seat in front of the fire.

She'd started to reach her hands out to the flames but stopped to look over at his face. "You can?"

Almost holding her breath as she waited for whatever axe was going to fall, she kept her gaze on him. Couldn't look away.

"Anything else would have been a lie."

Mouth open, she recognized the truth in his words. And waited for the bad part to fall. The part where, even though she'd been unable to just let him walk away from her, and where they'd ended together, soaring…it was just a dance.

An act.

A show.

Which summed up a lot of her life?

She looking at him. Waiting for more.

He was staring at the fire. "I talked to my mom today."

He'd said they had monthly calls.

Still facing ahead, he said, "She asked me to come home for a visit. A couple of days. She actually offered to take time off from the studio."

Heart leaping, Harper leaned toward him. "Oh my gosh, Nathan!"

And then, when she would have liked to hug him and hold on to the positives that were coming in their lives, he said, "I want you to come with me."

He what?

Her senses slowed. The night slowed. Aggie nudged her head under Harper's hand. She had to have heard him wrong. He'd spoken softly. The fire was burning. She was wound tight and, "You what?"

"I want you to come with me."

Yeah. There they were again. Excitement flared through her. And her walls shot up, too. "Why?"

"It's a piece of this—" he pointed between the two of them "—that needs to happen."

He was looking at her and she looked right back. Settling inside as she recognized the rightness of what he'd said. "Okay," she gave the only answer there was. "When?"

She'd rearrange things. Work it out somehow. Help him get the last piece of his life in place.

"Depends."

"On what?"

He looked back at the fire. "At how the rest of this conversation goes."

Tension grabbed her again.

There was more.

It was Saturday night. Her wine night. She clung to the thought, to avoid any others. Jumped up. "You want a glass of wine?" she asked him, already on the way to her back door, key in hand. She was going in, whether he chose to join her in libation or not.

"About two hours ago," he told her. "It's Saturday night."

Frowning, and yet, eager for the moment's repast, she worried about what was going on with him as she went inside. Opened and poured the wine.

And noticed that Aggie had stayed out with Nathan, rather than following her in. Curious.

Because the girl sensed that he needed her more?

She was already taking a sip from her glass as she handed him his. She didn't feel like toasting to an end.

But neither could she just sit there in silence, waiting for the world to cave in. "What's the rest of the conversation?"

"I realized tonight that there's been a shift in my future."

Her heart thrummed, with as much dread as not. Nerves on edge, she took another sip of wine, thinking she might have been better just to swig from the bottle.

Something she'd never even considered doing before in her life.

"Okay." And then horror struck as she put that statement together with calling his mother the day of the show. Going to see her. Wanting Harper along. "But if you're about to tell me that you're going back into dance, then just stop right there, Nathan. As much as I would give to have you in my world, there is no way on earth that I will ever believe that it's right for you. Nor will I see you waste your life living where you don't belong." A lot of words. Said in a rush. And straight from the soul.

"Just for the record, if I did choose to 'waste my life' as you put it, it would be on me, not you. I'm a big boy. I make my own choices."

Right. She almost thanked him for the reminder. She nodded, instead. Needing the conversation done, not prolonged.

She stared into the fire. Heard, "There is no longer a wife and child in the plan."

And froze. Caught her glass just as it was about to slip from her fingers. "I'm not following," she managed. Barely.

"If yesterday didn't make it clear, tonight most certainly did."

Her entire being was on the edge of an emotional cliff. She had to jump. Didn't dare. "I'm not following."

"Yes, you are."

He was right. She stared at the fire, and said, "The feelings between us..." Had to stop. To try to find a way to tell him that love didn't mean all souls were meant to join in day-to-day lives.

"I can't give my whole heart to another woman, when you already have it."

Tears filled her eyes. And a small spurt of joy sat on her heart. Mostly, she just knew anguish. All he wanted was a wife and family. The traditional home he'd never had. Something she couldn't give him. "It's not supposed to be this way," she told him.

"I think it is." His tone had changed, and she glanced over to find him staring at her. Intently. "I think it's been meant to be this way from the beginning. Two souls that touched each other, waiting to find each other again when the time was right."

No. She couldn't... "How can you say the time is right when it means giving up your life's dream?"

He shrugged. "Dreams shift. And who am I to question? My bottom line is that I cannot lie to myself. I didn't choose to love you. I didn't even look at you as a potential woman to date. Quite the opposite. I don't know why my heart chose differently, I might never know. But, tonight, when you reached for me onstage instead of finishing as choreographed, everything in me lit on fire. You don't argue with fire. You do and it burns you."

She knew then that he'd been on fire to leave dance long before he had.

And there they sat, in the strangest love scene ever written. Acknowledging that their spirits were so deeply connected, their hearts so strongly belonging to the other that there could be no one else. And yet...with an impassable abyss between them.

Might as well be the flames themselves.

"So where do we go from here?" she asked, feeling lost.

"You want to dance?"

She looked at him, and slowly started to smile. Without

a word, she stood, followed his lead as, phone in hand, he took her hand and headed down to the beach.

She stood in the sand, shivering a bit, as he touched his phone screen a couple of times and then set the cell in the sand. One of her favorite old-time love songs came on and when Nathan opened his arms, she stepped into them.

Let her body meld into his, as he led them in a slow, rocking circle, one step at a time. Followed by just rocking, lifting one foot than the other, in place.

She put her head on his shoulder.

Felt his hand slide up her back, resting just behind her heart.

"Let it go," he whispered into the hair glued up on the side of her head.

And slowly, as a wave she couldn't stop rose in her, she did.

Nathan held on. He felt the sobs wracking her body, and he moved. Slowly. In the sand that she loved. With the soft instrumental love tunes sharing the space with the ocean rolling in the distance. He didn't have their answers.

He wished he did.

But he knew they'd never find them until a lifetime of walls broke inside Harper. They'd been cracking since the day she saw him on the beach.

He'd figured it all out slowly, over time, with the last dance finally giving him clarity.

She loved him and knew that he loved her.

She didn't know how to love. Or let love in.

But she'd seen the love in her heart, just the same.

He had no idea how much time passed before she quieted. She didn't pull away. Just kept dancing. Taking on more and more of the movement herself.

Until she was leading, and he wasn't.

The dance changed from a sweet surrender, to something more. Something hungry. Grinding her hips against his hardness, he knew she'd figured out that he was in need of a replay of the afternoon before.

And couldn't let that happen again. Not in the same way. Not without...more.

Pulling away, he cupped the sides of her face and almost nose to nose, looked into her eyes. "I don't know," he told her, shaking his head at the unspoken question standing between them. "Do we live apart and see each other when we can? Do we live together and see each other when we can?"

With brows raised, she lifted lashes wet with tears, to look at him fully. "It makes more sense to live together, since the *when we can* part will be easier to accomplish."

He smiled. He couldn't help himself. Harper with her very different, very honest way of looking at life...pulled it out of him. And just like that, he was keeping his cottage. Her place was too small for the both of them and Aggie.

"And...maybe...we get married, too," she said then. "I mean, it *was* your plan, and while, granted, you're losing the dinner-at-home-every-night part, doesn't mean you have to give it all up."

He stopped moving. Stared down into her eyes. And then lowered his head to kiss her. Long. Gently. And then harder. Stopping when the next second would have had him dragging her down into the sand and making love to her right then and there.

"And...it would also work better that way if...say...we go to that clinic and, you know, donate our stuff, and nine months later show up at the hospital to claim our baby..."

His entire system went into Park. He stared.

Meeting his gaze, she kept talking. "Because the thing

is, when you came down here last night, thinking I might be pregnant…for the first time in my life, I was devastated that I couldn't be. Strange, huh? But there you have…"

Nathan didn't wait for the rest of whatever she'd been going to say. He lowered his head to hers and kissed her like the desperate, starving man he was.

One who lived deeper in his emotions than some men. Who felt every nuance of the dance. And one who was strong enough to move mountains, too.

Her walls weren't going to come down in a night. He'd have to find his boundaries for how much time he spent in her world. They'd need to figure out how the two of them raised healthy children.

The mountains of obstacles were not going to prevent him from living, from loving, as deeply, as intensely, as the universe intended.

And with that acceptance, the answer was there.

Breaking off the kiss, he looked at Harper's face in the moonlight. The mascara stains, makeup that had run unevenly with her tears. And lost his air at her beauty.

At the depth of her that she was exposing to him.

The honesty in every interaction they'd shared.

Taking a deep breath, he said, "The incredible work it takes to be a dancer, with a single mindset and a lifetime of dedication attached—makes for one who can do the hard work to make a relationship work."

He had his clarity. And saw by the widening of her eyes, that she had hers.

Truth was, they'd found it together. Starting from the beginning. With that very first dance. The one she'd seen him perform. And the time he'd sat in the dark all alone, watching an angel.

Their hearts had been opened to each other, and the future had been waiting for them to find it ever since.

They were dancers. They'd been doing the work since childhood. Better than most.

And just like the next piece she'd choreograph, the next deck he'd design, the rest would come.

Because love, the source of all beauty, was the strongest dancer of all.

* * * * *

Get up to 4 Free Books!

**We'll send you 2 free books from each series you try
PLUS a free Mystery Gift.**

Both the **Harlequin® Special Edition** and **Harlequin® Heartwarming™** series feature compelling novels filled with stories of love and strength where the bonds of friendship, family and community unite.

YES! Please send me 2 FREE novels from the Harlequin Special Edition or Harlequin Heartwarming series and my FREE Gift (gift is worth about $10 retail). After receiving them, if I don't wish to receive any more books, I can return the shipping statement marked "cancel." If I don't cancel, I will receive 6 brand-new Harlequin Special Edition books every month and be billed just $6.39 each in the U.S. or $7.19 each in Canada, or 4 brand-new Harlequin Heartwarming Larger-Print books every month and be billed just $7.19 each in the U.S. or $7.99 each in Canada, a savings of 20% off the cover price. It's quite a bargain! Shipping and handling is just 50¢ per book in the U.S. and $1.25 per book in Canada.* I understand that accepting the 2 free books and gift places me under no obligation to buy anything. I can always return a shipment and cancel at any time by calling the number below. The free books and gift are mine to keep no matter what I decide.

Choose one:
- ☐ **Harlequin Special Edition** (235/335 BPA G36Y)
- ☐ **Harlequin Heartwarming Larger-Print** (161/361 BPA G36Y)
- ☐ **Or Try Both!** (235/335 & 161/361 BPA G36Z)

Name (please print)

Address   Apt. #

City   State/Province   Zip/Postal Code

Email: Please check this box ☐ if you would like to receive newsletters and promotional emails from Harlequin Enterprises ULC and its affiliates. You can unsubscribe anytime.

Mail to the Harlequin Reader Service:
IN U.S.A.: P.O. Box 1341, Buffalo, NY 14240-8531
IN CANADA: P.O. Box 603, Fort Erie, Ontario L2A 5X3

Want to explore our other series or interested in ebooks? Visit www.ReaderService.com or call 1-800-873-8635.

---

*Terms and prices subject to change without notice. Prices do not include sales taxes, which will be charged (if applicable) based on your state or country of residence. Canadian residents will be charged applicable taxes. Offer not valid in Quebec. This offer is limited to one order per household. Books received may not be as shown. Not valid for current subscribers to the Harlequin Special Edition or Harlequin Heartwarming series. All orders subject to approval. Credit or debit balances in a customer's account(s) may be offset by any other outstanding balance owed by or to the customer. Please allow 4 to 6 weeks for delivery. Offer available while quantities last.

Your Privacy—Your information is being collected by Harlequin Enterprises ULC, operating as Harlequin Reader Service. For a complete summary of the information we collect, how we use this information and to whom it is disclosed, please visit our privacy notice located at https://corporate.harlequin.com/privacy-notice. Notice to California Residents – Under California law, you have specific rights to control and access your data. For more information on these rights and how to exercise them, visit https://corporate.harlequin.com/california-privacy. For additional information for residents of other U.S. states that provide their residents with certain rights with respect to personal data, visit https://corporate.harlequin.com/other-state-residents-privacy-rights/.